TWICE BLESSED

TWICE
BLESSED

A NOVEL

Ninotchka Rosca

W. W. Norton & Company
New York London

The text of this book is composed in Electra
with the display set in Poster Bodoni
Composition by PennSet
Manufacturing by Courier Companies, Inc.
Book design by Chris Welch

Library of Congress Cataloging-in-Publication Data
Rosca, Ninotchka.
Twice blessed : a novel / Ninotchka Rosca.
p.   cm.
I. Title.
PR9550.9.R64T85   1992
823—dc20   91-25401
ISBN 0-393-03091-1

W. W. Norton & Company, Inc., 500 Fifth Avenue, New York, N.Y. 10110
W. W. Norton & Company Ltd., 10 Coptic Street, London WC1A 1PU

1 2 3 4 5 6 7 8 9 0

ACKNOWLEDGMENT

When *mala suerte* overtook the original title of this work, Harry Newman came up with a new one.

N.R.

TWICE BLESSED

1

The formal ball usually begins with the *rigodón de honor,* a quadrille by seven couples, six along the hall's length and one in the middle, underneath a ball of mirrors spinning on its axis, piercing space with the pink, blue, yellow, and purple of reflected light, reflected images, its harsh brilliance an insubstantial waterfall spilling upon the dancing pairs, all drawn from high society, provided of course there are enough who can dance without tripping on their feet or causing the help to titter under their breath, otherwise dancers will have to be pulled in from the Women's School, where they train future society-page ladies and discreet prostitutes. But if the ball is to be opened thus, as tradition decrees it should be opened, when will Herself make the grand entrance? One step, pause, one step, pause at the marble staircase swerving down to the ceremonial hall of the palace, which isn't a palace but a humbler summer retreat, two hundred years old, of Spanish governor-generals long departed. Too bad the real one disappeared in the rubble of the last war—or was it the war before that? And if Herself makes her entrance at this point, should the music stop to allow the Boys Town Orphanage tots to toot the fanfaronade while she slide-steps, slide-steps, down the staircase, careful of the train of her *terno,* and the stiff butterfly sleeves, the garment weighing around forty pounds, what with the seed pearls and the silk embroidery? How can she walk in stiletto heels with that load?

Endless problems. Even with the battalion of servants at one's command, a presidential inauguration is a complicated affair; and though responsibilities have been divided—Katerina in charge of the reception invitations, since she *had* to be surrounded only by those she found amiable; Hector to the official functions and functionaries, which led to inevitable clashes with his sister, since to him politics aren't a matter of whom one likes but whom one can use; Armand to physical requirements, like the Luneta Park stage—still Teresa Tikloptuhod, childhood friend and official confidante of Katerina Gloriosa Herself and her twin brother, His Excellency (to-be) Hector Basbas, has to hover over the entire preparations like a hawk surveying the landscape, ever vigilant about details. Will the moon be properly full, be clear overhead—or will it be necessary to send aloft propeller planes to huff-puff dark clouds over to the horizon towards the China Sea? And if Herself, as Katerina has come to be known nowadays, makes her grand entrance at this point, should the *rigodón* music halt for the fanfaronade, and if so, how then can the dancers do the traditional Salute without music? Bah, endless problems. But Katerina wants everything just right, perfect, symmetrical, she says, making a double circle—mindful of her inch-and-a-half refrigerator-white plastic nails—with thumb and index finger of both hands. Nothing untoward, nothing unusual, nothing out of place, because, as Teresa knows, she has a mania for harmony, for order, arising from the constant disruption of her life; a longing for the precise which grows and gathers like dark cumulus in her chest, just beneath her throat, to be disgorged, once in a while, in the form of an incoherent, uncontrollable rage.

Such as possessed her three days after the Commission on Elections announced the final vote count and proclaimed the triumph of Hector Basbas, henceforth to be called His Excellency (to-be), sir, even in his bathroom and the twins' San Juan residence with its artificially aged adobe walls filled up with well-wishers. The town mayor had decreed a holiday—discreetly, justifying it by citing some allegedly scholarly findings at the Dead Sea (which was half a globe away and thus unverifiable for cynics) which proved that the town's namesake and spiritual patron, Saint John, had been beheaded in November and not in summertime per the church calendar. Wherefore, by virtue of powers invested in him, the mayor, and so forth and so on, he called for the celebration of the Day of Saint John the Baptist, *now*, thus satisfying with a single proclamation his desire to pander and his need to appear nonpartisan. At which bands of ragamuffins and watch-your-car boys deployed themselves about the Basbas residence, at street corners, between parked cars, behind trees and even up electric posts, thus showing they knew very well what this was all about, with their feast-day paraphernalia of water hoses, water pistols, pails, tin cans, because Saint John was honored by dousing the unwary in mock baptism. Faucet water, canal water, pothole water . . . while through the Basbas gates, past the dark-blue uniformed security guards now augmented by presidential guards in funereal black, streamed a literally streaming throng who had to be tendered fresh towels and pushed towards various bathrooms. Among them came dear, dear and least-liked, cousin Matrimonia Basbas, now the Grand Matriarch of the clan though she was still unmarried, having attained the honor by virtue of attrition, with so many relatives overseas or dead or gone insane, which was why this afternoon it was she who brought the clan's respects, batting her eyelashes and flicking her fingers despite the splotch of water which had ruined the bodice of her pink dress, stitched by seamstresses of the couturier Romero, whom, said Matrimonia, Katerina simply must try for her inauguration ball gown. Over your dead body, Katerina thought, noting how cousin Matrimonia was revealed to be as flat as a wall while she managed, through many eyebrow archings, moues, and head-shakings, to convey the impression that dear, dear cousin was always welcome, no matter how she looked, while all the time pushing her towards the main reception room, without benefit of towel and mirror to repair her ruined toilette, and there she found herself, stinking of canal water, amidst the glossed-to-the-hair-roots denizens of *alta sociedad*. But not before Katerina had deftly extracted from her fingers the congratulatory gift, a rosary of pearls, each bead the size of a man's thumbnail, the Hail Marys of pure white, the Our Fathers bruised blue, and the Crucifix a hefty twenty-two-karat gold, at least four inches, mind you. Looping the rosary firmly about her right hand, Katerina repaired to an upper-floor landing, the better to watch Matrimonia's discomfiture, for this was the cousin who, many years ago, when she herself was at the Women's School and had been chosen Lantern Queen, had lent her with malice aforethought a pair of shoes from among the fifty or so pairs in her closet. The oldest pair, many times resoled, repaired; perhaps with the cheapest glue or maybe not glue even but with hardened floor wax, crusted leftover cream of chicken soup, or crushed rice grains. What with Katerina's exertions as she danced the Queen's Waltz and the December humidity, the soles came loose and punctuated "The *Blue Danube*" with a flap-flap, flap-flap-flap-flap, flap-flap, flap-flap while the Consort, the most eligible only son of a sugar baron, grew red in the face and glanced at his pants buttons as suppressed giggles in the darkened hall rose to thin squeals of laughter. A misstep; Katerina stumbled and fell heavily against her partner, who, caught at the instant he was rising to his toes, lost his balance and landed on his butt. He arched forward and sprang to his feet at once, like a *karateka*, but his eyes had been brought to ground level and he'd seen the indecent black tongues sticking out from underneath Katerina's white shoes. With a strange smile, he wound his arms about her again and led her back to the dance, but not before whispering into her ear such a phrase that, when it was uttered, knives and blood were drawn. *Patay-gutom*, he said. Oh you dying-of-hunger you. Trembling, frightened, and turning all colors of humiliation, Katerina allowed him to twirl her and turn her, left shoulder forward, right shoulder following, left knee bent slightly, dip! to the last waltz note, after which he clicked his heels, bowed with irony, and disappeared from her life forever, *flap-flap*.

Grimly, Katerina watched Matrimonia as a small space bloomed about the woman, an emptiness which swallowed her elegant nods, her brilliant smiles, as men and women sidestepped away from her pleasantries, for the scent of canal water could be vicious to those who were awakened by maids spraying the morning with water and crushed jasmine petals. She smiled, sliding the pearls of prayer between her fingers, breathing her gratitude to a God who'd allowed her this moment of pleasure—in a life, she would add to Teresa later, largely devoid of joy. But she wasn't stupid enough to believe that the fickle heavens wouldn't make her pay for this tiny moment, and so as not to tempt fate, from here on she'd make sure she had a pair of shoes to go with every dress, every coat, every handbag, every bra even in her wardrobe, and would never travel again, even to the corner grocery store, without a crate of footwear, heaven help her. She could be grateful to God, but trust Him?

She did trust Teresa Tikloptuhod, who, if truth be told, was certainly no childhood friend. Katerina was already thirty-two when they met; Teresa, then twenty-four, was spending a fifth year of terminal boredom at her father the Provincial Governor's house, having been "finished" at the Women's School, the first of her clan to be so civilized, not that—as the gossip went—that helped at all. No one came to sue for her hand, since her hard-headedness was legendary and she was, to put it bluntly, down-right ugly, being dark, thin, scraggy-boned, and awkward, not to mention flat-nosed and slit-eyed. That would not have been as much of a drawback to the ambitious young men of the rising

tobacco-and-garlic clans; wives after all were for establishing con-
nections and breeding children, and a half-dozen mistresses
would suffice to gratify any male's yearning for feminine pul-
chritude. But Teresa's sexual preference was also suspect, there
being that merest hint of a scandal when she was at the nuns'
secondary school. The northern clans were too new at power and
wealth to take on such risks, though to hear them talk, one would
have believed their forefathers rubbed elbows with the Adelantado
Miguel López de Legaspi himself when he conquered Manila.
Except for an occasional sneer, Teresa exhibited no chagrin at
the situation, not even when her two younger sisters were formally
bethrothed, though custom dictated they couldn't marry before
she did.

"Their wombs will pucker up," Teresa told her father, "if they
wait for me."

The youngest eloped and broke the taboo. Two weddings were
planned immediately, the Provincial Governor throwing up his
hands at Teresa's intransigence, but her sisters assured her she'd
be maid of honor, that they'd throw the wedding bouquet in her
direction, and that they'd search the whole province for a gallant
escort, two escorts or more. She didn't have the heart to tell
them she couldn't care less.

She was quite content to remain by her father's side, needling
him with her not too little wit, cutting ribbons at inaugural events,
hosting parties, since her-mother-his-wife had died five years
before and his mistresses were unacceptable at certain official
and upper-crust gatherings. The local newspapers duly noted her
presence at this-that affair, baptizing her the "Black Beauty"—
which sobriquet she read with amusement, knowing the provincial media to be on her father's payola. But then again, they
could've been simply calling her a horse. She took to puffing on
foot-long hand-rolled cigars like the matriarchs of her mother's

time, because, as she told everyone, horses at least didn't smoke. Her father was appalled and threatened to strop her with his belt, she wasn't too grown up for that, but she crinkled her eyes and reminded him of *his* mother, who, in prewar days, spent all her waking hours rolling tobacco leaves against her thigh in the dimness of the old thatch-roofed warehouse, her own lighted cigar parked thriftily on a cracked Ming plate salvaged from the odds and ends of porcelain unearthed in the cemetery behind the cathedral when the grave for Teresa's mother had been dug, this mother dying with her mouth inflamed and mute because of a monstrous multipetaled tumor growing on her palate. So there.

An unbroken line of matriarchs trailed from Teresa to the vagueness of those times when the tobacco-and-garlic clans were no more than a handful of warring families jostling one another for quotas and favors from the Spanish authorities who administered the tobacco monopoly. It was only during the chaos of World War II, the Japanese occupation, and the devastation of Manila that the clans managed to loosen somewhat that city's control over the archipelago's economy and politics. The warring tribes became a regional alliance, dedicated to carving out a larger share of power for the north—which wish came true with the coming of huge, American-licensed cigarette factories and the export of garlic to exotic places of Southeast Asia. Such hypocrisy, Teresa said, blowing cigar smoke into the air above her father's head; smoke and spice had always been the north's attraction to the world, and they still fueled the rise of its warlords. If such an explanation was not sufficient to deflect her father's anger, she added calmly, she'd give up smoking and take up instead where she'd left off when she was in high school, one vice for another, fair trade, no?

Smoke yourself to the grave, was her father's reply, and he

added what he thought was the supreme rapier thrust: "Too bad you're female. With your cold blood, you could become head of the family." He went away laughing.

Ha-ha. Nice but predictable, Teresa thought as she laid out tarot cards in the rear breakfast room of her father's mansion, which, praise the Lord for the Governor's simplicity, did not pretend to have been there since time begun. Indeed, the house being new, its internal climate was of the smell of drying paint mixed with the garlic and tobacco perfume of the flanking warehouses. Servants walked through this odoriferous fairyland with dim and lost eyes; they were nubile fourteen- and fifteen-year-olds, conscripted from outlying farms, with auras so intense that Teresa had flashes of prescience whenever they hovered about her.

As she turned over cards and spotted the Hanged Man, the Clown, the Queen, Teresa couldn't help thinking of how the Provincial Governor was too shallow really to understand why his eldest daughter, who'd been a calculus whiz at the age of eight, should choose such an idle life, not even bothering to bend her considerable intellect to the keeping of account books as every family matriarch did, hunched over stained ledgers spread out on the dining table as soon as the dishes of the day's last meal were cleared out. Truth was, Teresa couldn't forgive her father for having sent her to a boardinghouse in Manila to attend the Women's School, where she was trained in the mind-destroying arts of how to walk, sit, talk, or in other words, How to Carry Yourself; How to Be Provocative Without Appearing to Be Provocative; Small Talk and What to Serve With It; How to Manage Maids and Assorted Help and Thereby Organize Your Life . . . at all of which she failed miserably, excelling instead in math, geometry, trigonometry, and algebra, which inspired the dean of students to ask, in the full hearing of her entire class, if she could check the physical paraphernalia of *Señorita* Teresa Tikloptuhod, just to make sure she was really a female.

She was chuckling over that when the roar of a jeep engine destroyed the silence, to be followed shortly by her father's bellows. Since there was nothing else to do, Teresa sipped the last drops of her coffee, stubbed out her cigar—it had lost its shock value—and gathered her house robe about her to follow the spoor of her father's anger. There on the front porch, a lieutenant and two constabulary soldiers stood at attention beneath the twin onslaught of her father's yells and salivary rain.

It seemed that but an hour before, the soldiers had come upon a woman in black laving her feet at the ancient and moss-covered fountain of the central plaza in front the cathedral. Asked what her intentions were in the area, the woman had said she was on her way to God or Bhutan, whichever crossed her path first, and she'd walked all the way from the last town of the neighboring province. A pair of battered black sandals and a stained black leather suitcase lying in the plaza dust confirmed this statement. When one soldier picked up the suitcase and balanced it on the fountain ledge, preparatory to forcing its locks with his butterfly knife, the woman had added that she was the twin sister of the Senate President and had better not be interfered with, as she had the rank of ambassador extraordinaire and plenipotentiaire and her mission was official, very official. They did not believe her, not until the suitcase lid sprang open to reveal wads and wads of brand-new, crisp hundred-peso bills tumbled in among black shirts and skirts, black undergarments, and an extra pair of sandals.

The woman said she wore sandals in honor of her great-grandfather, who was a Franciscan.

The Provincial Governor was nonplussed. He remembered suddenly a wire from Manila warning all points north of the city to be on the lookout for the Senate President's sister, who had inexplicably left their home, which, at the time, was a modest three-bedroom bungalow in a newly developed residential section of Cubao, a suburb of Manila.

"Why here?" Teresa's father demanded, smelling the coming scandal, the enmity of a powerful political leader, Hector Basbas, who everyone said would be president someday since he was already wooing and, it was said, had already sewn up the backing of American experts at that mysterious office known only by the acronym JUSMAG.

"Tell her God's moved, what the hell, to the next province," he said, thinking that if he could unload this embarrassment on his political rival . . .

But Teresa, propelled by an abrupt conviction that her destiny had come for her, stepped forward. She would take this danger off her father's hands, provided she was equipped the way the woman was—meaning black sandals, black clothes, a black leather suitcase, and . . .

"How much money was in the suitcase?" her father asked the lieutenant, sweat already forming on his brow.

"Twenty, thirty thousand pesos."

"You lie!" he shrieked. "You've never seen and will never see that much cash in your life." Silence. "It can't be more than ten thousand," he added after a while.

"Twenty," Teresa said decisively. "Every time we hit town, any town, I wire you and you wire the military post in the area to look out for us. That way we'll have a measure of security."

He scratched his head.

"You call"—she pointed to the just-installed telephone, one of only six in the province—"the brother and tell him your sane daughter's taking care of his demented sister . . ."

Ah. This he understood. Favors to such a man would come in handy someday. "Very good," he said, smiling. "You'll be a prime asset to your brothers. If you stop fighting with them."

Teresa shrugged. Her opinion of her two brothers, who were engrossed in building their private armies—recruiting, smuggling in weapons, pitting one enforcer against another—was not flattering. "Trust them," she'd told her father, "and they'll be your ruin." But he'd turned away, dismissing her words as so much envy. He was right, of course, for he stayed on top of the quarrelsome heap of his clan and family by stirring them to compete for his favor and approval.

This was the way Teresa met Katerina. The military jeep dropped her a block away from the plaza, and ostensibly footsore, weary, dragging the suitcase, which the soldiers had scuffed and dirtied vigorously, she made her way through the yellow dust to the fountain and thrust her feet into the water, breaking the algae coat of its surface and mentally crossing her fingers in the hope that nothing vile lived beneath that oily green slick. The woman on the other side of the fountain leaned sideways to snag her with a look.

"And where," the woman asked, in the crisp accents of a city-trained mixed-blood society matron, "are you going?"

Teresa then could thank her stars for her quick brain, for she plucked out of the soldiers' welter of words that phrase which was password and signal, bond and recognition: "To God or Bhutan, whichever crosses my path first."

2

The *architectural plans* for the inaugural stage were finished overnight, though Congress still had to meet in joint session two weeks hence to declare who was president-elect. But Armand Gloriosa wasn't the type to wait till the last minute. He was a *segurista*, a man who liked things guaranteed, as he explained to Teresa Tikloptuhod, handing her a neatly typed row of figures, the cost of the stage construction. Teresa's breath snagged when she saw the bottom-line amount. She'd never grown used to the way Hector, Katerina, and Armand dealt with money, wadding small fortunes in envelopes and paper bags each morning and returning late at night penniless. Armand, supposedly the businessman of the trio, advised her to think of it as investment, with returns at better than three hundred percent. But Teresa was a child of the frugal north, where a ten-centavo coin would be fished out of offal, and she could barely contain her panic at the thought of all that cash, of handing out bags of money. She was comforted only when she noted that half the cost of building the temporary inaugural stage would go to the woodcarving and wrought-iron guild traditionally owned by Armand's family. That kind of a giveaway she understood. But perhaps, given the cost, a permanent structure could be built . . . ?

"Don't be silly," was Armand's reply. Considering that the president greeted the parade at the same spot every Independence Day, a permanent stage would throw away an annual profitable enterprise.

She had no answer to that.

Armand rubbed the side of his nose with a forefinger, the better to hide his smirk. The stage floor, he said, would feature two huge designs of fragrant sandalwood: one of a stylized Malayan sun, its eight rays short double-edged broad swords, and the other a plain circle, delicately pale. "See here where Katerina sits, to the left of the stage, the moon will be under her feet," Armand said, "while Hector's chair will be right at the sun's center. So we have the symbol of the twice-blessed. . . ." Unlike the arrangement at previous inaugurations, a cleared space would separate Hector and Katerina from the guest dignitaries. Since Hector was a bachelor—the first to be elected head of state (but then wasn't his life a matter of being first always: born ten minutes before Katerina, most decorated war hero, first at the bar exams, first lawyer to be defense secretary, youngest senator and the only one to become senate president in his rookie year, and now youngest and only unmarried president ever?)—his twin sister was to be both First Lady and Official Family. Teresa, hiding the twitch of a smile, asked on what would Armand's and the three children's chairs be placed, four minor stars?

She regretted the joke immediately, as they were friends and it was still a wonder to her to be considered a close associate of the fabulous Armand, the only son of the wood-and-iron Gloriosas. This was no clan, only a singular family bearing the name, for unlike their Spanish friar progenitor, the Gloriosas were oddly and notoriously infertile. They had managed to keep the purity of their Caucasian blood intact for two hundred years, through the simple expedient of importing blond whores from Macau, introducing them to high society as the Duchess de La-de-da or the Marquesa de So-and-So, locking them up in the ancestral plantation south of Manila, and breeding children as soon and as fast as possible. Unfortunately, after three children at the most—usually two girls and a boy—the women's wombs would

seem to be stoppered and there was nothing left to do but send
them off with a sum of money to a quick divorce in Hong Kong.
They were quickly forgotten, except in the family's official ge-
nealogy, where they were listed with their fake titles. Every other
generation, the Gloriosas married their first cousins, ensuring
the consolidation of their genes and inheritance at one stroke.
This was why they remained a family, refusing to spread out into
a clan, and like a closed fist, they burrowed their way up the
integument of the archipelago, unearthing Spanish royal land
grants which gave them ownership of entire villages, huge city
blocks, acres of fallow land fortuitously adjoining the perimeters
of an expanding metropolis. No one dared ask how it was, a
hundred years after the end of the Spanish empire in the Pacific,
the Gloriosas continued to brandish these land grants from the
king of Spain, even though that country had been ruled for what
seemed like forever by a military dictator. In any case, the royal
land grants enabled them to evict neighborhoods wholesale in
the name of real estate development, their moonlighting team
of ten off-duty constables first class efficiently burning down
shanties and nipa huts, backyard gardens with their chicken coops
and pigsties.

A rare few of the imported women chose to stay, as Armand's
mother did, and quicker even than the divorce they had forgone,
they lost their minds. As Armand's mother did, before death
delivered her from an obsession which made her dose Armand
periodically with tablespoonfuls of attar of roses, ruining forever
his childhood and digestion. When he was ten years old, she
took to sniffing and smelling at him, her nose quivering as though
to draw out that most precious of Gloriosa legacies without which
no inheritance, no power, no formal recognition would be made
by the head of the family—for by some chemical quirk of their
bodies, the true Gloriosas exuded a scent of dried roses, a sweet,
irresistible pheromone which disturbed she-dogs, she-cats,

mares, and women. In the old days, the presence of a Gloriosa
in a closed parlor room sufficed to inspire a fainting epidemic
among the women present. And if truth be told, that was where
the Gloriosa fortune had its origins: in the service of that secret
niche which naked women instinctively shielded from strangers'
eyes with a fragile gesture of both hands one atop the other laid
on their loins. Armand chuckled when he dug up this bit of
history for Teresa, confessing that it had never been talked about:
how his many-times-removed grandfather had bedded a Chinese
merchant's daughter and thereby gained the key to the Celestial's
treasure box. For the life of him, said Armand, he couldn't
understand why this smidgen of oriental blood in their veins was
considered a gross secret, since if more truths were to be told,
his many-times-removed grandfather was a direct descendant of
a Spanish family of Judaic origins. They should've been proud,
he said, that they'd survived the Inquisition. In any case, with
perfumes and deodorants no longer a rarity nowadays, the scent
had become commonplace. But that had been no comfort to
Armand's mother, who, trembling in fear of a possible apostasy
by her husband, took to smelling the saliva stains on her child's
pillows, sweat stains on his shirt, skidmarks on his underwear.

She died before his puberty and was no longer around to
celebrate the scent's arrival—stronger than that of any other
Gloriosa, potent, aphrodisiacal, which led to Armand's being
dragged, starting at the age of fourteen, to the uppermost room
in the attic of the impossible Gloriosa mansion with its huge
double front doors stolen from a seventeenth-century church
somewhere, its layers of carved, embossed, nacre-overlain beams
and eaves and walls of wrought-iron leaves, grapes, apples—
everything ornate, rococo, crowded except for that tiny (oh, tiny!)
punishment room where Armand had to drop his pants and have
the living daylights walloped off his butt by his irate father to
cure him of his *dee-praved proo-clii-vii-tiies!* Until one day he

realized the irony of the situation and felt a tickling and a giggling underneath his throat, a ha-ha laugh which spewed out of his mouth still ajar with cries of pain and ha-ha rode the waves of rose scent gamboling towards the lone, small window high upon the wall.

He was civilized, nevertheless, Teresa could grant him that, remembering how at the first Manila party to which Katerina had taken her, a year after the two had found each other, Armand had come up to her neglected self, lost among the crush of chiffon and perfume and smooth bare flesh, to ask for a dance. Oh, but she couldn't, didn't know how, she said, horrified at the idea of all those eyes weighing her awkward bones. He insisted. It was easy; surely the principal lass of the principal tobacco-and-garlic clan had had a dance master. His fingers were delicate and impersonal against her hand and on her waist. Follow me, he whispered, eyes laughing as the small orchestra swung into the rhythm of a sweet, slow song. Left foot, right foot; turn. Show your profile, pirouette. Shoulder forward now, turn once, turn twice . . . She found herself floating on the music, on his confidence, and was besieged by intense visions of herself as a ballerina. Dip, he said, right arm curving into a cradle for her torso. Applause. Oh, they applauded—and Teresa, eyes hot as stars, clasped her hands modestly before her, bowing slightly to Armand's bow. As Katerina, wearing a headdress of bananas and hoop earrings, commanded the dance floor and everyone's attention, Armand led Teresa to the bar, obtained a rum and Coke for her, and steered her gently towards the terrace, enfolding her in the perfume of his sweat.

"Now, what really happened?" he asked, as soon as they were comfortable on the wrought-iron settee of the lawn. "Katerina refuses to talk about it, but shit, woman, the two of you were gone for a whole year."

Somewhat deflated, Teresa sipped her rum and Coke, a frown

settling on her forehead. Looking back now, it seemed like a lark, the year of unsurpassed freedom, but there had been difficult days, weeks even, for Katerina was subject to sudden attacks of melancholia during which she would not stir from wherever they were—at a mangy *pension* or rental room or a peasant hut—and would weep for thirty-six hours nonstop. In a lucid moment, she'd explained she was giving herself the luxury of grieving for all those times when she couldn't, because it was unseemly or because it could be construed as a sign of vulnerability or because she was in too much of a hurry, or all of the above.

Thus she wept for the death of a mother she'd never met, the wise woman dying at childbirth, and the death of her father when she and Hector were ten.

She wept for the day their uncle took them in, plucking them like weeds from the garage of the old family house and transplanting them to the ancestral house in the middle of a coconut plantation.

She wept for the forced separation of the twins, Hector and Katerina, at the age of fifteen, as punishment for some "child-foolishness," he to be sent to a military school and she to the Women's School.

She wept over the casual cruelty of the sugar princesses she endured for four years at the school, and the spiteful neglect of teachers and administrators who knew she was there for appearance's sake.

She wept over how aunts, uncles, and cousins had pressured her into this arranged marriage with Armand Gloriosa and how she'd run away, determined to find a job and somehow lay down the foundations of a normal existence for herself.

She wept over her relatives' perfidy, since one and all called on each of her prospective employers and talked every one out of giving her a job, to save the clan the embarrassment of having a working woman.

She wept over the wedding ceremony, which had been designed by her aunt, the Grand Matriarch, who insisted on festooning the open garden reception with palm fronds and bulging coconut bunches for good luck.

She wept over the births of her three children, one episode apiece.

But most of all, she wept for her twin, her brother, who was the only one who knew her and would know her until her death. She wept over his departure for the military school, his thin shoulders underneath the rough ramie shirt stinging with welts from the terrible whipping his uncle had given him. She wept over his disappearance when the war broke out and the four years of great silence when nothing, no news at all, was heard about or from him and everyone conceded he'd perished along with the rest of his class, who'd singly and collectively taken to the hills to become anti-Japanese guerrillas. But she wept the loudest and longest over his reappearance, four months after the Japanese surrender in the Cordilleras, showing up at the plantation gates with two servants, each bearing a wicker chest stuffed full of jewels—diamond necklaces, emerald bracelets, ruby brooches— as incredible as his stories of unsurpassed courage and patriotism as he waged a one-man war against the Japanese Imperial Army. She wept and laughed over his private tales to her, of how he slipped away from school as soon as bombs had fallen on the American base Fort Stotsenberg, and with only his wits for capital, plunged into the buying and selling of foodstuffs in famine-stricken towns and cities of the war, accepting as payment only gold and silver and gems.

Having wept, she was washed clean, like a glass pane after a sudden rain. She would then tax Teresa with preparations for the continuation of their journey, because, to be honest about it, Katerina inclined toward laziness, her big sensual body with its somewhat thin legs readily succumbing to languor at the first opportunity. Teresa, the bony, the hard-fleshed, sought out possible lodgings, spotted likely meal places, hired jeeps, buses, vans, or water buffalo sleds as the need arose, and furthermore made a beeline for the telegraph office in each town so as to send news of their whereabouts to her father, messages she felt compelled to sign inexplicably with the first three letters of her ancestral surname: TIK.

There was no lack of the unusual during the journey. She and Katerina encountered a desultory Lenten procession of peasants and watched as a young man was nailed to a cross and hung against a seared sky for three hours, with only the ropes about his chest to support his weight and keep him from suffocating.

Once, they cowered inside a chapel, crushed among the unwashed bodies of frightened peasants, as a typhoon outside peeled roofs off houses, strummed electric wires, and pummeled mango trees to the ground to the tune of a wind caterwauling over rice paddies.

And once they chanced upon a small hamlet at dawn where the villagers dressed as papier-mâché trees in an annual ritual without logic. Katerina had to slip on a light and attenuated lanzon tree, with sticky bright green and brown paint, while Teresa had to wear what was either an overgrown fern or a dwarf palm tree. For an hour and fifteen minutes, as the sun singed the farside hills, inching up a sky as blue as God could make it and at last spurting light all over the rolling moist green land below, they marched back and forth in the forest. At some discreet signal the two never discovered, all the villagers took off the costumes, returned them to a storage hut, and hied back to their homes for breakfast and their daily business.

Quite often they would be the only women in cockpits large, medium, and small at villages whose names weren't on any map and would sit fanning themselves with their hands and calling aloud their bets as men worked themselves into a frenzy of blood-lust over two roosters with razor-sharp tiny steel swords taped over their spurs. When the roosters caromed into battle, beaks thrust forward, wings half-spread, legs working like pistons, Katerina would scream herself hoarse, betting hundreds of pesos, and Teresa herself would break into a sweat as much from the men's scalding glances as from the excitement of gambling. On a whim, Katerina bought a victorious rooster for an intolerable amount of money, brought it to the pension where they were staying, had it butchered and stewed with ginger and green papayas. It took some four hours, but the hired cook of the moment finally managed to reduce the champion cock's muscles to a semblance of tenderness. Katerina ate the breast and thighs greedily.

And once, they found themselves on a seashore at day's end, with the sky so blood-red that waves flamed with the reflection of a sun going down in rage. They were convinced they'd walked off the edge of the earth straight into hell.

But they made the journey back, didn't they, no worse for the wear and tear, and carrying an elaborate bird cage made of a thousand fitted slivers of pale wood from Paete, and with Katerina saying as much to herself as to Teresa that henceforth no one could tell her anything about this country ever again since no one could know it as well, as intimately, as she did.

Which was a perilous conclusion, Armand had said; the three of them—himself, Katerina, and Hector—could never presume to know enough about anything, precisely because they had to know everything. He fell quiet momentarily, mulling over his own words. In the warm silence, the scent of dried roses overwhelmed, and Teresa thought she heard the indignant buzzing of a bee in the hedges. Then, in a strange lost voice, Armand told her of having seen a photograph of a sculpture, a marble rendering of a man wrapped in the coils of an enormous serpent whose head he barely held away from his own head. The man's face was a compound of terror and indomitable will, his expression both a surrender to fate and a defiance of it. "That's us," Armand had said. "Myself, Katerina, and Hector. Encoiled, trapped, but struggling, struggling, struggling. Wanting to let go but not daring to because we can't. We'd die, otherwise. We'd be finished. Kaput. We've gone beyond, overstepped the boundaries set by men and gods." And he'd laughed.

That was how it was in this country, Teresa told herself; everyone lived in terror, not daring to stop, not daring to look back if only to check whether the adversary was far or near or indeed if there even was one, not daring to take stock lest the little havens of safety they'd patched together over their heads came crashing down.

And what, she'd wondered aloud, was her role in this equation?

"You're Katerina's friend," Armand had answered, defining immediately her role and her destiny. "She has none at all except you. Not me; certainly not her brother, Hector. Only you."

But of course. Certainly. How could it be otherwise, Teresa decided. The moon will have to be under Herself's feet.

Only sixty more days to the inauguration, Armand reminded her, and what with all that Katerina wanted, the work had had to proceed nonstop, twenty-four hours, making a mess of the public works department's budget. Using Hector's franking privilege at the senate, they had sent notices to every department head of every government office, advising them of the advantage and benefit of the entire staff's being present at the formal oath-taking, said employees to be in the assigned colors, of course— blue for foreign affairs, red for public works, yellow for finance, green for social security, and so forth. Little marker flags were to be laid at the proper spot for each department, and just to be sure, a dress rehearsal would be held the weekend before the ceremony.

"The cardinal, two Protestant bishops, and the head of the

Church of the Mystic Limb . . . but what is the matter?" Armand looked at her in surprise.

Pursing her lips in distaste, Teresa asked whether it was necessary to include such a primitive sect. Armand gave her a playful nudge and confessed himself one of the sect's Twelve Wise Men, with authority to wave about its holiest symbol, a petrified acacia branch. "Hector arranged it," Armand said. "Years ago, when he first ran for the senate. The Mystical Limb has blessed all his campaigns with large donations. Cash and manpower."

Well, that being the case, the acacia branch indeed had won the right to be at the inaugural stage. Armand laughed but after a while conceded that invocations by four religious heads could be a little too much—"but backing is backing, and considering what's about to come down, we need all the support we can get."

That was how Teresa came to know that the lame-duck loser president was about to release his thunderbolt at the Basbas campaign.

3

"Not *until the fat lady sings,"* said José *"Blackie"* Domínguez y García, who had not only lost the presidential election
but also led his entire slate to a humiliating total defeat. Nevertheless, until the December inauguration, he remained Head of
State, President, Commander in Chief, His Excellency, sir! and
had to be taken seriously. Besides, his cryptic remark, in a country
without operas, rendered his refusal to concede unusual; otherwise, it would have been dismissed as merely the croaking of
frogs after a cloudburst; after all, no one in the archipelago had
ever conceded defeat since time immemorial. But as it was,
rumor and speculation metastasized; everyone was convinced that
the Basbas campaign organization had been infiltrated by a
Blackie moll, a fat one at that, presumably unattractive—and
such stupidity on the opposition's part was unpardonable.

Blackie Domínguez y García, so named for his ash-blue complexion, filed thirty-two petitions before COMELEC, alleging
that Basbas campaigners had committed fraud, terrorism, ballot-
box stuffing, and cheating both at vote counts and vote tallies,
as well as having seriously compromised the integrity of the
electoral process itself by accepting huge donations from foreign
companies, governments, and personalities and underworld so-
cieties. He asked all at once for a recount and recomputation,
for the setting aside of votes in five major provinces and 280
precincts elsewhere, for the election itself to be declared null and
void and its results set aside, and for a new presidential election

date to be scheduled at the convenience and pleasure of the commission. "Take as long as you want," Blackie said magnanimously. "I'll gladly serve until then." He would provide proof of all his allegations at the opportune moment—but in the meantime, the Basbas headquarters should be a little circumspect with their riotous victory orgies since, as the *Amerikano* was fond of saying, "it ain't over until the fat lady sings!"

In the ocher-painted corridors of the Legislative Building, Armand was cornered by reporters, photographers, and television cameras and could not avoid giving a statement, since he was his brother-in-law's general campaign manager. Nose in the air and wearing the famous Gloriosa half-smile, Armand gracefully held up two open hands and said, "Boys . . . and excuse me, lady . . . this is between His Excellency (was) and His Excellency (to-be). But I can tell you all the women in the Basbas campaign are lithe, slim, and svelte. We don't have a fat female campaigner . . . uh, not that fleshy girls aren't succulent." In the guffaws that followed, he made his escape to the senate president's office, lightly tweaking his collar and pleased by his own wit—though, as he told Teresa, he was damn worried about that Blackie announcement and had grabbed a telephone as soon as he was in Hector's office. Calling his two aides at the campaign HQ, he'd ordered an immediate sifting of all personnel to isolate overweight ladies and subject them to interrogation. "Put a Diablo at it. Better not to take chances."

Teresa mulled that over and decided not to explain Blackie Domínguez y García's allusion, so as not to discomfit Armand and everybody else. It didn't do to tell the media that one was more knowledgeable than the strutting columnists and editors of the Op-Ed Page. Instead she busied herself with stuffing plain white envelopes with ten hundred-peso bills each. With rough waters looming ahead, they would come in handy and protect everybody from the indignity of giving and receiving cash. Just envelopes; nothing but envelopes.

At each of the four toilets reserved for the use of congressmen and senators, Hector had already installed a Diablo "brother"— members of a secret society formed by ten veterans of the past decade's counterinsurgency war, who'd been trained in covert operations by the 'Kano's intelligence service—with three card-board boxes stuffed full of 10 × 13 manila envelopes which in turn bulged with hundred-peso bills. All four did brisk business, handing over clean copies of Hector Basbas's dignified "An Open Letter to His Excellency, President José Domínguez y García," two or three copies atop each envelope handed over to a con-gressman or senator about to answer a call of nature.

"We're being bled white," Teresa told Armand. "That damned Blackie, I'm sure, knows what kind of hole he's opened. Where's he getting the cash?"

"He doesn't have to fork over anything," Armand said. "All he has to do is stay in the palace and let us do the scrambling to get him out. He's exercising his right of eminent domain."

Teresa cursed and shoved another envelope into the shopping bag at her feet. "The presidency's not property," she shouted. "And what about the right of imminent domain?"

"Uh, yes and no," Armand corrected her. "It can be bought and sold, after all."

He'd settled himself in a soft leather armchair (also white, because Katerina had this preference for blank walls and what she called the *tabula rasa*) and was cradling the ornate white-and-gold living-room telephone on his lap. In the doorway to the dining room, the three children had lined up by height and age—Epee (thirteen years old), Inè (ten), and Marmol (eight)— and watched him intently. When Armand begun dialing, Inè moved to the white Steinway to bang out *"Chopsticks,"* Epee floated out to the balcony to shriek repeatedly (poor child, Teresa thought, her menarche was forcing her to emit these shrill bird-calls), while Marmol turned into Captain Marvel, kicking at the furniture as *whams, bams, pows* spurted from his mouth along with saliva. Armand gave up, made an ineffectual wave of his right hand, and rose to his feet. As though at a signal, the children stopped and lined up again to watch him leave, the black spears of their eyes lunging for his back.

"Don't bother your father," Teresa said aloud. "He's off on important business."

Marmol snorted, Inè giggled, and Epee brayed with laughter. What strange kids the Gloriosas had, Teresa thought and immediately castigated herself for the traitorous idea. As though divining her discomfiture, Marmol sidled up to her and pressed his face against her right arm. *What you doing, what you doing, Tita Te,* he murmured, nostrils flaring as he pulled the shopping bag close to his face.

"Oh, it smells so good," he said after a while. "So gooooood."

"It's only money."

That made the children laugh again. Teresa patted the head of Katerina's only son, remembering how the afternoon they'd returned from their year's journey, the baby had been lying in his play pen out in the yard. Katerina had handed the bird cage to Teresa, pressed a hand to her chest as though to ease a pain there, and rushed forward, scooping up Marmol, who was shaking a rattle and chortling mightily. Perhaps she had frightened him or maybe it was an accident, but as Katerina was about to lay the child against her, turning his head upward towards her shoulder, the kid had drawn back his knees and kicked. Bam, bam! Two blows, each centered perfectly on a breast. A short scream from Katerina; the abrupt drop of the baby on the (fortunately) padded pen and Marmol's toothless, wet laughter. *The beast*, Katerina had said, hyperventilating. *The twice accursed, twice blessed beast.*

Watching the kids now take an envelope each from the shopping bags, open the flaps, and thrust in their noses, Teresa had to admit that they were decidedly strange—which wasn't wholly unexpected, considering their parentage. . . . She hastily blanked out her thoughts, stabbed by the fear that the children could read her mind. Resuming her work, handing the two girls a bundle of cash to divide into the correct amounts, she had to grant that each of the three was unique, each with a rather uncanny talent which endeared them to their uncle and terrorized their mother. Inè could will herself into such immobility—on her feet, sitting down, hands over piano keys, or just leaning against the wall— for hours on end, not even blinking, not a hair ruffled by even the strongest wind, that at such moments she easily passed for a statue. One could enter a room where she was, frozen like a fossil, and not detect the slightest sign of her presence, no not even a breath's faint susurrus nor the subliminal echo of heartbeat and bloodpulse which betrayed a human being. In this manner, she eavesdropped on conversations and arguments in various houses and offices where she was visiting, accumulating a formidable storehouse of exotic facts which she would display at her uncle's prodding and for his entertainment. Private telephone numbers, who was sleeping with whom, what perversion was enjoyed by whom, who kept his servants underfed and underpaid, how much was missing in what office and where it went, what plans were afoot, who was friend and who foe . . .

Epee, on the other hand, was by all standards not handsome, favoring her uncle's features, her face gross and sullen with a lantern jaw, but she was blessed with the peculiar ability to turn a man's head, any man's head, given a moment or two of togetherness. She inspired strange affections, earning for herself surprising gifts at holidays and during her birthdays, and at parties was always trailed by a man or two, usually fifteen, twenty years her senior. They told her what they wouldn't tell mothers, wives, sisters, and girlfriends, compelled somehow to reveal their secret shamelessness. Thus, at thirteen, Epee had more than a passing acquaintance with the sexual peccadilloes of two dozen powerful officials, as well as the location of brothel houses and call girls they patronized and the particular services they required—black leather and whips, Bo-Peep dresses, lace corsets and water pistols, blond pubic hairs, nuns' habits and priests' robes . . . She and Hector had a roaring time talking about the majority floor leader, the chief of staff, the chief executive officers of the top one hundred corporations, various consuls of the U.S. embassy, the political officer of the British embassy, and so forth. Teresa, often overhearing the conversation, would feel herself overwhelmed by the tedium and unimaginativeness of such evil.

Marmol was too young to catch the attention of Hector's political circle, but that his vocabulary was no match for his intuition Teresa had known since the boy was three. Out of nothing, save perhaps an instinct lodged deep within the chaos of his primitive childbrain, Marmol could come up with a seemingly incomprehensible sentence or two, totally without bearing to whatever circumstance he found himself in at the moment, which, later turned out to be succinct, direct, and infallible solutions to the problems confronting the Basbas household. Last year, Teresa recalled, when Hector was twisting in a high wind of indecision, wondering whether the time was right for a stab at the presidency, arguing aloud with and against himself—he was too young; he was outside the power circles; he had no money; the 'Kano would back the reelection of Blackie Domínguez y García; et cetera—Marmol, who had glued two beetles back to back with chewing gum and was watching them roll over and over on the living-room floor, struggling against each other's desire to have their feet on the ground, suddenly looked up and said to his uncle: "You have to."

What? What? Have to what?

Adding, "There's no one else," Marmol bent his head back to the two beetles and, perhaps tiring of their Sisyphean fate, swatted them away with the back of his left hand. Two days later, when a formal, cold-blooded "evaluation of the situation" by the Basbas twins, Armand Gloriosa, Teresa Tikloptuhod, and a dozen of their top aides and assistants ended, Hector had to admit that Marmol had been right. The opposition had no serious potential candidate, and their moneybag clans, from sugar to mines, would finance Hector's race for the presidency, provided he could pull off the trick of disaffiliating from Blackie's party, since he was or had been (thank God no one remembered any-more) a Domínguez disciple. He, on the other hand, had no other path to tread on; if he didn't run and Blackie won a second term, the president would destroy him for his perfidy.

It was done. Hector rewarded Marmol with a very real .22 caliber silver-plated and pearl-handled revolver, the señorita, as it was called, but refused to give him any bullets until he came up with more predictions.

Teresa examined Marmol intently, wondering whether she should ask him about the latest crisis, but the kid was intently smelling the envelope of cash in his hands. "Sooo gooood," he said, raising his head and aiming the black bores of his eyes at Teresa. Then, bam! "It's what the man needs," he said, and Teresa jumped, sliding to her knees as the kid dropped the en-velope back into the bag and took off, yelling with delight at the new game.

Her fingers snagged the tail of his shirt and she drew him back, fighting his laughter and squirming. What man? What man? "The black man at the gate," Marmol screamed in glee, and as though scorched, her fingers let him go. Oh, to have an imperfect oracle was so frustrating, but as soon as he was old enough, articulate enough, he would read the palm lines of the Basbas destiny with deadly accuracy. She rose to her feet, mentally chewing over that phrase about the black man, wondering whether it referred to Blackie. She glanced through the always open front door and saw, far down the driveway, beyond the gate and across the street, a man on the sidewalk indeed, the neighborhood beggar and bum on his regular rounds of the fortress-houses of the rich neighborhood, asking for scraps of food, a coin or two, discarded clothes.

Was that it? Teresa weighed Marmol's words. The bum or the president? Was Marmol's child speech a reference to this instant or to something else, bigger, more important? The boy had run to the terrace and was calling out to someone or something in the garden. She thought of calling Armand, of asking him to help decipher the enigma, but she knew he would be locked in a back room of the Gold Cup Café with Mr. Naguchi, John Smith, and Go Pue Wan.

At such an hour, three in the afternoon, the café on what had once been considered the most beautiful boulevard in the world, following the amiable womb-shape of Manila Bay, would be forlorn, with only half a dozen men in frayed, long-sleeved shirts and carrying worn-out vinyl portfolios for customers. Such men lingered for hours, over endless free refills of coffee, scattering sugar powder on the tabletop as they negotiated deals and talked of schemes involving millions of pesos and travel to the most exotic places, only to search gingerly in their pants pockets for the two coins to pay for what they'd drunk. Armand was recognized, of course; a shudder of excitement ran through the café; three or four men scampered to their feet, hands clutching wildly at papers and portfolios; Armand walking in was opportunity presenting itself. But a nod from the brother-in-law of the president-elect—a nod and a sidling away of the eyes—telegraphed the message that he was busy, had come for a specific purpose, had no time to consider proposals, was headed for the back rooms and woe to anyone who delayed him.

Beyond the curtained doorway wedged between the men's and ladies' rooms was a separate area of cubicles the café maintained for private conferences. Each cubicle had a table and four chairs, plastic fern fronds, a telephone on the wall, paper and pencil and inner locks on the booth doors. Soundproof, safe from prying eyes, as intimate as a confessional. In the last cubicle—a wise choice, since it wasn't hemmed in and more difficult to bug— were the three men. Mr. Noguchi. One bow. John Smith. A handshake. Mr. Go Pue Wan. A slight incline of the head.

Taking his seat, Armand slipped out of his shirt pocket a tiny folded piece of paper. Before leaving his own office, Armand had written on the paper a certain amount. He held this up now to the three men's eyes. Smith whistled. Go Pue lowered his eyelids. Noguchi peered at the figures intently.

"That much?" As expected, it was John Smith (nicknamed Sunday by the locals, for his stated desire to do absolutely nothing like God on this day), Armand would tell Teresa later, since who else but the representative of the great race and nation could be expected to haggle? Whoever said that bargaining wasn't a western habit?

"This is war, gentlemen," Armand said, pocketing the paper again. It didn't do to leave evidence around, written, oral, or other.

Go Pue traded glances with Noguchi. Both nodded. Uh, uh. Armand's eyebrows rose. The two had conferred, added and totaled, considered and padded, and had come up with an amount close to Armand's. Shit, Armand thought; he should've bloated it by ten, twenty, maybe even thirty percent.

Noguchi opened his fist, pale gold fingers spreading, and a key dropped to the tabletop. He pushed this towards Armand and said, "Far East Bank." Armand picked it up, noted the safety deposit box number stenciled on its broad, flat head. But Go Pue was already sliding another key forward. "Our share," he said. "Continental Bank." Armand then looked at Sunday Smith, who'd gone red in the face and was squirming in his seat.

"No sweat, no sweat," the man said, right hand groping at his back pants pocket. "But there are other details, hey, listen, two or three things . . ."

Armand lifted his eyes to the ceiling, thinking the man just had to be garrulous, had to hang your breath a little bit, show you who's who and who's what, the son-of-a-goat bureaucrat. Truth to tell, he would say to Teresa and Katerina later, he hated this—so gross, so vulgar, so petty, when it was clear anyway what was going on and coming down. Besides which, everything had been worked out beforehand between Hector and the political officer. But Sunday was eyeing the other two, and it was obvious that some exchange had gone on among them before Armand's arrival.

"Two things, uh," Smith began again, having the grace to be shamefaced. "One, your enforcers . . . they can become a liability over time. We have a simple solution to offer. They could be recalled, uh, to the military and sent with a battalion over to the war."

Noguchi and Go Pue were expressionless, eyes hooded, conveying thereby the message that since the interests they represented had steered clear of that war, another one in Southeast Asia in which the 'Kano had embroiled himself, this was between Armand and Smith. So what had the Diablo Brotherhood got to do with it?

"Just a suggestion, just a suggestion," Smith said hurriedly at Armand's frown. "If the troops are sent—well, there's all kinds of arrangements which can be made and you can take care of that problem at one stroke. They can be a liability. We know.

We trained 'em. What we thought would be perfect is to have them train a second batch and then ship the first off. This kind of round robin would make sure Hector has fresh help always, without the arrogance of the old-timers. Fresh and hungry and therefore dependent. Obedient. Reliable. Not too cocky, not too knowledgeable, not too aware of authority . . ."

Armand closed his eyes at the unpardonable error of having Hector's name mentioned at this table. He inhaled-exhaled audibly and said that would have to be worked out between the proper—uh—individuals, when the time for such arrangements came. He was on private business here, namely the sale of next season's crop . . .

"Second," Smith said, not letting him finish. The other two looked very sharp, very interested, of a sudden.

Uh-uh. Armand swallowed his words quickly.

"We got samples from his—you know—his last physical. Cost a minor fortune, but we thought you should know. . . ." And with a delicate movement, he slid over a folded piece of paper. "In the short term, maybe it means nothing. But in the long run . . ." A shrug; a glance at the other two. "Maybe, everything. We do have to protect our investments."

Armand touched the paper delicately, with the tip of a forefinger, pressing down its lower edge so the words printed therein would be legible. Steroids. Oh, the fool. The fool. The physicians will have to be fired, he thought furiously, the damned hospital closed down. He forced himself to smile, saying, well, we'll take this under advisement, maybe the doctors or whoever pulled a scam and gave you someone else's samples. *He's* in perfect health, a physical-fitness fanatic. Doesn't smoke, doesn't drink, doesn't eat meat. . . . Illogical that this, this, should be in his blood. Ha-ha, they put one over you, man, those doctors can be clever, ha-ha.

And practically snatching the third safe deposit box key, stopping long enough to note Sunday Smith's hurried words "United Rural Bank, in the first daughter's name," he made his exit, escaping thereby the blade of their eyes unsheathed by disbelief. Still he had to admire the thoroughness with which the Caucasian saw to his deals. A rural bank would be a place Armand, who had coconut plantations, would visit, and it was natural for him to have valuables stored away for Epee.

"They're very thorough," he told Teresa and Katerina, over dinner, over the voices of the children riding the breeze from the smaller dining room. "But what do we do now?"

Katerina, eyes dreamy, smiled and said forget it; it was all a mistake, she was sure; while Teresa didn't dare look at her, thinking of the appetite depressants and diuretics which Hector was demanding, making his sister take. She was beginning to grow, Katerina was, nibbling at all hours of the day, her impeccably polished inch-and-a-half fingernails ferreting among plates and silver dishes, pushing a spoonful of *leche flan*, a handful of grapes, half an apple, a square of chocolate into the elliptical gap between her red-painted open lips. Eating, eating, eating.

4

Ten o'clock Saturday morning and all prime-time soaps over radio and television were rudely cut off to accommodate a paid simultaneous broadcast of Hector Basbas reciting from memory his "Open Letter." It was frightful expense, Teresa had protested vigorously, pointing out that her own project, a news-analysis-cum-talk show called *The Fearless Enquirer*, run by her two favorite hacks, was still going strong. Despite its being secretly financed by the Basbas campaign, it had garnered several awards for most impartial reportage, one from the Catholic Church communications center itself. "Precisely," Armand had snapped. "It's so subtle no one gets what it's supposed to say." He felt that a more direct approach was needed and ordered his assistant to set up a "dirty tricks" department. "Flood the country with caricatures of Blackie. Have him drawn as a black and ugly horse," he snapped and failed to note Teresa's sudden discomfiture. Katerina, on the other hand, was convinced that the sound and sight of Hector would sway the whole country at once to his cause. "He was always Best Debater, since elementary school," she said, soothing Teresa. "After winning, he'd challenge his opponent to trade sides and win again. He's just so good." Hector's eyes shone at the prospect of speaking to the whole archipelago, without commercial interruption, for a full forty minutes.

Therefore, there he was on television, a white wall behind him, dressed in black pants and a smartly tailored embroidered shirt whose traditional design had been altered by the master cutter of a newly opened Parisian boutique. Katerina, checking the bureaus in her bedroom for things to wrap, things to leave behind—in case the move to the palace materialized—gave the TV screen fond glances and murmured, "Oh, he's really good." Frankly, Teresa was appalled. It was so sophomoric, she said. There Hector was, insubstantial as a ghost, his arms closing and opening, index finger jabbing—point at the horizon, point at the floor, stab at the open palm of the other hand—like a high school orator at one of those perennial Voice of Democracy declamation contests sponsored by USIS.

"But what would you have him do?" Katerina asked.

"Be firm. Issue short definitive statements. The contest is won. Either this is a democracy or it isn't."

Katerina laughed. "Nothing's as simple as that." She glanced through the list of servants who would join them at the palace and who had to be placed on government payroll. "It's a pity their wages are so low," she muttered. "Why don't we put them down as private secretaries? His, yours, mine, Armand's . . ."

"All eight of them?"

"Eight of them."

Teresa swallowed her protest, not wishing to disturb Herself. Despite rumblings from Blackie about some private scandal involving Hector, Katerina was like a ship becalmed. She drifted through the Basbas house trailed by a maid with paper and pencil and pointed to this and that—her white armoire, the Baccarat glasses, matching oils of her parents drawn from old photographs—and this and that, designating thereby what was to be packed and what wasn't. The children steadfastly insisted on bringing everything, ant farm and water pistols and raggedy dolls, saying they weren't coming back. They had made a list of all their friends, their uncle's friends and enemies, evaluated their suitability as palace residents, and rejected everyone. No one else deserved to live in the palace, they declared, and therefore the Basbas family would never move out. Katerina looked at them in sly amusement, her eyes going blind with tenderness.

"How could a child of mine be so ugly," she murmured now, picking up Epee's gold-framed photo off her dresser table. There were four there, of the three kids and Hector, forming a backdrop to the jars, boxes, lipstick tubes, brushes, and powder puffs.

Teresa's eyebrows rose as the thought whipped through her mind like a snake: how a child of *his* could not help being . . . Uh. She tossed away the idea with a quick shake of her head, noting how Katerina was running the tip of her index finger over Epee's face.

"It may not be hopeless," Katerina said, after a while. "The nose can be lifted; the cheekbones made more pronounced but the jaw—oh, dear—it will have to be realigned." She fell silent and then added, in a lower voice: "Broken and realigned." She smiled, eyes downcast.

Teresa shivered. She knew she should remonstrate, should turn Katerina's mind to something inconsequential, at this very minute before the idea took root and became immutable conviction. But she dared not, knowing that in the Basbas household, Katerina rendered all judgment pertaining to beauty or the lack thereof. If she said Epee had to be, uh, rearranged, then that was it. Poor kid. She would spend months in pain, hidden in various clinics and hospitals, from Brazil to Switzerland, until Katerina was satisfied. Perhaps some good would come of it, Teresa thought; her being far away from home would help perhaps, for the child was becoming too close, much too close, to her uncle, onto whose lap she snuggled, whenever his schedule gave her the opportunity.

"We've always been so . . . like this," Katerina said, veering off on another tack, thrusting forward a clenched fist and blocking Teresa's view of Hector on the TV screen. He'd just reached that portion where he was calling for "statesmanlike behavior" on the

45

part of the incumbent, who "should heed the voice of the people," and his own voice had grown impassioned.

"We've always been like that, you know," Katerina continued. "Wrapped around some goal. Myself, Hector, and Armand. First, it was law school and the bar exams. Then an official appointment. After which came the senate. And in the last two years, this—the presidency. Armand already has a team working on the reelection. But after that? What happens? Shall we loosen? Scatter?" And she opened her fist, spreading her fingers. "I'm the only one who worries about this. About the hereafter, the beyond. . . ." She stared at the back of her right hand. "And I don't mean afterlife, either." A pause. "Of course, we could always become royalty," she said and laughed, as if to say she found that ridiculous. But in that instant, Teresa divined what Katerina meant the future to be for Epee.

Oh, poor vicious child, lost pretentious child who made a major headache of something as ordinary as a menarche. Teresa saw her dragged, sent off, to the meat markets of Europe, Asia, the Middle East, displayed in the expectation that a royal title would turn in her direction and claim her for his own. Sighing, Teresa assuaged her guilt by telling herself it wouldn't be such a bad life. If only Epee weren't so smart. . . .

"Well, at least it will give us something to strive for," she told Katerina gamely.

Katerina shrugged, picked up Hector's photo, and studied it. "He was getting old," she said. "Look at him now." In the photo, Hector was bare-chested and flexing his biceps.

Katerina set it down beside the TV set, her eyes moving from one image to the other. Her right hand crept to her belly and kneaded the flesh there. "I'll have to watch it," she said. But to defy her own fears, she went to the intercom and ordered the kitchen help to send up coffee, butter cookies, jam-jelly-and-peanut-butter. "And some cold cuts!"

From the side garden below the open windows, the children's voices rang out. Katerina stretched her neck to look. She giggled, squealed, "How cute!" and beckoned to Teresa. On the green grass about a whitewashed fountain—the same which had stood, Teresa remembered, at the plaza of her hometown's cathedral, and which had been dismantled and moved brick by brick to the Basbas residence—Epee, Inè, and Marmol were engaged in a sack race. The children had discovered and appropriated the canvas money bags in Hector's office, bags deflated by the cost of the *simulcast*, as the newspapers called it. Forty minutes of Hector yakking his head off, saying in public what could be said to Blackie in four words: "Get out of there." Or in two, if the local language was used. Teresa took her defeat in the matter badly.

A soft tap on the door and Armand entered, followed by a uniformed maid wheeling in a chrome food cart. Armand had decided to let Hector handle the broadcast by himself; it was being taped, anyway, at the Senate office, which had been transformed into a studio, with lights, cameras, recorders, and whatnot. "So as not to complicate the security requirements," he explained to Katerina. "Besides which, Hector can run circles on this producer-director. The guy hadn't even heard of belladonna to make the eyes sparkle." He snorted. "State of the art's quite primitive yet."

Instead, he'd spent the morning packing for his trip to Hong Kong. Smith, by some sleight-of-hand, had managed to arrange for new money, some ten million pesos, to be printed with neither the government's knowledge nor consent. "One disadvantage," Armand had said to the women, grinning broadly, "of not controlling your own mint and having your cash printed elsewhere." The money had been placed in a London repository which had coughed up a draft to the amount on an Italian bank which in turn rolled it over to a Spanish account which issued it as a loan to a Hong Kong–based corporation which opened an account in the original London bank and then withdrew the pesos and brought it to its vaults in Asia, where it awaited Armand's appearance. "A neat trick," Armand had commented. He was already thinking of how to prevent its being pulled on Hector four years hence, and corollarily of its being pulled by Hector. He prided himself on how the Basbas organization learned quickly, learned from extrapolation, and never made the same mistake twice.

Katerina threw him a cold glance and signaled the maid to bring in an extra cup. She hadn't liked the idea of Armand's going off alone to sit—literally, for the money was being flown in by chartered plane—atop that wealth. "Teresa should go with him, at least," she'd said to Hector. But this was man's work, His Excellency (to-be) had decided, ending all arguments, while Armand, in the flush of victory, had stuck his tongue out at his wife—but only when Hector's back was turned. Teresa couldn't help smiling at the memory.

"I'm off," Armand said, settling on the bed's edge and pouring himself a cup of coffee, not even waiting for the maid's return. "In two hours." He flicked his wrist smartly, turning up his watch's face.

"That's Teresa's cup," Katerina said.

"I can wait," Teresa intervened, forestalling a quarrel.

Katerina shrugged and pulled out a sheet of paper from the pile on the bed. "Since you'll have twenty-four hours in *that place*," she said, tossing the sheet to Armand's lap, "you might as well do some shopping for me."

A noncommittal noise from Armand as he picked up the paper. It was followed immediately by a scandalized "Four hundred! Four hundred single-strand Mikimoto pearl necklaces! *Hijo de . . .*"

"Wash your mouth," Katerina shouted back. "They're not for

me. They're for the benighted wives of the benighted Manila Stirrup and Polo Club!"

"But, Lord, woman, four hundred . . . and thirty-two dozen Charles of the Ritz makeup kits, a hundred gold Rolex watches . . . Holy bananas!"

Katerina shook a fist at Armand. "You listen, you . . . Single-strand, doesn't have to be expensive. Cheap, single-strand, so long as the Mikimoto tag's there. And makeup kits at bargain basements and Taiwan-made Rolex . . . hear that? Taiwan-made, you in your stupid London-tailored silk shirts and suits and pants and three fittings apiece for every item of . . ." She sputtered into incoherence and turned away abruptly, showing her back to Armand.

"Buy everything," Teresa hissed.

Abashed, he folded the sheet and tucked it into his shirt pocket. "Seems to me," he said in a forcibly light tone, "we can arrange it so that I don't become the shopping maid here." He picked up his cup and drained it in one gulp. A scent of dried roses filled the room.

Teresa, sighing in fatigue, pinched the bridge of her nose. Light flashed painfully behind her forehead. She had a vision of Armand in some vague future, pursued by a shrieking mob, cowering, knotting his body into the smallest ball possible in the sanctuary of a black well of shadow, not knowing he was already betrayed, had been betrayed from the first step of his flight, by the rose scent of his cells. "That'll be the death of him yet," Katerina had said once, in answer to Teresa's comment about Armand's body odor. She had no reason not to believe it.

He left without saying goodbye, and it was only then that Katerina raised her eyelids to follow his exit with a mournful look. "The doctors said I shouldn't distress myself," she murmured, half-smiling at Teresa, who nodded. Upon their return from that insane journey, Hector had assigned Katerina two psychiatrists, so she would not have to seek a second opinion, and between them, Katerina had an ample supply of tranquilizers, depressants, relaxants, sleeping pills, and amphetamines. Because it kept her tractable to some extent and enabled her to deal with the interminable and faceless crowd filling up Hector's life, Teresa's initial objections had petered out to a mild foreboding. These past weeks, though, had been a trial.

Six times now, Katerina said, she had had to move residence, the first time to Armand's decrepit ancestral mansion in the first year of their marriage. Though no amount of scrubbing could confer a pristine shine to its sanded granite floor, it had been such a still and quiet place that Katerina had not minded being there at all. But when Hector finished law school and set up an establishment of his own, he'd arranged with Armand for the couple to move in. He had no intention, he told Armand, of marrying. "What for? Women are available at all hours of the day," he'd said. He could not countenance, a partnership which required that he be on call, as it were, because he was "pursuing a grand design—which was, is, Katerina's goal as well." What that was, he'd never spelled out, but with the linking of the Gloriosas with Hector's fate, Katerina had found herself trailing the spoor of her brother's political career. The modest suburban two-story wooden house was replaced by a slightly larger three-bedroom bungalow when Epee was born. An even larger residence, with a rose garden, came when Hector assumed the post of defense secretary, and it was here that Inè arrived. When Hector ran for the senate, skipping the usually mandatory lower-house post since he already had national exposure, the demands of the campaign and his new office required even larger accommodations. Thus Marmol was born in a quasi ranch house on five acres of rolling land where party ward leaders and petitioners could gather in impromptu fiestas and barbecues. By Hector's second term, the whole family had moved to a huge instant-antique two-story nineteenth-century-type house, its lower floor of cool white marble-inlaid cement, the upper floor of pale wood and white paint, the whole place referred to as the Basbas San Juan residence to distinguish it from the Forbes Park compound of the Basbas clan. Though the houses had been progressively bigger, more sumptuous, more elegant, each move had caused Katerina pain, for there was the inevitable discarding of things accumulated, the acquisition of new odds and ends, and disruption.

She hated disruption. "To think that all we wanted, when we were kids, was to have a place of our own," Katerina said. "Peace and quiet, in a little room. Far from everyone's eyes."

Living in the clan plantation had been hell, she had admitted to Teresa, for though the two kids, age ten, were relatives, still they weren't actually of the Montelibano-Basbas branch which had taken them in. Not out of the goodness of their dried coconut husk of a heart, Katerina said bitterly, but merely to spite the Locsin-Basbas branch, who were "sugar, Teresa, but certainly not as sweet." It was direct rebuke, for the L-Bs had perpetrated a slow-motion scam on the twins' father, who was addicted not to gambling but to get-richer-quick schemes.

In the short decade the twins spent with their father, they'd witnessed not the meteoric rise but the meteoric fall of the family fortunes. It was an L-B who planted the fantasy in Hector Basbas Segundo's head of breaking the power of the Laguna Chinese-Filipino lanzon distribution network by establishing plantations of the highly desired fruit in Cebu island. One city rental block owned by the elder Basbas was duly traded for a hillside in said province. Alas, the land was more rock than soil and rain came in the form of typhoons which knocked down trees for miles around, with the exception of the banyan, which, in the moist after-storm air, extruded huge penis-shaped roots and threatened to take over everything. Another minor L-B wife drew Basbas

Segundo into investing in a steam-powered-car deal, which enterprise cost him his share of the coconut plantations. This was
followed by heavy investments in the manufacture of ramie,
envisioned to take the place of cotton in the world market. That
took away the rest of the city rental blocks, which were saved
from the auction block only by the cheap intervention of another
L-B. At this point, Basbas Segundo became frantic to recoup his
losses and went full-scale for mining schemes, oil exploration,
treasure hunting, and so forth. By the time a stroke felled him
dead, the twins were ten and living with their broken father in
the garage of their old mansion, which a bank had taken over.
It was an L-B bank, of course.

As to why Basbas Segundo never wised up to the L-B tactic,
Doña Perfidia Basbas y Montelibano, Grand Matriarch, was quite
explicit. "Vanity," she said, rapping the boy Hector on the head
with each repetition. "Vanity, vanity, vanity. Those clever ones
made your father feel clever—as if he could do anything. But
everyone knew he was a fool. A retard. The clan retard. Vanity
(*thonk*), vanity (*thonk*), vanity (*thonk*)." She forbade Hector from
tacking a Tercero onto his name, "to break the curse." On the
other hand, by taking in the twins, the M-Bs could raise their
noses a notch higher. Doña Perfidia herself had been heard to
declare to guests in her parlor that "at least, no one can say we're
not charitable."

Katerina was handed over to the *mayordoma* for training as
parlor maid while Hector became general factotum to uncles and
cousins. He polished their shoes and belts, brought them Coca-
Cola and thick cocoa after their horse rides, and suffered without
rancor the occasional knuckle rap on the head from the younger
males and the pinch on the buttocks from the long-fingernailed
women. His uncle preferred belt-stropping and administered it
liberally, as a form of exercise. Oh, the twins were better-treated
than the ordinary servant, but they were servants still, make no

mistake about it, and had to spend hours in the grip of a stuporous hunger, for Doña Perfidia was so militant about the family budget she kept an accurate count of the lima beans in the pantry.

Katerina, being female, could be said to have had an easier time, for her cousins, with the exception of the tightwad Matrimonia, tossed her no-longer-wanted clothes, underwear, and shoes, with the proviso, of course, that if they wanted the stuff back, they could have it. Besides which, she had only one major duty, which the M-Bs one and all said was really a special honor. She had to care for an invalid member of the household, someone kept in a little house down there, tucked away in a discreet corner of the yard proper, guarded over by two killer Dobermans chained to the front porch. Katerina had to bring food trays three times a day, as well as wash-wipe-powder and dress this . . . uh, *thing* . . . a boy, judging by its shrunken equipment, or perhaps a man. It was difficult to tell, for the invalid looked like an albino frog, with stiff, spike eyelashes, no eyebrows, and absolutely no forehead, only the top of a bald skull sloping back an inch above the pale gray staring eyes, *madre mia*. It was the unfortunate result of who-knew-how-many generations of first-cousin couplings—an obscene, deformed, unhuman product of aberrant genes, which was carefully hidden, for, make no mistake about it, had the plantation tenants and the town known what kind of an abomination lived among them, they would have razed the estate to the ground and hunted down every single M-B to the death. To spite their own fears, the M-Bs had turned the mutant into an icon, ensconced in a room smelling faintly of incense and candlewax, with windows shielded by Valencia lace curtains and a Persian rug on the floor. There was a legend, believed with due fervor by all M-Bs, that the family fortunes depended on the survival and comfort of this, uh, thing—and thus, against all odds, they'd kept it alive, its delicate, almost translucent skin laved twice a day with the softest Mediterranean sponge and warm, perfumed water. Once a week, resident family members gathered in the little cottage and said a whole rosary, on their knees around the oversized cradle of their unmentionable relative. At which time, of course, they also checked on Katerina's work.

As soon as Hector became defense secretary, he arranged for the escape from the Bilibid Death Row of the notorious psychopath Sonny Boy, the killer with the angelic eunuch face, who was then provided with the wherewithal to eat, drink, and fornicate to his heart's content for six lovely months. After which the grateful maniac made his way to the M-B plantation by train, bus, water buffalo sled, and finally by horse, slipped past the private guards in the disguise of a tenant farmer delivering his quota of copra, hacked the two Dobermans quietly to pieces (how, no one knew) with a machete, and then entered the room-cum-chapel and with an abaca twine garroted the creature to death before security guards emptied three M-14 clips into his torso. "That's why," Katerina said, her eyes so blank it seemed she wasn't even speaking at all, "the Montelibano-Basbas have gone down in the world. Doña Perfidia would have called Hector and me congenital ingrates."

5

His Excellency Blackie Domínguez y García shelled and munched peanuts at his press conference, grimly reminding everyone how he liked the darn things dug up, cleaned, boiled, and eaten all within the hour. "Fresh and clean," he said, "with integrity intact." To make sure they understood what he meant, he had the palace help distribute handfuls of boiled peanuts, along with glasses of white Spanish wine, to the media corps, ensuring thereby one of the strangest presidential press conferences ever, one where the music of cracking nutshells accompanied official pronouncements. Five strutting mayors from the Central Plains flanked him in the study room and swore by God and by the blood of their mothers that the voters in their territories had been terrorized, electoral registrars bought off with fistfuls of money, the votes miscounted four times—at the precinct, district, city and provincial levels—and that if the election had been clean and the opposition honest, Hector Basbas would be shown to have garnered no more than a hundred thousand votes total for their area, instead of the reported million and a half. Except for one mayor's complaint that for a democracy the country had the most primitive paraphernalia for the election process, there was really nothing new said that morning. Nevertheless, the session provided the lead stories of news broadcasts the whole day and evening and much of the headlines in the papers the following morning.

"This is cheating on a grand scale," Blackie said, voice booming over the tinkle of the crystal chandeliers shuddering from the river's warm breeze, "and we must be grateful these gentlemen had a change of heart and decided to reveal the truth."

Hector, watching the evening television broadcast, pouted. Blackie, he said, had an intolerable liking for long sentences. "An affectation. To remind everybody he writes poems. Once in a while. Only thing wrong is they're never any good." He thought for a second, turned to Teresa, and asked if she knew of any poet-for-hire. It wouldn't hurt if he were to issue a volume of chaste love poems written for Katerina, since as everyone knew, the people of the archipelago were terminal romantics. Teresa said she would see to it at once—which was by way of saying they were whistling in the wind; without spending a single centavo, Blackie had just undone the impact of Hector's simulcast.

They were not really surprised when both senate and house voted to postpone the proclamation of a winner until after Blackie's protests had been resolved by the Commission on Elections. That altered Hector's demeanor. After damning senators and congressmen for the perfidious sons-of-goats that they were, he grew very quiet and went about with the expression of a man about to implode the world. "That bastard Blackie," he said to the world at large. "What the hell did he promise them?" Back and forth in the living room he paced, anxious for a call from Armand. "Can't do anything now," he confessed wryly. "No *gasolina*. And everybody's holding still, afraid of backing the wrong horse. That bastard Blackie."

Next day's news was worse. The northern provincial governors were getting restive, holding one meeting after another, while a Muslim mayor of the south-south laid the deaths of some twenty-five Blackie campaigners on Hector's doorstep. When Hector took to the air to deny the accusation, saying that his party, being out of power, had no access to the kind of weapons needed to wage terror in Moroland ("Only a man who commands the military—or part of it—can do that," Hector had said, deftly kicking the blame back to the mayor), a snitch at the international airport spewed this little secret about a cargo of high-powered weapons brought in posthaste a few months back by a certain individual. Who? Well, far be it for him to be a gossip; however, everyone recognized former Air Force Captain Julian de Naval, of course, the top honcho of the Diablo Brotherhood, who had flown his fighter plane over the Congo and Indonesia on missions whose secrecy he had blown afterwards during marathon drinking sessions all over Manila. Blackie followed up with a promise to show actual election certificates which had been tampered with and sworn affidavits of registrars as to who had masterminded the fraud.

Endless problems.

Hector to Teresa: "Call your father." Hector to Katerina: "Track down Armand." To de Naval: "Take care of that leak." To the elegant Ricardo Martelo, Armand's assistant: "Go to Civil Aviation and make sure Armand's plane lands and *unloads* without hitch. Give 'em your ass, if need be." To his private secretary: "Call the American ambassador and say I want to discuss far-ranging policies of my new administration." To the room in general: "Shit, we'll be forced to sell everything." To ex-Sergeant Emil Emilio, second-in-command of the Diablo Brotherhood: "I want those affidavits. I want those certificates. I don't care how."

After which he repaired to this exclusive spa in the business district where he had a private lounge and to which, Teresa knew, tall, buxom, and fair-skinned women with glossy blue-black hair, all nearly identical twins, were brought occasionally to help him whom the Diablos called the Boss-Chief relax. Beauty-contest aspirants, starlets, cocktail-lounge singers—the usual preference of politicians. Long after Teresa had noted this fact, she finally understood that the women's marginal social status was part of their attraction. The explanation mollified her somewhat. Besides, it would take a unique being to gain ascendancy over Hector; or rather, to overpower the image of Katerina which commanded his fantasies, for if the truth be told, all the women (Teresa made it her business to eyeball them at one time or another) resembled Hector's twin. The eyes of one, the mouth of the other, the jawline of a third, the voice of a fourth, and so on.

The twins, strangely enough, didn't even look alike, despite the "twice blessed" phrase which surfaced constantly in news stories which she and Armand planted with great skill in the media. The oddity had certainly inspired Armand's sun-moon metaphor. Where Hector was slim, straight, and dark brown of complexion, with black hair and black eyes, Katerina was fair and, though tall, inclined to plumpness. She had amber-brown eyes, and were it not for the fortnightly ministrations of a hairdresser, two skunklocks of gray hair would radiate from both sides of her forehead. But the hair was blue-black now, a duplicate of Hector's, in which there was no silver shimmer, despite his age.

The sun-moon. Ever since Armand had laid out the stage plans before the twins, they'd taken the allusion to heart. A long, intense debate over what kind of chairs they would use was settled only by Teresa's arbitrary choice of two designs: an intricately carved nacre-inlaid high-back mahogany chair with arms for Hector and a delicate pearl-festooned white rattan peacock chair for Katerina. Both were being fashioned in the Gloriosa woodcarving guild.

Teresa was amazed that despite Blackie's public protests, a section of the Basbas organization went on working on the inauguration, as though it were an unstoppable fate, ordained by the heavens. A greater wonder was how high society proceeded in the same manner, ordering ball gowns and gifts for the Basbas twins, covertly perhaps, but doing it nevertheless. As soon as it was known that Katerina would wear Valero's clothes at the inauguration, the modest couturier was besieged with entreaties from wives of the rich. Oh, four gowns for one, three for another, while a rather ungainly Spanish wife of a real estate developer, "a closet you-know-what," Valero confided, wanted her entire wardrobe redone. Valero was overwhelmed. He waived the fee for Katerina's five gowns (all in shades of moonsheen white) and Teresa's two costumes (in royal blue, as Katerina wanted).

It was actually Valero who started the fashion of referring to Katerina as Herself, passing on the honorific with the chocolate and vanilla bonbons served to his customers in the pink-and-lavender parlor of his shop, through which echoed the raucous cries of a dozen or so combat roosters penned in the backyard. Cockfighting was Valero's vice—a strange one, he would say, for a homosexual. But, he'd amend that quickly, he was "an unconflicted faggot," easy and without agonies, which was more the pity, because as everyone knew, only the agonized attained true genius. "All I have is abominably good taste," he would say, "and I'm a good craftsman. But a real creative artist? Bosh! I'm too happy to be a genius." The fighting roosters brought him good luck, he said, balancing the too-yin essence of his clothes shop with their yang. "That's Chinese, you know."

What Teresa did know was that Valero's parlor was a disguised communications center. Information walked in and out of its doors, hand in hand with gossip, rumor, and speculation. This way, he was able to provide Katerina invaluable service, acquainting her with the current attitudes of the upper-crust women and enabling her to prepare for her running confrontations with the matriarchs and the little princesses. Katerina would not attend a major function without checking with Valero first; he had proved his worth early in the game, by advising her not to attend an annual ball of the sugar baron wives. "You'd be turned away," he'd said, "at the door, because Blackie's wife doesn't like you."

A terrible humiliation. Fortunately, on the night of the party, a fire had broken out in the city's waterfront, where the shanties of the poor huddled shoulder to shoulder. Teresa arranged for Katerina to be at the relief center past midnight, and thus it was that the front pages of newspapers that morning bore two photographs: one of the dancing sugar baron wives, the other of Herself, soot on her cheeks, embraced by a woman and her four children who'd lost everything in the fire. The Basbas retinue had gloated for weeks.

"And is it true," he asked now, the feigned innocence in his voice making Teresa sit up and look over to where three seamstresses on their knees folded and flattened and sewed on a marvelous piece of chiffon draped about Katerina's body, "is it true that the *Reina Elena* Matrimonia Basbas, your esteemed cousin, will have a seat of honor at the inaugural ceremonies from start to finish?"

"Whatever gave her the idea?" It was Teresa who answered, popping a bonbon into her mouth and garbling her words.

Katerina laughed, nudging one of the seamstresses with her knee.

"Why, it's a sure thing, she claims. The invitation's in the mail. You cannot *not* do it, she says, because were it not for her, you wouldn't"—Teresa almost jackknifed from the chaise longue to signal frantically, but it was too late—"be able to bring with you onstage a priceless, prized Basbas heirloom."

Katerina shrieked, and her body's sudden pirouette scattered the seamstresses.

"Is it torn?" Valero goggled at the women who were scrambling forward on their knees, hands groping for the gown's skirt.

"It's not," Katerina shouted. "And who cares? I'll drop a planeload of this infernal cloth on your head. Attend to me now!"

"Katerina, First Lady, Yourself." Valero picked up the silver dish of bonbons and offered it to Katerina with both hands. "Control, madame. Control is the first sign of civilization."

"What heirloom?"

"Why, a rosary." And now too late, he glanced at Teresa, who glared back at him. "Of pearls. Three hundred years old, she tells *everyone*. It's a lie, no?" He widened his eyes innocently. "I just wanted to know—because you'd assured me she wouldn't be there. I didn't want her to waste money."

"What money?" Katerina's voice ripped through the room.

"For the gowns, *hija*. She wants three gowns, and she wants them as close to the design of yours as I dared. At whatever cost. The world has to be shown, she said, your blood affiliation."

"That . . ." Katerina mouthed a filthy word.

A short silence. Valero shrugged daintily in answer to Teresa's look of anger.

Then Katerina smiled. "Accept her commission, darling. And add to her bill whatever you were going to charge me—shut up, Valero, or you're ruined—for these gowns. For Teresa's, as well. Say I said she'd be happy to pay, being my grand-cousin."

"Oh, she'll pay." Valero put down the dish. "Am I to understand then that she'll be onstage?"

"Hell, no." Katerina gave an evil laugh.

"Oh, but . . ."

"Shut up. I have to think about the rosary." She pressed two fingers against the side of her head.

"But that's no problem, is it?" Valero looked a query at Teresa, asking for her agreement.

Katerina looked in turn at Teresa, whose eyes went blink, blink. She had no idea what Valero was talking about.

"What d'you mean?" Teresa rasped.

"Oh, I . . . well . . . a rosary's not really a rare object, is it? I'm not a Catholic, but I have the impression there are rosaries galore in this archipelago. Or that it's possible to make rosaries galore."

"It's an heirloom."

"Who says? Besides, heirlooms are manufactured by the tons in Ermita. I'm sure there are many who'd be happy to lay heirlooms at your feet. Not only of pearls but . . ."

"Valero!" Teresa's hands fluttered. Too late again. A beatific light had broken out over Katerina's face.

"You are a genius," she said, extending her right arm as though to touch Valero with a sword. "You're hereby proclaimed as one."

Teresa raised her eyes to the ceiling in surrender, expecting rosaries to come tumbling down any moment now. Of onyx. Of emerald. Of topaz. Aquamarine. Ruby-red. Diamond Hail Marys. Lord, the scandal.

But Valero was entranced with his own idea. "Many, many heirlooms—which should make your cousin's heirloom nothing to brag about."

Alexandrite. Malachite. Gold beads. With thumb and index finger, Katerina picked up a bonbon off the dish and gently licked its top before placing it between her lips. Oh, sweet. Oh, good. "No one in the whole wide world will ever have such a collection." She laughed. Valero laughed. And in that instant, Teresa's heart begun to hammer so strongly she had to leave the parlor, calling out over her shoulder that she had to make a call. She sat at the antechamber desk, muttering to herself that there had to be limits; this fooling around with religious objects wasn't to her liking. It would bring them the worst of luck, the worst possible luck. . . . And the vision of herself used up and discarded by fate was so overwhelming she nearly wept.

In that instant, Hector's voice echoed in her head. "Fear," he was saying, "fear is what you have to think of. It is the single, most powerful constant among the people of this archipelago.

We're raised to fear everything. Fate, gods, the elements of nature, authority, even joy." She searched for and found the memory: Hector in one of his philosophic moods, speaking before his aides and family, even the children, at six in the afternoon, his words taking the place of vesper prayers in his home's study room. "We must separate the fear from ourselves," he said. "Let others fear, but we must never be afraid." Her breathing returned to normal, and for the life of her, she couldn't understand why she had been so angry. Rosaries, whether of plastic or pearls, were merely part of the game played in the archipelago. On impulse, she picked up the phone receiver, dialed the long-distance operator, and gave her father's phone number. It would take a while, she was told. The operator would ring back.

When the call went through, she heard her father shouting at the operator to cut it out, he was in hurry and what the hell, it would take only a few pesos to pay for the call anyway, so what was all the rigmarole about? Of course, of course. And then she was on, talking to him after nearly six months of silence.

"Well, so you remember us once in a while, don't you," he said, knowing immediately what would upset her.

The last time they'd met, at her mother's death anniversary, he'd pointedly ignored her, fussing instead over his sons and grandchildren.

"Tell Basbas he's in trouble," he went on, without preliminaries. "If he doesn't know it yet. But I—you and I—can swing something in his direction. You understand? A dozen mayors here are willing to consider backing him. Got that? Say it that way. Precisely that way. Willing to consider backing him. Not considering backing him but two steps away from it. Willing—provided they can come to a mutually beneficial agreement."

"He has to invite them over?"

"Nothing doing, no. They won't leave the region in this uncertainty. Blackie's playing for keeps; have to hand it to the old man. He's got guts. The question now is: does Hector Basbas?"

"He has to go meet them?"

He laughed. "Are you mad, child? You want to ruin him? Of course not. He and I talk. Then you go walkabout the territories of these mayors and bind them to me."

"But . . ."

"No offense meant, but your patron isn't from the region. He'd offend them with his posturing and his bragging and end up being challenged to a duel, *mano a mano*. You come. In his behalf. You speak the language, and even I have to grant it, you have an instinct for the politically just-right. And because you're a woman, no one can challenge you. On the other hand, you can bring along some real men—you understand what I mean —to resolve whatever quarrels you may encounter. Also, to dispense some favors. You know what kind of currency's acceptable here."

"But—"

"No buts. I've been a politician all my life. And in this god-forsaken part of the world. This is one instance you're lucky you're a female. But bring along your warriors, if you can find some. If not, I'll give you six of my bodyguards."

"But what about . . ."

"I'll speak to the senate president about my fee, of course. And yours, too. Don't worry about it. Move fast. Time is of the essence. And to console your *padrino*, tell him that while Blackie moves well and decisively, he doesn't have real gasoline, only promises. You understand? I'm assuming, of course, that Hector does. If he doesn't, he'll have to have it. And soon. That's all. Come visit me. If and when you have the time and inclination."

He hung up, leaving her open-mouthed. Not a word of inquiry about her well-being. She tongued a filthy word and dropped the receiver. It was so like him. Never again would such a moment come when she'd consider saying to him, "Father, I want to come home." She shrugged. So be it. He'd given her that much to bargain with, and in a world of scratch-my-back-and-I'll-scratch-yours, it should be enough. From the backyard came the intermittent crowing of Valero's champion roosters; from the parlor, peals of laughter. Suddenly, without reference to anything at all, a great sadness overcame her. She remembered her mother, how the dead woman's skirts smelled of tobacco and rose water whenever the young Teresa laid her head down on that comforting lap, during moments of confusion. She missed the old woman, wished she were still alive, were there to guide her through the madness of life. The stooped slight woman in the faded pink housedress, puffing on a foot-long cigar with lips blackened by heat and smoke, had been hard as nails. Her eyes, though, had been exact as spotlights. She had only one wisdom to her life. "Keep the granaries full," she would say. That simple admonition had built the family fortunes and molded her husband into a power. *Keep the granaries full*, Teresa repeated to herself.

When Katerina came searching for her, saying it was her turn to be fitted, Teresa begged off. She could only take so much, she said to Katerina, and heard the hysteria in her own voice. A gnome seemed to have parked itself behind her forehead and was battering her brain with a pickax, shattering her equanimity. Could she please go home for a few hours, to her own house, which she'd managed to visit, in the past four months, only long enough to change her clothes, glance through her mail, and check on the servants?

"Foolish girl," Katerina said, pinching her left cheek. "Take all the time you want—but be at the house for dinner."

In good humor, Herself strode out of the salon to the limousine parked at the curb, forgetting that Teresa hadn't brought a car.

"The maid will call a cab for you," Valero said, handing her a glass of iced water and two aspirins on a silver saucer. "A good move, girl; always opt for a longer leash. Opt for a little freedom. You have harsh masters." Chuckling, he went inside, calling loudly for a servant.

Teresa sighed.

At least there was good news that evening. A fire had broken out and gutted the international airport, burning all documents (incriminating and otherwise) within, as well as the snitch, three other men, and five women. Private air traffic had to be diverted to a smaller airfield in Cavite, which, being in the territory of a Basbas ally, ensured the peaceful arrival of Armand's plane. Nevertheless, scenes of the devastation, shown on TV, were of such stunning gore that even Hector, sitting on the white Italian leather sofa surrounded by the family, aides, and assistants, had to turn to the ex–air force captain to comment: "Shit, Naval, nine dead! That was excessive. Thorough but excessive." De Naval blushed, lowered his eyes, and looked pleased.

6

Gasolina. *Whoever had decided* that the word was adequate description for whatever inspired men, moved cars and mountains, eased procedures, and kept the world turning was wise indeed. From car fuel to alcoholic drinks, bribe money, and women-of-the-moment, from food to cash—that was *gasolina,* something certainly more than the meaning of the original word. It arrived with Armand in the quiet of a Sunday midnight, the dead hour allowing him to load unremarked two crates and a cardboard carton into a van guarded by four jeeps crammed with a dozen submembers of the Diablo Brotherhood, each cradling an assault rifle and wearing two bandoliers of ammo. While Armand found such display of weapons distasteful, he couldn't fault de Naval's precautions. The provincial governor had arrived in his black Mercedes-Benz, and as the men labored with the crates, he offered to ride shotgun—"but only to the border. I don't want to touch off a war with my neighbor." Armand nodded. The governor then pointed to a dark mass at the horizon, the shadow of a low-slung hill outlined by stars.

"A reservation," the governor said. "Lying fallow."

On the road, as they passed comatose houses whose residents knew enough to ignore the midnight rumble of vans carrying bales of marijuana to and crates of imported cigarettes from the airport, the governor said he knew exactly how to make the watershed reservation profitable. "Logging, first," he said, thin wisps of smoke from a hand-rolled cigar following every gesture of his right hand. "Once cleared, the land can be terraced and flattened for an exclusive housing subdivision. The way we have babies in this place, it's a hundred percent guaranteed. Manila will overflow soon and that"—the cigar glow was aimed at the horizon—"will be prime real estate, with an amazing view of the bay. But it's public land, of course." He looked at Armand with mild eyes.

The governor had foresight, Armand would grant to Teresa later; but being as astute, Armand could only give vague promises, prefacing his statements with as many clauses as he could manage, leaving them unfinished and letting the governor interpret them as he pleased. "It is an art," he said, "which you should learn, Teresa. You're too direct. You have to give people the chance to construct their own hopes."

By the time the caravan nosed into Manila's southern border, the governor was thanking Armand profusely, insisting that the latter promise he wouldn't hesitate should further services be required and so forth and so on, because truth to tell, one's thoughts had to turn to something legitimate sooner or later. "Never fails," the governor complained good-naturedly. "Open a new line of business, make a little money, and overnight, you've got half a dozen competitors." His most profitable enterprises were being threatened by several marijuana plantations set up in Palawan island and the Cordillera range, while along the un-patrolled shoreline of Quezon, smugglers' coves were mush-rooming. "You wonder sometimes why we're so good at aping others," he said, laughing. Unfortunately, until something equally injurious and as easy to vend as cigarettes and marijuana came along, he was stuck. He laughed again and waved his farewells at the Diablos as Armand transferred to the third jeep's front passenger seat.

Wouldn't do, Armand said to Teresa later, would it, for him to be in the lead vehicle had they run into an ambush?

Storing the crates was a problem, as each was the size of a medium-scale freezer. Hector's desk in the study room had to be jammed against the wall to make room for one crate. The second was installed in the kitchen storeroom, whose door had triple locks. A smaller box, containing the items on Katerina's shopping list, went to the children's den, for lack of space. It stayed there forgotten for almost a week, next to a pile of Inè's music scores, until Katerina discovered that the three children had pried the staples off its top with a screwdriver and had burrowed among the packages. Epee had laid out about a hundred pearl necklaces on her bed and, stripping herself naked, had rolled over and over them, gaining nothing for her efforts but red marks and bruises. Marmol dismantled four necklaces, slipped the unstrung pearls into his pockets, and used them in a game of marbles during recess at school, nearly precipitating a heart attack in a teacher. Inè was more circumspect, merely taking six watches and jamming them about her slim ankles, three on each. She managed to convince her schoolmates that they were the latest in Paris fashion. Katerina was livid.

It was all straightened out eventually, and Teresa thought the whole household breathed a little easier, particularly when half of the contents of Crate #1, as Hector referred to what had been stored in his study room, had been neatly divided and stashed into plastic shopping bags. "Take one each," Hector told de Naval and two Diablo aides who'd been helping with the work. "Before you even begin. One each. But that's all." Oh, yes, sir; yes, sir. The men beamed, rubbed their hands together, and thanked His Excellency (to-be, for sure) extravagantly. Hector laughed, clapped de Naval on the back, and said: "Shoot anyone who takes a second bag. Including yourself."

Well, isn't that nice, Katerina said in disgust when Armand, nibbling at the now ever-present snack cart in his wife's bedroom, praised Hector's profound insight into human nature. She kicked a pile of soiled underwear out of her way and marched without a by-your-leave into her twin's bedroom, catching him trimming his nose hairs. Without preamble, she let loose with a tirade about how men were simply like that, patting one another's shoulder, rewarding each other while taking women's work for granted. "Teresa and I wore our fingers to the bone," she shouted. "Counting, wadding, stuffing. Next time don't even bother calling us."

"Oh, hey!" Hector raised his hands in surrender.

"And it had been such a beautiful morning," Katerina said and was suddenly silent, for that at least was true. She'd been awakened by a touch, a subtle caress, it seemed, of fingertips upon her cheeks. She'd opened her eyes, smiling. Except for the scent of frangipani blossoms seeping in through an open window, the room was empty. Nevertheless, the feeling had remained with her, this certainty that something important was coming her way.

She could take a bag, two bags, what did he care, Hector was saying, there was no need to upset herself over such trivia. "Isn't all this for you, for Epee, for the others? You think I like it? If it were only up to me, why, I'd be happy with a small office and a lawyer's shingle. . . ."

She looked at him with disappointment. When did he begin to lie to her, she wondered. It was almost grotesque to remember now that once upon a time, they had opened their eyes at the exact same instant in the morning, hands immediately groping for the other's hands, so that their first awareness of the day was that of their fingers entwined, of hands steepled together, negating the somber damp of the pale gray room beyond the kitchen to which they'd been consigned by Aunt Doña Perfidia. Compared to the memory of that room, this house, with its seven bedrooms, three study rooms, two guest rooms, living, dining, breakfast rooms, its front and back porches, its balconies and azoteas, was

a veritable palace, the same as all the other houses (except one)
Katerina had lived in. But why, she asked herself, an ache knotting itself in her head, did space grow smaller and smaller over
time; why did space itself press in upon her even as the demar-
cations of what the Basbas twins owned and controlled expanded
continually, geometrically? She would have to think about this,
find the time to pursue the thought before it was lost the way all
her thoughts were lost in everyday details.

Hector was saying, "Take three bags, four . . . take half a
crate . . ."

He'd learned to lie to her with a straight face. A lawyer's
shingle, indeed. Irritated, she slammed the back of her right
hand against his taut belly. "I'll take what I want," she snapped.
"Don't you go telling me what I can and can't have."

"Within limits," he said quickly. "Within limits, of course.
We're still subject to . . . you know. I'm a politician, dependent
on votes. As yet. But soon. Soon. Be patient. . . ."

Et cetera, et cetera. She sat down at the vanity and tucked a
straying hair strand back into her coiffure. Not too bad, she
thought, staring at herself in the mirror. The nose was pert but
the eyes were beginning to be shadowed, the flesh underneath
swelling faintly. Her chin—was it sagging? She thrust her jaw
forward, feeling with her left hand at the soft flesh on both sides
of the esophagus.

"Putting on weight," Hector declared, confirming her fears.
"You have to watch it. Can't have you heftier than I am. How
would we look side by side? And those cameras add ten pounds
at least!" He turned to eye his body sideways. "Whatever happened to that official portrait?"

Her lips pulled back. She inspected her teeth—large and
square, clear white. Behind her, Hector was combing his hair
and grumbling about the Diablos. They were costing too much,
he said, but were only about sixty percent effective. True, they

got the airport but they couldn't locate the proofs, Blackie's proofs, despite several discreet raids on the other campaign headquarters. Done at dawn, Hector said, when fatigue rendered everyone just that much more careless. "We need to see what Blackie's got," Hector went on. "Can't underestimate the man, you know. He's been around a long time."

"The last of his kind," Katerina agreed, echoing a familiar sentiment. The Basbas campaign had worked out a propaganda line, not far from the truth, which had been subtly nurtured until it had become the dominant idea of the entire election, providing the codicil by which the two candidates could best be understood. Blackie was the hothouse politician, a traditional gentleman-leader with a firm base among the clans and with a family political heritage. The Domínguez y García family were political animals, having been in public service for over a hundred years. Hector, on the other hand, was the upstart, a maverick, young and modern, independently clawing his way through the political maze of the archipelago, acquiring his power base through marriage (that was Herself with Armand) and the favor trade, and expanding his economic base through public corruption. The scenario was a mix of half-truths and lies; had anyone bothered to think seriously about it, he would have understood immediately that Hector couldn't have reached this stage without backing from the clans. But for some reason, no one did, and his six years as a Blackie protégé faded beside the ferocious campaign mounted against his former mentor.

The genius of the propaganda line lay in its simplicity and, as Teresa pointed out, its archetypal characters. She'd explained it all detailedly to the Basbas family and was thus surprised when the twins and Armand swallowed the thing whole and began to see themselves within its context. She had to shake her head ruefully, noting the dangers of fudging around with myth and reality, and accepted that this was what happened in the world of politics. She'd tried to warn Katerina, who had ended Teresa's tirade with an abrupt "What do you care? It's to our advantage, isn't it? Blackie's traditional; we're modern. Hell with it."

Teresa's reply—"So what's postmodern?"—came to Katerina now as a twinge of anxiety. To deflect her fears, as Hector had taught her to do, she picked up a bottle of cologne off his vanity desk, took a sniff, and abruptly sprayed the mirror. "Terrible stuff," she said. Musk. Civet-cat musk. Heavy, cloying. Why men believed it to be a pheromone she couldn't say. Perhaps it had a testicular smell. She gave a brittle laugh and was surprised when Hector joined in. She caught the tail end of his words and realized he'd been talking about Blackie's campaign manager and the Diablos' attempts to get to him.

Everything had failed, including the six-foot-four German blonde brought in from Hong Kong, a woman with such fierce blue eyes, muscled arms, and huge mammary glands it was all de Naval could do to keep himself from drooling on her spike heels. The ex-captain, who was short and slight of chest, had a fetish for Valkyrie types, and since Blackie's campaign manager looked like de Naval, it had been assumed he would have the same taste in women. The "tender trap," as the Diablos not unexpectedly coded their plan, suitably baited, caught de Naval instead. It was pitiful to watch him try to control himself, to suppress his impulse to howl, pant, and throw himself with tongue lolling at the blond German's feet as soon as she appeared. She was so big, so tall, so huge, it was only a matter of days before de Naval began demanding that he savor the bait as well, and worse, have her exclusively.

"De Naval's an idiot," Katerina said. "I would've sent a fifteen-year-old virgin."

Hector's eyebrows lifted. "Oh, you know nothing about it," he said.

"Don't I," she said, smirking at herself in the mirror. "I was

a fifteen-year-old virgin. You're as much an idiot as de Naval."
She rose to her feet, balancing the weight of her hips on her feet
grimly. Ten pounds extra, even twenty—she was tall enough to
get away with it. But more? Uh-uh. "Blackie's people are way
behind you all in decadence. Give the man a virgin."

Hector sighed. "I'll tell the captain."

"And you'd better start thinking of what you'll do with that
bunch afterwards," she said, stopping Hector from walking to the
bathroom and thereby evading her. "First we had two Diablos,
then ten, and the ten recruited ten more. We'll have a whole
army if we don't watch it."

He demurred. "Never know when we'll need an army."

"You'll have an army when you're president. And an air force,
navy, police . . . What will you with the Diablos?"

"Leave it to me."

"No. Come up with a plan now—or I will."

His chin went up. "I'm the president, remember?" he said.
Then, mildly: "Oh, I've been studying the problem. I'm going
to create a postal police. And hide them there."

She had to grant him the cleverness of the solution, she said
to Teresa afterwards. A postal police, with practically unlimited
authority to make raids, seize property, conduct investigations.
"It'll be the only postal police in the world with enough weapons
to launch a war," she said, amused.

"They should have a communications room," Teresa said,
joking. Sometimes it was difficult to take the twins seriously.

"That's it! With radar, bugs, mikes, wiretaps! Oh. State of the
art. Donated by Japan. We'll listen in to everything." And she
hustled Teresa off to the living room, where His Excellency's
"inner cabinet," as he called it, was gathered.

In the days to come, they would be grateful for this impromptu
assembly. It gave Hector the chance to set down, concisely and

succinctly, their guide to action, so that when he disappeared, the organization continued to function though bereft of his guidance. Automatically perhaps, without enthusiasm, but act they did, keeping at bay, Teresa thought, the wolves at the door, the tigers at the windows. Had they faltered for a single moment, their enemies would have torn them to pieces—figuratively speaking or maybe not—and they would've become truly the orphans they felt at the time. Years later, in a foreign land, unpacking and making an inventory of all that she had managed to snatch from disaster, Teresa would recall this moment and her eyes would water when she thought of how magnificent, decisive, and iron-willed Hector had been.

He looked tired—all of them undoubtedly did—as he stood beside his mahogany desk and surveyed "his men." They were going to the people, Hector said once the assembly was complete. Armand with two aides; de Naval and two aides; Katerina and Teresa. Nine all in all, nine men and women to stop Blackie's offensive and make certain that the power which Hector held but tenuously at the moment remained in his hands. "We'll take our case straight to the nation," Hector declared.

To which effect, Teresa was to do a grand tour of the north, accompanied by four Diablos.

"Two cars then?" Teresa asked, already scribbling in a her little notebook.

"Don't be silly. Hire a helicopter. And three light planes. Six- or seven-seaters. One for Armand. You go to sugar and coconut, since you speak their language. One for Katerina . . ."

"I can't go without Teresa."

"You will. De Naval will go with you. You go south."

"Muslim land, too?"

"Yes. They won't kill a woman. Load up on guns. They're street money over there. Now, I—I will do the Central Plains."

He looked at them, letting his eyes rest on each of their faces for a split-second. "We each contact the mayors, governors, and military commanders of the areas we visit. I need their support. Give them what they want; promise them everything. But I need their commitment. On paper." His lips pursed towards a carton before a bookcase. "Over there are copies of a petition to Blackie, calling on him to concede and avoid unrest, instability, and bloodshed. I want everybody's signature on this petition."

"You're kidding. That's only paper. No one will take it seriously." Armand said.

"We'll have to make sure they do," Hector said, frowning. "Being newcomers"—Teresa winced at the phrase—"we have some convincing to do. We have to make people believe we'll plunge this whole nation into chaos before we give up what is ours. If we manage this at this time, then we won't have to do anything else hereafter. All we'll have to do is bluff and threaten and everything, everyone, will fall into place." He sighed.

"Blackie's had four years on us," de Naval said. "And before that—so many years of politics. Prewar, during the war, after the war. Plus his family's history."

"We have to be excessive," Hector said, "like our captain here." He sighed again. "I don't like excess. It's messy and leaves loose ends. But for now, it's unavoidable."

"We'll run into major PR problems here," Teresa said.

"Deny!" Hector barked the word out. "Deny everything. If they say your grandmother's name is such-and-such, deny it, though your grandmother be staring you in the face. Firm, absolute denial. Force the other to doubt his eyes, his ears, his own mind. Confuse him and you can create your own reality. Do you understand?"

"What about the media?" Katerina asked.

Hector laughed. "Sometimes, dear sister, you can be pedestrian. But you will dazzle them, my twin. Dazzle and blind them and force them to see only you. So the rest of us can function freely."

"How?"

"Oh, be inventive. A scandal. Gossip. Armand having an affair." And here he laughed long and hard, so that the assembly was obliged to titter while Armand flushed. Hector wiped his eyes and swallowed the tail of his amusement, his lips working. "Have a miscarriage. Or turn Inè into a prodigy. Or . . ."

"I'll be the town fool?"

"Only for a while, only for a while. Then maybe we can drop all this pretense and be what we really are."

Which was—what? Teresa found she could not complete the thought.

"What happens," Katerina blurted out, "if we become what we pretend to be?"

Hector was genuinely surprised. He studied his sister and then shrugged. "So much the better," he said after a while. "It won't be such a strain anymore."

Only then did they realize how the fight had drained, was draining them; how Hector kept himself and them together by the sheer force of his will. They looked at him, he looked at them, and Teresa felt the circle lock into place. This was the world now and all outside was illusion.

"Go work out the details," he said. "We have barely a week before COMELEC meets. I want the petition signed; and I want those who signed to understand that we won't let them back out. We'll kill first before we allow them to betray us." He exhaled audibly. "Maybe we won't have to; maybe we will have to. No matter. As long as they're convinced we will." He hesitated. "There was something else. What was it?"

It was the official portrait, and though Teresa argued that that was impossible now, Blackie would never, never allow them into the palace grounds, Hector was adamant that it be done. Katerina seconded her brother and listened as Teresa called the palace social secretary, the protocol officer, and Blackie's private aide. It was no use; no one dared take the responsibility of allowing the Basbas people in. Katerina, exasperated at last, yelled for Inè to come up to her bedroom, and once the child appeared in the doorway, demanded the number of Blackie's private line. The girl rattled off six digits, her eyes hot with pride and contempt —was contempt, Teresa wondered, the children's strongest emotion?—and whooping with laughter, turned around to fly downstairs.

"I don't believe it," Teresa said.

Katerina, ignoring her, picked up the phone and dialed. In two seconds flat, she was talking to Blackie, saying, well, Señor Mr. President, there's this problem, we all know, between you and my brother, but this thing's men's work, men's disagreements, whereas "myself, as Hector's twin, can only attend to minor things, being a woman and concerned with the unimportant . . ." and so on and so forth, for ten minutes nonstop, not allowing Blackie the chance to cut in abruptly with a negative. When she replaced the receiver, Katerina had a bemused look. She told Teresa to ready everything; they would be allowed inside the grounds—only the grounds—by the morrow.

"What did he say?" Teresa asked, breathless.

"He said he was a gentleman," Katerina replied, frowning. "And that prevented his being rude, even to monsters." She licked her lower lip. " 'Be here at eleven,' he said, 'tomorrow. You'll have exactly two hours for your fairy tale.' He said." She bowed her head and considered the tips of her shoes for a second. Then: "His wife—what does she like?"

"Antiques, from what I hear. She collects antiques from all over the country. They have an old house, of which she's very proud. She comes from an old family line, pre-Hispanic chiefs, it's said."

"I shall own the oldest house in this country, Teresa, mark my words. I shall own the best, the most astonishing, the most recent, antiques in the whole wide world."

Teresa laughed. "Whatever for? Money's a better investment."

"So that one day I can offer all of it, everything, house, furniture, collection, everything, to Blackie's wife—for free, provided she grovels at my feet." She sighed, exhausted by her anger. "I wonder when this will end."

"Or how." Teresa shrugged and began gathering papers off the bed.

"Don't tell Hector," Katerina said quietly. "He might kill Blackie. Don't say anything. I'll take care of it myself."

Teresa threw her a black look. Secrets had a way of coming out in this archipelago, Teresa thought as she hooked her handbag strap over her shoulder. Births and deaths, loves and feuds . . . everything. She could bet that Blackie was even now bragging about Herself's discomfiture, not understanding what inspired the twins to murder. At the foot of the stairs, she found Epee, hair disheveled, wearing a loose dirty housecoat and sobbing her eyes out. In near-incoherence, the girl said she wanted to go with her uncle because she knew enough. Enough.

"Like what?" Teresa asked, ringing for the nanny to take the child to her room.

"Smith's stupid," the girl said. "It's possible to increase money without actually increasing money."

"Oh-ho! An economist." That was Armand, holding an empty overnight bag for dusting in the kitchen. "And how do we do that?"

"Same serial number," Epee snapped and broke out into a thin, high wail at her nanny's entrance. She flung herself at Teresa, saying something was going to happen, she knew it, just knew it, knew it, and for a few minutes, there was a ruckus as the nanny shushed and tugged and pulled and the girl clung with all her strength.

"Not a bad idea," Armand said, after peace was restored and Epee was led away. "Should make a note of it. And are we on, is it true, for tomorrow?"

Teresa nodded. Someone had turned on the TV set in the parlor and Blackie's voice was coming in strong and unequivocal. The election, he said, had been compromised and couldn't be taken seriously.

Armand, glancing towards the sound, snapped a foul word in its direction and, turning to Teresa, said: "Come help me choose what I'll wear for the photo."

Teresa could congratulate herself the following morning, when the caravan of two stretched limousines (one white, one black), three patrol jeeps, and one van stopped before Gate #4 of the palace. Two guards, already sweating though it was only ten o'clock, saluted the lieutenant colonel in the lead jeep and drew back the wrought-iron gates without hesitation, causing Teresa's heart to give a skip. They were in—past two low buildings which housed the presidential bureaucracy (social secretaries, speech-writers, information officers, and assorted hangers-on), beyond the front gardens to the inner residential section, which was set apart by another low wrought-iron fence, a guardhouse, a gate, and an air of isolation so intense that beyond the demarcation between the compound's public and private wings, all noise turned mute and only the rustle of the wind among trees and shrubs could be heard.

The caravan nosed into the crescent-shaped driveway looping up from Gate #1, opened only during state events, to the moon-sheen facade of the summer retreat of Spanish governor-generals now long gone.

From the black limousine stepped President-elect Hector Basbas, his body unfolding into that familiar ramrod-stiff posture (head high, shoulders back, stomach in). With a swift arching glance, he scanned the grounds. He wore a translucent shirt of the palest pineapple fiber cloth with the presidential seal embroidered on its left breast, black pants, and black shoes.

From the white limousine stepped Katerina Basbas Gloriosa, formal and—by her own estimate, conveyed to Teresa—regal in a pale rose tailored suit with a modest hemline and black patent-leather high heels. She was followed by Armand in a white silk long-sleeved shirt and brown pants; daughters Epee and Inè in identical pink lace dresses, white socks and white shoes; and son Marmol scowling over a blue bow tie and starched white shirt.

The twins may not have looked alike but that they did think alike was obvious in their simultaneous pivot towards the palace, by the double rise of their noses towards the fluted roof, as though they were peering at an invisible pennant hailing them from an upper window. After a second of hesitation, Armand joined them at the driveway's curb and looked up as well.

The rest of the entourage, mystified but respectful, waited out what seemed to be an eternity of instinctive obeisance. Nothing moved, except for the leaves of the compound's trees, which were busy swallowing traffic noises, children's cries, a hawker's pleas.

When the three turned around, Teresa barely resisted the impulse to cross herself. They wore identical expressions: a loathing so profound it slammed against her chest. She would swear later that this was when the twins acquired the ability to lower the temperature of their environs by as much as ten degrees. And the same moment when she herself, Teresa Tikloptuhod, who asked for nothing more of fate than her fate realized, acquired a sense of time so acute that she began to be able to unravel the future from the skeins of the present. Much good it did her, since no one listened, anyway.

How to sit the Family, with its two heads (Hector and Armand;

or Katerina and Hector?), had been the subject of an intense discussion between the photographer and the protocol officer the night before. Finally, they had agreed that though the Gloriosas would be, by default, the First Family, still they were not the equal of Hector's own wife and children (if he ever had them) and officially at least could not occupy seats at the same level and of the same design as his.

Thus on the half circle of the front lawn, a lawn whose apex was speared by a flagpole, a transparent plastic sheet had been spread. On this, at the center, was a high-back mahogany chair, simple and yet elegant, which would not draw attention away from the person sitting on it.

His Excellency would take the chair and the Gloriosas would be seated at his feet: Katerina to his right, Armand to his left, bookending the children, who would be in front. Such an arrangement would satisfy protocol and still be symmetrical, formal, symbolic, and pleasing to the eye.

The photographer gave a thumbs-up signal and went behind the camera, now set on its tripod. It was perfect. Basbas in the chair; the children on the grass between Armand and Katerina; the plastic sheet invisible; sunlight slanting gently through the trees as though a gate in the sky had opened; the palace in the background and the flag waving overhead. Such intensity, the photographer whispered, smiling momentarily at Teresa; look, look. Such energy. Such singleness of purpose. Like a statement: *Deal with us if you dare.* No wonder they won.

Teresa, listening to the man ranting under his breath to himself, wondered what the hell he was talking about. All she could think of, as she watched the Family, was that Hector and Katerina were home at last. Finally. Only the presidential palace could have contained the twins.

7

When she left her father's house, Teresa Tikloptuhod was prepared for a one-way journey, without regret, she might well have added as she shook the dust of her birthplace off her shoes. At the time, she already knew there was nothing much else the province could offer her, and when she discovered, upon arrival in Manila, that rural warlords from all over the archipelago were building or had built their own forts in the city, she was gratified. She felt herself to be part of an insidious assault on the metropolis and its almost exclusive control of both history and modern times, with its airports and docks open to the world, its horizons bristling with buildings and neon, and its gallows-like electric posts which enabled residents to enjoy the most recent of conveniences. The assault was the more successful for its being unremarked, and she relished the secret belief that the city was losing its homogeneous character as a preserve of urban folks. Unfortunately, the pleasure did not last long; as the migration of the rich proceeded, so did that of the poor, and in both the central district and the peripheries of the city, the mushroom-pale shanties of desperation sprouted with breathless fecundity. She began to feel she was dancing on grounds which cracked slowly and inexorably with seismic tremors occasioned by the weight of the human mass pressing in on the city. She had moments of rage when visions of massacres comforted her. Because that was politically unwise, she kept her disgust at the explosion of humanity about her a secret.

Six months after she and Katerina surfaced in Manila, her father had come to visit, having made an appointment first, as was proper, through Senate President Hector Basbas, in whose house Teresa stayed.

Grinning with satisfaction, the Governor brought his daughter a dozen hand-rolled cigars and an intact ribside of pork, cured and deep-fried, wrapped in waxed paper, "just in case Teresa was pining for her hometown's specialty." He'd then spent two hours lecturing her on the need to protect and affirm the family plans. Nothing, said he, could be done in the name of and by an individual in the country, there was no escaping that, life here being so ambiguous, inexact. Resources and loyalties had to be pooled, so that in the interminable scraping of this or that family's interests against another's, a person may have protection and defense. There was no helping it; having sprung from a motley of tribes, the nation was governed still by the old ways of pacts and alliances, of fealties and obligations, remember that word *please*. "The only thing we don't do anymore," said the Governor, "is the blood compact."

Though she felt him to be wrong, she also knew he was right and for that reason did not argue. Blood was blood, he went on, and so forth—and what the hell, for whom was she laboring, anyway, since she was unmarried, had no children, and, chances were, would never build her own family line, so sorry. "Let's be blunt," he said, "since you're not a stupid female." He stopped long enough to spit on a rosebush guarding the entrance of the Basbas garden kiosk. She twitched away but he pulled her back, catching the right sleeve of her dress.

He disapproved of her stay at the Basbas house; it placed him under obligation to the Senate President. On the one hand, because this Basbas was shaping up to be a formidable politician, that was okay; but on the other, he liked to make his own alliances. So, he would build her a house, though the north would always be home, not in the same area as the Basbas residence, heaven help the cost of it, but elsewhere, not far away, still in the city. Teresa granted the wisdom of this but was perverse enough to insist that her house be of bamboo, with wicker and rattan furniture.

"People will think we're poor," her father had exploded.

She wouldn't budge. She hated the instant adobe bungalows copied from the California model, and she knew of an architect willing to experiment. If she was to have a house, much as she resented the thought of being trapped that way, it might as well be to her liking. She was a simple person and that was that. After a while, when it became clear she would not change her mind, he agreed, handing her a bank draft for a not-so-modest sum. That was how her house was built and how she lost her claims to the family fortunes, for the Governor extracted in return her quitclaim to her mother's legacies. Six months after the work was finished, the Governor was gratified to find out, through Manila magazines which had traveled northward, that it was considered a marvelous innovation, a study in the grace of bamboo, which, properly treated, turned out to be stronger than steel. "I built it for my daughter," he told the reporters in his province.

This was Teresa's HQ, as Hector referred to it teasingly, though after the housewarming party, no one was invited back ever. Teresa kept a household of four servants and five fierce dogs, a growing collection of Ming and Tang Dynasty porcelain, and, discreetly, a ward or two—girls from far-off provinces, orphaned either by parental death or neglect, who stayed for a few months and then were sent out to the world. In the interim, they were trained rigorously in service and gave her a bonus pleasure. She soon became known as a source of perfect housemaids.

It wasn't noticed how she was building, through the maids, her own modest network within and among the rich, and in an embassy or two—though for what, she herself couldn't say, as she had absolutely no ambition. Through the years, she had entertained an idea or two about her Future, but somehow, her father's Perfect Question, one he constantly asked of any proposal for a new enterprise, had stymied her each time. What for? he used to ask. She was studying painting? What for? Was there money in that? Discrete numbers? What for? A campaign to popularize bamboo? What for? She soon grew used to gauging instantly and first of all the cash value of any undertaking; in the end, because she had all she would need, could ever need, a sense of futility dulled her interest. She maintained the mission of training housemaids but resisted her father's advice to turn it into a business. That he did himself, financing a School for Perfect Domestics in his province, whose graduates, he claimed, despite the school's rocky start, would become a nifty export item, mark his words; the time would come, what with the birth rate and land accruing to fewer and fewer families, and so forth, when there would be no recourse except to send out all surplus human beings. Teresa shrugged, allowed him to recruit two of her own trained servants to run the school, and promptly forgot what her father called a monument to her acumen.

But she had returned to his house a half-dozen times since, for holiday reunions and celebrations, for consultations, since as Hector was borne away by the horse of his presidential fate, he trusted her more and more to keep the restive north on his side of the fence. Though he viewed her as essentially his sister's, he was not averse to helping himself to the resources Teresa commanded.

To Katerina, she was family—her one shield and one victory against the importunings of Hector's Diablos and Armand's "technocrats," young men of impeccable lineage and graduates of overseas business and law schools. Teresa was not unaware that both Hector and Armand chided Katerina for her choice of an awkward and, let's face it, downright ugly rural lass as administrator, but with time, they learned that Teresa was efficient, did not panic, and asked for little. "She has no ego to subvert her sense of duty," Armand once said to Katerina, in grudging respect, which words his wife took to heart, often taking liberties with Teresa, even with her self-respect, on the theory that the latter had none to damage. Teresa let all that pass because, truth to tell, she enjoyed the importance which her association with the Basbas twins conferred, enjoyed even the whispered mockery of voices which baptized her as being "twice blessed," meaning she was in the favor of both Hector and Katerina, trusted and used by the two. She enjoyed the sudden tension in a room when she entered as though she carried invisible weapons. At such times, she felt herself come into her own, no longer a stranger and almost a member of the inner circle. Besides which, wrack her brain as she might, she couldn't find any goal for herself which she could pursue with the same obsessive passion as the Basbas twins felt for Hector's career.

Today, the dogs patrolling her yard had been caged and the maids were packing her clothes while two Diablos stood beside a car parked behind her own car in the driveway. The presence of strangers was so unusual that the servants, including two wards of the moment, were subdued, not raising their eyes from their work. Teresa calmly finished the list of chores for the *mayordoma*, shoved cash into an envelope for the household expenses, locked her safe and her bureau drawers, and warned everyone never to forget to turn on the security alarms while she was away. She gave her living room, with its coordinated wicker and brass furnishings, its twelve priceless paintings and six small antique jars, a last look. Who knew when—or if ever—she would see it again? The question was a cold whip of wind; she became aware that the house built on a whim had become a home, a sanctuary, and that she would miss it grievously, painfully; miss its four perfectly designed bedrooms, its cozy study room, its master bathroom with the black-and-white tiles and sunken bathtub, its little breakfast room where she could unwrap and light a cigar while having coffee and calling forth from the sleep-fogged continents of her mind images of her childhood meant to ravish her with nostalgia; would miss it years from now when she was pinned down, immobilized, disgraced, and exiled in a foreign country.

But what, she wondered, would she be doing overseas?

She shook off the sadness and boarded the Diablos' car. One of the men seated himself in the front passenger seat, beside the driver; the other, beside her, in the backseat. Hector, for some reason, had feared for her safety—which was hogwash, Teresa knew, as Blackie wouldn't dare anger the north by killing a northerner and a woman at that. Besides, Blackie had no track record for murder. Indeed, he was considered by many still too soft for politics, since it was known that his older brother had been the anointed as far the Domínguez and García families were concerned. Only the brother's unexpected death from a heart attack, precipitated by a fishbone lodged in his throat, had caused Blackie's instant conscription as professional politician. But Hector had decreed that Teresa should be so guarded, and thus, with the men, she rode in silence to the domestic airport, where a helicopter waited with its load of *gasolina*. The aircraft wasn't a small one, she discovered when they arrived. The Diablos had managed to pry one of the air force's latest acquisitions off their military contacts. The first stop, obviously, would be her father's house.

After forty airborne minutes, interrupted by a hysterical radio call from Katerina, who'd misplaced some documents, they spotted a circular patch of red earth behind the town hall. They landed perfectly. No dust cloud rose to protest the aircraft's weight, since the ground had been lightly sprayed with water. Despite experience, the soldiers of the north feared each aircraft landing, half expecting a catastrophe and everything to burst into flames.

San Custodio, the Diablo team leader, was the first to disembark. He accepted the constabulary commandant's greeting and signaled his men to spread out and inspect the two cars and three jeeps awaiting their arrival. The Diablos' fanning out unnerved everyone, and even the commandant muttered hastily that they were loyal, loyal, ma'am—to which Teresa replied with an apologetic shrug. San Custodio ordered two Diablos to ride with her in the white Toyota while he boarded a patrol jeep with his aide. The other vehicles, he told the commandant, could go before and after, as shields. No one argued.

Under her father's rule, the province had acquired a harried look, with clusters of new two- and three-story buildings seemingly dropped, full-grown and gleaming, from the sky. They appeared alien among rickety low wooden structures and warehouses stained almost black by smoke, their rusting corrugated iron roofs bloodied by the sun. The streets showed the same haphazard and whimsical evolution: a dirt road would suddenly straighten out into a cemented four-lane highway and just as abruptly disintegrate into naked earth with mudholes and cogon weeds. Pedestrians and motorized pedicabs mingled in reckless chaos with jeepneys and brand-new Japanese cars. She was cheered by the sight of the *ratiles* tree at the mouth of her old neighborhood; it had survived, if a little horizontal, no doubt due to the weight of innumerable children scampering up its supple trunk. But it had managed to spread its green crown over the rusting hulk of a derelict truck in which she and her playmates had once set up a clubhouse. The inexorable eradication of this memorabilia of her youth pleased her unexpectedly.

As she should've known, a virtual fiesta was taking place in her father's house. The colored bulbs atop the high white gate walls were on, swinging as much from the rock music within as from the wind. Food, drinks, music, dancing, talk. Much like everyone else in the archipelago, the Governor preferred to turn the commonplace into a ritual. That way, as he'd explained to Teresa, the anonymous were accorded special status; bonds were renewed; everyone was reminded of obligations and everything acquired significance.

"We're grounded for the night," she told San Custodio bitterly.

The usual thirty-foot table had been spread between the warehouses in the backyard, which thirty meters farther sloped down to the garlic and tobacco fields. To one side, a six-man band played tinny but enthusiastic rock music while three girls in shorts and sequined halters jerked, bumped, whirled their torsos. It was hard going for them, Teresa saw; grass and earth were not hospitable to spike heels.

The Governor was shredding white chicken meat onto two plates. For the Pomeranians, he explained happily, thrusting greasy chunks into his mouth, grinning at the dozen or so of his associates present. Servants brought chairs for Teresa and the Diablos while the local soldiers melted into a silent row of tenants standing at the field's edge, watching. As Teresa seated herself, she noted how the Governor's shirt strained about his belly and how his hands flailed, fingers groping, feeling for the glass of scotch that was never far away, for bits and pieces of food plucked brusquely from platters and conveyed with greedy impatience to his mouth. He'd put on weight, was putting it on visibly, as he shushed Teresa and ogled the dancing girls, his dentures gleaming.

That night, before he allowed her to retire to her old bedroom, the Governor confirmed her fears. He'd called His Excellency (to-be), he said, and given him to understand that he, the Governor, was very interested in acquiring an exclusive license to import the raw material needed for cigarette filters. Exclusive, he repeated, chortling; since that was the only adequate compensation for favors given and about to be given, evidence of which would reach Manila, in due time, by special messenger, in the form of telegram copies signed TIK.

She pitied him, Teresa did, looking at him calmly in this instant when he was most pleased with himself, though seeing him on a Sunday, one Sunday into the future, in his beautiful hand-tailored suit, getting up from his knees at the cathedral to walk to the communion rail as a priest and an acolyte came forward with the cup of holy communion, the Governor not noticing the nondescript young man who crowded behind him as he knelt at the rail and took in the thin wafer of his salvation, the same young man firing one bullet into his brain as the Governor's throat worked with the passage of the blessed host down his gullet. It would be a clean kill. Her father would be assured of instant entrance into heaven as the young man leaped over the rails like an ecstatic ballerina and disappeared into and beyond the cathedral's back rooms, leaving behind a bloodpool on the white marble floor and a chaos of the devoted, who'd automatically thrown themselves flat on their faces or ducked behind pews.

Oh, she pitied him—but she could do nothing for him. She did not have the talent to save anyone who came too close to the Basbas twins. And listening to him at this moment when he felt the most affection for her, feverishly and drunkenly grasping her hand and saying how happy he was to be sending the shrewdest member of his family to the neighboring provinces under the aegis of the Senate President, she knew herself for the most despicable person alive, one of those true-blue intellectuals so to speak, who could eyeball the worst catastrophe with pitiless detachment. His murder would never be solved, she understood, and its scandal would linger but for an eyeblink. "You will bind them," the Governor said, "to him and to me."

Top of the list was Gloria Aldaza, better known as the Widow. Now sixty years old, the Widow had held on to her husband's territory, a town of limestone quarries and fishing villages, after he died of a stroke occasioned by the hottest summer the north had ever felt. Since the oldest son was a mere stripling at the time, untried in the game of politics, bets had been laid as to who among and how the neighboring power clans would move to engulf her inherited fiefdom. But the Widow, marshaling her husband's private squads and calling on a network of obligations her husband had built over the years, had herself elected and proclaimed mayor. She managed to hold off the rival clans, so successfully in fact that the oldest son could go overseas, to the Wharton School of Finance, for a graduate degree.

The Widow was in trouble now, for a new rival had risen, a brassy, psychotic ex–army captain whose one claim to glory was having beaten up his own sons so thoroughly they were all brain-damaged. Because the Widow's other children were too young or too fey, and the captain's reputation had terrorized all possible challengers, he had taken over the local *beto-beto* and bingo gambling joints easily. He might be moving slowly but he was moving surely to dispossess the Widow. His military past helped, for the mystical camaraderie of soldiers protected him from reprisal.

San Custodio took care of that problem, barely an hour after the helicopter landed in the Widow's territory. As Teresa joined the Señora Gloria Aldaza in the contemplation of the accumulated loot of the limestone clan—an unimaginable wealth in antique church reliquaries, from ivory saints with ruby-and-emerald studded gold halos, ciboriums of such delicate artistry that their value as art overwhelmed the value of their metal and precious gems, to pearl-and-gold-thread-encrusted velvet gowns of the Virgin—San Custodio took a jeep to the town square, got off ostensibly to see the sights on foot, bumped the ex-captain by accident, traded insults involving their respective parentage with him, and then cheerfully admonished the man to be at the town basketball court in two hours "if fear doesn't drop your balls so low you'd be stepping on them."

As the Widow and Teresa consummated their agreement and a Diablo delivered a dozen assault rifles to the Aldaza house— for the woman had refused other forms of compensation, saying that everything else would naturally follow from the possession of guns—the nearby villages had emptied, its residents trekking to the basketball court to spill among the sparse bleached seats and onto the grass at the asphalt edge. San Custodio was already there, his body swathed in elastic bandages beneath his fatigues. It was an old amok trick, this. The bandages would hold in his innards in case of a gut shot and would slow down hemorrhaging, giving him time to dispatch his rival. It would also enable his men to bring him to a hospital before he bled to death.

The ex-captain wasn't as well versed, it would seem, in the art of dueling. He came alone, holding his .45, and from the way he moved, was unprotected. In ten minutes flat, to the abrupt roar of the onlookers, San Custodio drilled him neatly through the forehead with a single shot, uncapping the back of his skull neatly. Beer bottles popped open, gin gurgled in abundance, and the impromptu town celebration was not even dampened by the discovery that San Custodio had taken a bullet in his left leg.

It was nothing, the Diablo hero said, refusing to be returned to the city and accepting only the most cursory ministrations from the province's only doctor. The *médico* shook his head and advised immediate surgery, but helped by his men, San Custodio boarded the helicopter after Teresa. Duty was duty, he said; there were still half a dozen places to visit, and what the hell, he hadn't had such a good time in years, not since the advent of peace. "You will never know, you women," he said, "how it feels. When your blood's pumping at high pressure, adrenaline flowing, and your brain's intent on only one thing. One and only one thing: to pull that trigger."

Teresa shook her head, seized his forearm, and gripped it in appreciation, for the doctor had been, as he said, frank with her, and though he was only a general practitioner, there was no helping it, the leg would be lost, it seemed to him. Teresa had a vision of meeting San Custodio some time hence, on crutches, earning his living the way the maimed, the crippled, the hand-icapped earned their livelihood in this world: by forcing a happy tune out of a harmonica while passersby dropped coins into an empty tobacco box at the unfortunate's feet.

But she could not afford to waste more thoughts on the injured Diablo. The helicopter radio was crackling with a message from Katerina, who'd taken off for the south and was shrilly demanding that Teresa meet with her somewhere, immediately, for Herself couldn't take this anymore, no, not anymore, the presidency be damned.

8

Wealth *didn't bring* automatic immunity from what she dreaded the most, Katerina Basbas Gloriosa was discovering. Hitherto, she'd considered public humiliation to be poverty's natural by-product, but having been snubbed, flatly and thoroughly, in a succession of three cities and five towns, she understood that powerlessness was equal to being poor in the archipelago. Because the Grand Alliance, which had been formed from a merger of the Basbas organization, the opposition party, and splinters of other groups out of grace with Blackie, had no official access to the political structure, local ward leaders had to beg and plead for appointments for her with governors, mayors, and other officials. She couldn't be refused because Hector was still senate president. But they didn't have to, didn't want to, in actuality. Instead, Blackie's people seized at the chance to let her know how unwelcome she was, even while she was being welcomed, forcing her into reception lines with the world's most minor personalities: barrio councillors, municipal treasurers, heads of sanitation departments, building custodians. In one town, two or three hours' drive from the urban center, the officials dragged her on an incredible walking tour of the main road, which was a pothole-plagued dirt street moist with pig and horse droppings and the morning rain, ravaging the impeccable white of her shoes and the hem of her rose—her favorite!—pantsuit, perdition take them all. And all the while, as though to remind them of his true loyalties, the mayor held a brown bag of boiled peanuts in the shell and kept tossing them like confetti at a phalanx of mangy kids, three to ten years old, who trailed them with laughter, impertinent remarks, and pleas for food and "give me money, five centavos only," having mistaken Herself, Katerina Basbas Gloriosa, for a Manila movie star. Shit, double and triple shit. Each time the mayor's arm arched like a hawk on the wing and the solid raindrops of peanuts fell, the kids screamed and threw themselves one atop another, scrambling for the dark specks in the dirt, mud, and potholes. What a scandal.

To cap it all, the "official" women—wives, mistresses, and assorted female ghouls—had been gathered into this hot, stuffy room on the second floor of the wooden town hall smelling of rotting fungi. Here, Katerina was "entertained" by a soprano who sounded like ripping aluminum sheets but who nevertheless ignored applause and nonapplause with equal aplomb and delivered five—yes, count them, one after another—five interminable arias and then nodded to Herself as if to say, "Top that, if you can." She had obviously heard of Herself's talents for entertaining.

Katerina Basbas Gloriosa, still game though wilting in her tight stays and shoes, rose and sang a traditional love song, a *kundiman*—and that was when she realized how intense, how uncompromising, how utmost, the hostility was. There were no calls for an encore. Frazzled but unfazed, she forthwith announced she'd brought some "arrival gifts, *pasalubongs*, in the tradition of a returning relative," for that was how she considered herself; though born elsewhere, she thought of herself as "kin to this island, this city, this town, ha-ha," and in the stony silence, opened the door and walked to where de Naval, Hector's most trusted, uh, *excessive* bodyguard, waited with proper rectitude, guarding a box of goodies, "nothing spectacular, just perfume and gold trinkets and packages of made-in-Hong Kong Cardin shirts, you know."

Katerina, impatient to be up and away, thrust in her hands and, cradling an armload of the merchandise—"it had to be dry goods, Teresa; they wouldn't take guns because the benighted officials each had his own small weapons factory in the outskirts, wholly illegal, of course"—walked back to the room and tripped. Tripped, stumbled, barely saved Herself and her dignity at the cost of what she was carrying, which spilled over and scattered on the floor. At which, would you believe, that horde of women rose and shrieked like hysterical birds, whirled once, the batwings of their arms and shawls flung up, and then threw themselves to the floor, scrambling for . . . oh, mortification! Even the Grand Matriarch, an eighty-year-old specimen of drool and drooping flesh flaps, heaved herself out of her chair and dove, a geriatric Olympic swimmer, into the helter-skelter of cellophane packages, boxes, tubes, and what-nots. Katerina was just thinking with sweet pleasure of doing this "accident" at all the hostile receptions when the governor, their governor, chose to make his entrance, catching her standing there, a bemused half-smile on her face, while the women writhed at her feet, clutching this-that package. The rage on his face was a pleasure to behold, though politically speaking it presaged a new disaster. This governor, who'd refused to be at the airport on her arrival, a Blackie man if she ever saw one, was hard put to protect his self-respect at the sight of his women—Switzerland-, Manila-, Boston-finished; local and imported—kissing the floor before her, so to speak.

He turned adamant. No, he would not sign the petition; no, he would not call on Blackie to yield; no, he didn't think Hector Basbas won the election and furthermore didn't think he'd make a good president. "For one thing, he didn't even know enough not to send *you* here," he said bluntly, waving at a constabulary aide to pour him another shot of brandy, two fingers please. "Not to give offense, but we don't do politics with women."

The hell you don't, Katerina thought. She smiled—the slow, lazy kind of smile which began with the lip corners and ended with eye-crinkling and which she'd practiced to perfection in her vanity mirror—and leaned closer to blast him with her Nina Ricci *eau de toilette*, and she was about to say that being such a gentleman, of the old school at that, he would surely forgive Hector his error, committed in ignorance, because of youth and inexperience; she wasn't contesting his judgment of her brother; she couldn't argue with him, of course, herself (not capitalized by that stress in the voice), being just a woman and he was so wise—"because, Teresa, that's how one does it with them; make 'em feel so, uh, omnipotent that like God, they can afford to be merciful and throw this, that crumb over"—when the door opened and his wife came in. That was the end of that. For the wife, an Australian frowzy blonde whom the governor had obtained ten years before to improve the bloodstock of his flat-nosed, moon-faced family, was squealing and whining like a pig whose throat had been cut, saying that everybody else got the pick of everything and all that was left was a chain locket filled with, ugh, cheap perfume cream going for a dollar each on any sidewalk in Hong Kong.

"Go to Hong Kong," the governor thundered, rising to his feet. "Buy what you want."

He was apoplectic. Apart from being his clan's singular pride, the woman was also a testament to his astuteness. Unable to marry her, for he was married to a cousin, he'd secured a husband and thereby a permanent resident visa for her. For a decade running, he'd been sleeping with the woman, who was techni-cally his chauffeur's wife and who now showed the effects of the local humidity and salty cuisine. Her fair complexion had curdled, her faint blush had turned into a dirty spray of freckles, and extra flesh, the color of unbaked bread, had gathered beneath her chin and on her upper arms. Tut-tut, Caucasians didn't wear well in this climate. Katerina was on her feet, rising as soon as the governor had—and there it was, reflected in the wall mirror of the municipal banquet room: Herself taller by two inches than the Australian; regal, slim, not a hair out of place, and smelling, excuse me, divine. It was complete disaster all around.

"No telling what will inspire envy," she said to Teresa later, cracking watermelon seeds between her teeth.

It was no go. She, de Naval, and the rest had to fly off to the next island and the next, until they reached the southernmost safe place, where the plane lurched down an airstrip of grass and gravel, *madre de cacao*, bumping and bouncing, so she had tiny blue bruises right there, on her unmentionables. This was Morolandia, and the erstwhile *datu*, a hereditary chieftain now suddenly legit as a mayor, met her at his house, a scaled-down bungalow with brass and plastic everywhere, including a sweaty, laminated, sticky table over which they conducted their negotiations.

De Naval had briefed her on this man, a tough septuagenarian with six wives, the youngest barely nineteen years old, and three sets of false teeth—one porcelain, one ivory, one gold—which he wore alternately, depending on the momentousness of the occasion. That he disapproved of her completely was immediately obvious, since he met her toothless, his lips pinched and his cheeks hollow. An impulse to slap him at the doorway of his sour-smelling house had nearly overwhelmed her, but she controlled herself admirably, reminding herself of de Naval's words. The old man had started out as pirate, an outlaw and rebel, a protégé of the dreaded Muslim rebel Kamlon, for whom the United States Army had invented the .45 because anything of lower caliber was useless against Moro amoks. He'd survived the siege, survived his brutal incarceration among the Christians, gathered up the remnants of *that* rebellion—"Ay, Teresa, how many dates and names of wars shall we have to remember?"— and built his empire, principally by turning a huge settlement of an ethnic pagan tribe into his personal labor camp. "What others do to us, we do unto others, no?"

As mayor now, he had the power to grant logging concessions, but he did so selectively, to such companies as would give him a share of ownership and to such companies as could trace the bloodlines of their owners to his. He grew rich, for he forced loggers to subcontract security arrangements to a company he owned, which in turn used the local military post as a source of free labor and matériel through the expedient of paying off the regional high command. Now and then, more to amuse himself than to convince the armed forces of the loggers' need for escorts, the *datu* would order his private bandit squads to launch ambushes, carry out kidnappings, and demand protection money. Thus he ate, as it were, from both sides of the plate and with both sides of his mouth.

With fake congeniality, he said to her that he could not decide on this matter alone, though the gift of assault rifles and frag grenades was much appreciated. It was lucky the '*Kano* was always at war somewhere nearby; his munificence spilled over to the archipelago. Nevertheless, he would have to consult his staff as to the proper action to take. "We're living in a democracy," he said, his lips working, "unfortunately."

He offered the hospitality of his house, calling in his women to minister to her—but at the sight of that clump of dusky females, Katerina's gorge rose. The dimness of the passageway from which they had emerged and which she surmised led to the women's quarters nearly caused her heart to stop. Thanks very much, Mr. Mayor, but she was religious and would he mind very much if she spent that time meditating in a nearby convent–

parish church complex? Not even de Naval's scandalized intake of breath could stop her from saying those words to the Muslim mayor.

He grunted and she took it for consent. Leaving de Naval to distribute trinkets among the house's residents, she made her way to the aforementioned place—"on foot, Teresa, because I would not risk my behind on those impossible roads!" And there, on the ultimate edge of the sea, it seemed, just before the globe inched up to the west again, she found this parish church presided over by a forlorn Irish priest, exiled by his good intentions and terrible ignorance, there to try to plant the banner of the Golden Lion in a wilderness peopled by Muslims.

The irony of it. The mother superior, wide as a warehouse door, met her at the low adobe wall marking off church property from the road, and since the priest wasn't around, though expected by dusk, she would do Katerina the honors of the parish. First, Herself was taken to the chapel. Though of stone and cement, it was small and smelled of moss and dried bird droppings. Here she was shown the chapel's pride and Christianity's glory in the area: a four-foot-high ivory Virgin wearing a halo of pure gold and, would you believe, over her burgundy velvet robe what looked like a hula skirt. On closer inspection, as Katerina made the sign of the cross at the altar's foot, the skirt turned out to be stringed matched pearls, alternately blue and white, incredibly beautiful.

"The devotees' gifts," the mother superior murmured. Pearls, of course, were harvested by the bushels from the sea all around—to which end slim young lads were conscripted by captains of large *praus* and in batches of ten or so were brought to the open sea, where ballasts of huge stones were tied to their waists. Then each was given a knife and a little rattan pouch and dropped overboard to glide and ferret among oyster beds. Heaven help the kid who returned without a pearl and with his ballast ropes cut, for the seamen required that stones be gently eased out of their harness. Kids were easy to replace but not ropes.

It had gotten about that the Lady, because she was a virgin, extended special protection to children (what the connection was, Katerina couldn't see). Every so often, a child would manage to hide a special pearl from his masters and bring this to the chapel, to be knotted alongside its twins, while the boy blissfully went away, comforted by his having made peace with the great powers. Thus it was that the Virgin acquired a priceless skirt which grew heavier and denser with the years.

Katerina was vindicated in her choice of accommodations. The church was full of, uh, longings which needed satisfaction. The mother superior had a lifelong wish to visit Rome and view the pope in all his glory—which her superiors considered a self-indulgent ambition, what with the cost of plane fare and all that. "Don't worry," Katerina said, "once His Excellency's in the palace, it shouldn't be difficult to get a free ticket from the national airline." The mother superior was properly grateful, saying that was all she needed, she could stay with her sisters over there . . . and so forth. The Irish priest, when he arrived, was also suffering the torment of an unfulfilled ambition: that of building a basilica down there, close to the waterfront, where all those huddled and desolate slum shacks had been built by the migrant poor and pagan sea gypsies. Katerina divined at once the magnificence of the priest's vision. A basilica here, at the very edge of Christendom in the East, would be a statement, a banner unfurled, a pennant of victory. It would make his superiors in Rome and Manila sit up and end his exile. "I don't see why not, father. There should be no problem as soon as Senator Basbas is president. We could launch a drive for donations among the rich." And so forth—but always, Teresa dear, prefaced by that phrase "as soon as," which was telling them to get cracking on it.

The good father understood and said that for the bishops to issue a statement might take some doing but he could call on favors done for this or that priest over on this or that island. Besides it was the church's duty to work for peace. While the mother superior offered her support by promising to bring in the nuns' orders. "We could have nuns fasting," she said, "for peace." By the time they went in to dinner, they were all friends, Katerina arm in arm with the mother superior on one side, the priest on the other. When the double doors to the mess hall were thrown open, she knew then that her choice of a sanctuary had indeed been correct.

It was a banquet to end all banquets. The buffet included two roasted suckling pigs, four kinds of vegetables, rice *a la Valenciana*, paella, the tenderest of beefs, which, as required by correct society, could be cut with a fork edge, chicken galantina, and so on, not to mention six kinds of dessert, wine, and the best coffee she'd ever had in her life. The priest said grace, of course, after which, perhaps pricked by a little guilt, he told Katerina that this was the way it was. "Life's blessings flow to those who give up everything," he said. Amen.

If one really thought about it, Katerina said to Teresa later, there was no better haven than the church, no? Free board and lodging; a perfect medical insurance system; job tenure and a pension without taxes. She was mulling this over in the pleasant little room assigned to her—de Naval and the others had to fend for themselves, since no males were allowed to sleep over, unless they were priests. The room faced the rose garden which novices cultivated, and thus, through the night, Katerina lay on a bed of fresh linen and breathed in flower scents and the tang of sea wind, as she thought of how much of a marvel it all was. How rich, certainly, this archipelago was, with such a variety of wealth. Coral and pearls in the sea; gold and silver and forests in the mountains; grain, sugar, and coconut in the plains; not to men-

tion the bounty of time, the pile upon pile of accumulated treasures scavenged from the China-Acapulco-Spain trade and later
the Manila–Hawaii–San Francisco trade. The whole problem,
she told herself, was that everything was hidden, locked up in
rooms, vaults, dungeons, homes and churches. . . . Though
there was enough to ransom a dozen kings three times over, the
loot was unused, locked away, its owners often growing so used
to wealth's presence they forgot its value, the possession of it
becoming the sole source of pleasure. She had just decided what
she would do, what her mission in life would be henceforth—
"If ever, Teresa, if ever we make it, I'll open up those vaults,
those rooms, and let all that wealth pour out. I'll force it to be
displayed, flaunted, thrown around, to show the world how much
we have to be proud of. Only thing is, if I do that, won't people
ask, well, if there's so much to go around, how come we don't
have anything? And what's the answer to that? You can't tell
them to their faces that it's because they're stupid, ignorant,
superstitious, and a bunch of cowards." She was reveling in
images of Herself crying out *Open, Sesame!* to a thousand stuffed
and overflowing thieves' caves when there was a shuffling outside,
a sibilant whisper, a knock. She rose, put on a robe, and opened
the door to a novice, pale and wide-eyed, who said de Naval was
outside, with news which could not wait till morning.

De Naval, limned by starlight, was there indeed, with an
expression so terrible he looked as if he'd drop dead any minute.
It was a while before Katerina pieced together his incoherent
words. An off-season typhoon had blown in from the Pacific,
sliced diagonally upwards through the Visayas, and struck the
Central Plains with barely enough time for warning. At a military
air force outpost, radar had been tracking the plane carrying
Hector Basbas and six Diablos, the phosphorescent green of the
blip-blip signal faithfully reflecting the plane's erratic course,
when the typhoon felled six electric posts. A transmitter some-

where exploded; lights and radar went out, and by the time the emergency generators kicked in, ten minutes later, the telltale green of the plane had disappeared.

His next words were a thunderclap in her ears: "The plane's down. His Excellency (to-be) is gone."

9

Sweet misery. Armand mouthed the phrase to himself, one used by plantation workers to refer to the sugarcane they had to tend, as he watched the guests arrive. The cars which wound down the road, volleying out from between tall sugarcane swatches, past the private golf grounds, were almost uniformly muted in color. Black or white, dark blue or maroon. Alien beetles among the jade-green canefields, under a blue sky, while down at the riverbank, sections of the chicken-wire fence were bladed with sunlight. It was a necessary eyesore, this fence; on the opposite bank huddled the unspeakable backsides of workers' barracks and shacks, spewing their sad effluvium into the river water brown with mud and fertilizer runoffs, where fish the color of caramel swam.

Armand's mission was kicking off with a gathering of his allies, mostly young men and women, second or third in line to the country's power holders, their sons and daughters. He fitted in with the group. They liked him, for their own private reasons. Perhaps because he affected their plumage—silk or fine cotton shirt of pastel colors, slightly narrow pants, glove leather or deer-skin shoes—or because his body knew, without having to be told, how to arrange itself into a hundred lissome attitudes. More likely, Armand thought, it was because he was on a first-name basis with a dozen jai alai *pelotaris*, a signal honor. The sport appealed to the younger set of heirs and heiresses, despite their having been educated, one and all, in the United States. It was a hearkening to a lost connection, Armand surmised, or an affectation of one; they turned their noses up at the national madness of basketball.

His brother-in-law, now, Hector Basbas, was an expert on cockfighting—a requisite in dealing with the patriarchs. *Their* language he spoke accurately: brandy glass in hand, left arm akimbo, belly thrust forward, voice portentous. . . . Armand had been told once by a young scion that the difference between himself and his father came simply to this: his father's generation derived their sense of power from being obeyed; his generation, from having attributes.

Hogwash. Give or take a few added years and the lithe young developed a paunch, acquired mistresses, bodyguards, brandy glasses, and the voice of command—all at once and at the same time. Hiking boots were tossed out, along with the theater, French films, and labyrinthine German philosophies, in a strange process Armand thought of as butterflies reverting to larvae. He chuckled at the metaphor and thought of how when the Basbas twins made it to the palace, he Armand would cause his friends no end of distress by becoming a basketball patron.

It was unfortunate Katerina had never acquired the ability to mollify the wives in the same way that Hector could deal with the patriarchs. To be fair, though, the matriarchs were a tough bunch, half insane with zealous jealousy over status and privilege; they didn't have much to occupy their time, after all. They could forgive Hector, being male, for having been born outside the proper cradle of pedigree. But not Katerina, who, being female, couldn't make up the disadvantage. That Hector's father had indeed been an idiot, a dolt, *tangengot*, as they say, was well proved by his having married and sired children on an unlettered peasant woman. Her prompt death made no difference. The matriarchs—and all women of the clans turned into matriarchs, sooner or later—visited on Katerina their affront over the personal

107

insult delivered by Basbas Segundo's choice of partner, an insult aggravated by Armand's marriage to Katerina, which was, in truth, precedent-setting, for the Gloriosas married only first cousins or foreigners. Had the matriarchs known it was possible for a Gloriosa to do this, they would have taken steps with regard to their own daughters. And what was wrong with Armand anyway, that he had to choose from an upstart family? What was wrong with the matriarchs' daughters, anyway?

Many things, Armand would've answered cheerfully; not the least of which was that they were boring. Oh, boring. Single, they did no more than cultivate and practice the art of self-importance, casting their eyes about for a likely heir to marry, while indulging themselves to perdition. And married, they bored themselves, oh, Lord, and were reduced to terrorizing their children and servants. Boring and bored, without even the imagination to help themselves. Wrapped in the same religious iron stays of their maternal forbears, they frowned in exactly the same manner as their mothers over the least hint of a—shh—scandal, while waging a war of subtle cruelties against one another and adroitly forgetting the scandalous escapades of their youths, even the sly abortion trips to Hong Kong.

Katerina, no matter what, exercised no such petty malice. She was silly, reckless, a glutton for attention, easy to anger and easy to mollify, but capable of real emotions. He'd never regretted marrying her, even in their worst moments together. She entertained him, he confessed to Teresa Tikloptuhod; she kept him on his toes by being on her toes constantly, alert to any obstacle to the family goals and interminably at war with her own husband over her brother's confidence and favors, at war even with her brother over the dispensation of his blessings. She was magnificent, at least, in this obsession.

If he'd married one of these—oh. His heart cringed at the

idea, even as he was running (lightly, dear feet) down the stairs, hailing the just arrived, his arms open, head inclined for cheeks to touch, mouth pursed for the chaste kiss-no-kiss which was merely an explosion of air—oh *hija* how well you look. . . . Someone fed a tape of the latest dance music into the stereo and three-four couples were frugging; six men were clustered near the sofa, inspecting one another's golf clubs and ruining the Taiping rug with the cleats of their shoes, even as the host, Don Andrés Villarta, was saying, "What the hell; if you can't afford to destroy it, you can't afford it," gamely dismissing his visitors' offer to go, ahem, barefoot. Armand greeted each and every one of the thirty or so who had arrived.

Bishop Camcam, grandson of the Church of the Mystic Limb founder and youngest of the sect's leaders, hovered among the visitors, grinning from ear to ear and loudly proclaiming his grief at having to forgo all this during his grad term at Harvard, where he was a nondescript foreign student and not of the master race at that. He gave Armand the three-finger salute (little finger, index finger, and thumb) of the church elect, embraced him, and, winking, asked in a voice that cut through the noise of celebration: "So what have you got for us today?"

At which everyone turned to Armand, lips stretched into smiles, mischievous eyes expecting him to provide excitement. He pointed to a stack of paper on a sidetable, shrugged, and said he didn't really have to explain; everything's been in the papers and so forth; so why didn't they just simply sign so they could get on with it? A shout of merriment; laughter and hand-clapping. A woman's voice said something about the "inimitable Gloriosa style," and good-humoredly, determined not to give the moment any importance, each secured a copy of the Basbas petition.

"My father will kill me," said a woman in halter top and jeans, the corners of her eyes crinkling. "But we've got to get the deadwood out, don't we?" She puffed on a cigarette charmingly. "Besides, the twins are preferable to same old Blackie. They're characters—or a character, no?"

Bishop Camcam winked again. He signed a sheet, peered at what the others were doing, and suggested that everyone affix a title by which he could be identified. "Do we have to?" a man murmured, brushing back his hair. "It's so much work." But he was already complying, and later, when Armand checked the petitions, he discovered that the majority had appended "Board Member" of this or that corporation after their names. What, he would wonder aloud to Teresa later, did they ever do on all those corporate boards?

"Receive compensation," was Teresa's succinct reply, "without taxes."

It took three or four hours to work off the group's excess energy: the men on the golf course, betting breathtaking amounts of money per hole; the women displaying their limbs in the swimming pool, ignoring an unfortunate replica of the Lourdes grotto which a misguided grandfather had had installed near the diving board. By dusk, everyone was back in the living room, dressed informally in cool cotton, listening to the bishop, who insisted on being called Andy, relate the plot of the newest Broadway show he'd seen—which discourse led naturally to a dozen or so deciding they simply had to stage the thing in Manila. "We could borrow capital from your bank," said a young woman who was certain she'd been born for the lead role. "Why borrow?" was the reply. "We'll sponsor it and write it off as a loss." There was a general clamor for paper and pencil as the group prepared to list what would be needed. Heeding the bishop's cry to "bring civilization to Manila," they set to work and to argue.

Armand wandered off to the dining room, out its French windows, and into the night air sweet with the odor of burning bagasse. He yawned, noting how his breath had soured and

wishing he could walk around, in the cool of the sugarcane—
but that would be extremely stupid. This spot of paradise, he
knew, was ringed by constabulary patrols, civilian guards, and
plantation security. Out there, amidst the gray on gray which
was the fields at night, under a vast black sprinkled with stars,
there were innumerable malcontents, rebels, bandits, and
whatnots—as his host, the seventh descendant of his family to
own·these fields, had found out.

The story at least served to amuse everyone for a spell: of how,
a year after his father's death, the new Don Andrés Villarta
decided to improve on the departed's hobby by increasing the
number of combat roosters in the plantation. He was going to
breed champions, he said, the likes of which had never been
seen in the archipelago. He would break the bank in every cockpit
from here to Bhutan and win the Champion of Champions
trophy at the national tournament. To which end he brought in
five hundred imported hens and a hundred imported cocks, Texas
and Nepalese, stashing them in an elaborate coop near a bamboo
grove midway between the plantation house and the canefields.

What kind of a devil possessed some miscreants he would never
know. Perhaps the cackling and cockcrow had been too much
for those who had to dine on mung beans and water spinach
tips, but one night of the new moon, the five guards and four
dogs of the breeding place all had their throats cut. By daybreak,
two-thirds of the fowl had disappeared. Totally, irrevocably, with
not even a feather to mark where they'd gone. Rumor had it that
the worker barracks feasted on fried, roasted, stewed, and *adobo*
chicken and that the children had enough wishbones for their
fancies for a whole week. Don Andres wisely chose not to pursue
the matter any further and simply took the precaution of (a)
moving the remaining fowl; (b) hiring more plantation guards;
(c) increasing the weekly allowance of the regional military command post; and (d) never braving the plantation dark ever again.

"Armand." The voice was cool. An arm fell and tightened about his shoulders; a weight laid itself against his back. The bishop, breath exuding the odor of malt, said: "A beautiful country; you find out only when you've been away." He sighed.

Armand made a noncommittal sound. This was standard melancholia of the church elect, delicately cultivated. Indeed, the sect was built on only one theological premise: the earth, heaven, the universe, and life itself had somehow fallen to the hands of the undeserving. The Mystic Limb's responsibility was to bring alignment, which would be complete when all decision, all resources, all thought, all power, belonged only to those divinely ordained for such privilege and responsibility. When he first heard the church thesis, Armand had guffawed—as he'd laughed at most other things the sect claimed, including the founder's "magic" third arm, of which there was abundant proof in the many, many prints of an amazing photograph.

But when Hector said that the church was important, Armand did not hesitate. He received training from the archbishop, listening to the ponderous lectures, avowed himself convinced, and declared his faith. It was a perfect match. Hector needed the sect's votes, and the church then needed something special with which to inaugurate its suburban capital, built by the grace of its members' dues. With its four minarets, central cupola, and piped-in sermons, it was the ugliest structure for miles around, looking more like a rectangular and badly proportioned cake than anything else. That failed to deter conversions, though. The new place of worship was huge—declaration enough that the sect was rich, was growing richer, and in the country of the poor, that sufficed for attraction. Besides, it had a state-of-the-art darkroom and an offset printing press which vomited thousands of copies of that "third arm" photo.

Armand's baptism was the first of two thousand others; being top of the line allayed his misgivings somewhat. At least it ensured the pristine state of the basement pool into which the archbishop, chanting an *oración* at the top of his lungs and with his hands firmly on Armand's head, dunked him, feet, body, head, and all.

Beneath the water surface, right at eye level, Armand saw the proper vision of the moment: the corpse of the founder, the archbishop's father and the bishop's grandfather, in full red-and-gold regalia, embalmed and in all likelihood stuffed, lying on a marble catafalque, guarded by four massive candelabras and illuminated by floodlights. With the archbishop's weight on his head and neck, Armand could appreciate the irony of the moment which confirmed and at the same time explained the rumor about the founder appearing at special church celebrations. He eyed the corpse in admiration, wondering how long it could last and whether the room it was in was refrigerated. The founder would be no food for worms, at least. When the pressure on his head eased, Armand came up smoothly, the taste of chlorine on his tongue and half blinded by the water. The archbishop pronounced him blessed, twice-blessed as a matter of fact, since he now had the protection of both church and state.

He was swiftly declared one of the sect's Twelve Wise Men and given his own quarters, a combination bachelor's apartment and office, in the cathedral and his share of the monthly tithe. He could count on a magnificent banquet every third Thursday of the month, when the leaders gathered in the archbishop's chamber and at which time the Wise Men were exempt from the church's admonitions against overeating, overdrinking, and other forms of self-indulgence. Such Thursday meditations were a joy to Armand, being an all-male affair, serviced by women. Moreover, the sect endorsed Hector Basbas's candidacy for the senate, kicked in a hefty contribution to his campaign war chest, and deputized its members as Basbas watchdogs during the vote count. This was no simple election, 'pañero; this was a holy crusade.

Nowadays, Armand had to struggle with his own growing conviction that the sect was right. Reality, after all, confirmed its thesis every minute of the day. For how, he would ask himself, was it possible that the "natives," as he called the dark-hued, anonymous crowd, go on living with such existential nonchalance? Feckless, Armand thought; almost mindless, not noticing the abundance about them, not asking why they had none, not even, so help me God, conscious of how short, indeed terribly short, earth time was. If it had been his fate to be one of them, Armand said, he would've killed himself on his seventh birthday, the stupidity of it all being so overwhelming.

It was Bishop Andy, the youngest of the sect's trinity, who resolved Armand's questions. "They're a people without destiny," he'd said.

Because profundity frightened him, Armand had seized the young man's hand.

"You and I have our fates," the bishop had gone on calmly. "Others don't. It's as simple as that." He'd laughed suddenly. "There aren't very many destinies to go around, you know." And because he had been educated abroad, he went into a long elucidation about how ninety-nine percent of humanity had been created simply for "critical mass, the means by which those with destinies work out their goals." His hand on Armand's shoulder had squeezed terrifically. "Anytime now, the truth will become the Truth."

None of those within the house were fated, Armand thought; he and Hector definitely had theirs. But Katerina and Teresa had their lives forfeit to the destiny of their men, as decreed by all the churches of the world. It seemed natural to divide those he knew into such categories.

"On the matter of alignment," the bishop was saying now, "we have a few important matters to discuss. You, me, and my father."

Whatever doubts Armand might have about the Mystic Limb, he could grant the sect's wise men the stamina of bulls. Despite the night's carousing, Bishop Andy was up and awake by six in the morning and hollering for Armand to come down to the pool. Midmorning found the two of them in a helicopter, being flown to a narrow island called Little Eden which was owned by the Mystic Limb. Here, among wild cogon grass, coconut and banana trees, and untrimmed purple, pink, and red bougainvilleas, the Mystic Limb had assembled its version of Noah's Ark. Imported and domestic deer, tigers, lions, antelopes, gnus, hippopotami, and a decrepit elephant rescued from a circus, not to mention a battalion of monkeys and a squadron of brilliantly feathered cockatoos and parrots, gamboled about a circular rest house which doubled as the archbishop's retreat. The animals did not have to fear poachers, for the island's shores were defended by every type of weapon the sect could lay its hands on. Armand wouldn't have been surprised to find a howitzer tucked among the stupendous purple of orchids hugging coconut trunks.

It was ferocious expense, of course, one which kept sect members sweating at two or three jobs. But for their sacrifice, they were granted the privilege of visiting the preserve once every four years. This small vision of paradise kept them going, it seemed, at the relentless drudgery of their lives. Armand conceded that, in a way, it was a minor miracle how the sect managed to keep its members after a glimpse of this paradise. He had to credit the sect's leaders for the skill with which they made sure none of their members opted out, either by apostasy or by death.

But that, Bishop Andy had pointed out, was the difference between ordinary people and the divinely ordained. Had his situation been otherwise, Armand would have launched a campaign to become a "wise man," he said laughing.

The conference with the archbishop, Armand was to discover, presented more dilemmas. The Church of the Mystic Limb, the old man said, wanted to hasten alignment, especially now that the presidency was almost in Hector's hands. It would be wise, said the archbishop, for every facet of the economy to be, uh, integrated vertically and horizontally. Andy had the plans for that.

"How?" Armand asked.

In the case of the coconut industry, for instance, such centralization of all its operations—and the support systems required—could be achieved with the establishment of one trading company and one bank, national in scope. Exporting, financing, and the inflow and outflow of monies connected with coconuts, as well as all documentation related to the product, would pass through these two entities.

"No waste. Efficient. Monolithic. And what's good for coconuts is par for sugar," the archbishop said with a smile. "Andy will discuss details with you. We've even gone through the list of clans and families to find the most likely leaders. Andy's good, you know. He'll have his M.B.A. pretty soon, anyway."

But . . .

"Oh, don't worry," the archbishop said. "It will take a while —a decade or two, perhaps. But in the long run . . ."

But . . . "Hector can only have two terms, Holiness," Armand whispered.

"Unless the elections are canceled and the constitution suspended . . ." The two aimed their eyes at him.

If he could, he would've cut off his tongue, torn it out by the roots, to stop himself from saying what he was, even at that moment, saying, for Armand believed in the power of words uttered at the proper time, in their ability to conjure a reality by description alone, and furthermore, as his mouth moved, his tongue wagged, he heard the snake-hiss of foreboding loud and clear in the chambers of his heart.

"But . . ." he was saying, sundered by the need to say it and by not wanting to say it, "that would require a state of emergency, a national threat . . ."

The archbishop smiled. "Just because it doesn't exist now doesn't mean it won't."

There. In perverse form, the Mystic Limb's greatest revelation. The archbishop could be dreaming of an illusion as phony as the "third arm" and the island of Eden, but hard on the heels of his words, from an immeasurable distance, came the whine of bullets, the whistling of rockets, the bull roar of a rampaging crowd as the flame blossoms of war sprouted among the green paddies under a blue sky.

Armand shook his head sadly. Sweet misery.

10

Blue heaven denied the existence of typhoons, one of which the radio had claimed to have swallowed the Beech King aircraft carrying Hector and his Diablos. Disappeared? Where to and how? Teresa lifted her eyes to the sky. Except for a slight moistness in the air, a wind smelling of new-cut grass, and a gravid cloud way up there, far away, nothing in the day warranted claims of a disaster. Impossible, she thought, to be lost in such transparent immensity. Perhaps it was a joke, only a joke; the plane would come swooping down from behind a sunray to bellyflop at her feet. Hector would stride out of its maw and demand an accounting. She would give him all that had been accomplished in her days of tramping to and from and through flea-size villages, her mind dulled by the monotonous topography. One plaza, one church, one town hall, and clusters of wooden and adobe houses lining the main road. Over there, to the back, far as the eyes could see, the fields—garlic, tobacco, an occasional vegetable patch—threaded by dust roads with bamboo-and-nipa huts, looking like exoskeletons of alien brown dung beetles. Who the hell said huts were charming?

Hours of handshaking, cheek kissing, and absolutely circumspect behavior on her part, herself pressing an elder's back-of-the-hand to her brow, so she could be drawn into the magic circle of kinship and be called child, daughter, *hija*, as she trapped each and every one by his most importunate need. Ah, did

Grandpa suffer from a rude young heir who, without a by-your-leave, had taken over the business of protecting bus drivers? Said young heir was promptly pistol-whipped in the town's full view. And this one could not persuade a young woman to be his bride? Said woman was abducted and delivered to the man's house, indeed to his bedroom and bed, and given to understand that if she valued her hymen more than her life, then certainly she would die. A municipal treasurer who insisted on going by the books? Well, he had to be made to understand that his boss, the mayor, forged all rules "or so help me God, civil service or not, I'll take away your job." The currency of politics had to be circulated, of course, which was a trying job, as Teresa Tikloptuhod hated but simply hated giving away anything, but so it went: weapons to a governor, cash to a military command post, the promise of public works funds to a mayor, a special assistantship to the son of another mayor, and even the ambassadorship to Lisbon to the son of a third mayor. Only the women, Teresa thought grimly, asked for little or nothing.

She had managed to do all that while dragging the albatross of a delirious San Custodio, whose wound had flamed into a fever which set his bones jiggling and jangling, as they flew, motored, walked from one settlement to another, *binding*—as her father called it—allies to the holy crusade. San Custodio, who clung to her and refused to be repatriated to the city, his Diablos unwilling to disobey his own orders, and all of them expecting a miracle from Teresa, as though she was Herself herself. Each morning, the blankets about the man were sweated through, as though his tissues were liquefying in the furnace of his body. Each morning, a fresh supply of sheets, blankets, and pillows had to be found. And each morning, Teresa did the unthinkable: she had his breakfast prepared and brought it with her own hands to his room. Per San Custodio's order, it never varied: coffee, plain bread, preferably *pan de sal*, and tart *kalamansi* juice. In this manner, the Diablo reminded himself daily of his impoverished origins.

She brought him breakfast so she could watch the miracle of his dying. She did it to etch in her mind forever the meaning of all the handshakes and cheek-touching. But even death failed her as its horror passed with each day that San Custodio managed to remain alive. As he grew weaker and thinner, though, the wrinkles and pouches of his face smoothed out; his lips swelled into fullness and time seemingly sloughed off his cheeks, a ruddy flush taking its place. When he was awake, his eyes glittered with the rage of his fever. He was becoming young again; and though his youthfulness was a false one, it differed little from the real, since San Custodio had lost the thread of his days, reverting to a childhood spent among the after-storm fireballs, *ratiles*, and banyan trees of the swamp of his birthplace. Her soft, lotioned and perfumed right hand caught between his sweating hot palms, he poured out to her the story of his life, a litany of fragile terrors. "A man can't afford to be fearful," he said once, his eyes fixed and glittering. "Terrified at being terrified, he becomes fearless. Ay, Teresa, I'm done for." Her name in his voice made her eyes water.

One night he was convinced a *buruka* had wrought witchcraft upon his body, transforming his leg into a giant python. "It's swallowing me," he shouted, nearly wrenching himself off the bed. The Diablos, a superstitious lot, ran for Teresa, who had to leave her host's dining table, impressing everyone with her dedication to her men. She quieted the bodyguards, calling them fools for succumbing to San Custodio's delirum. With a rigid spine, she walked to the back room of a mayor's house where San Custodio had been stashed away and felt his forehead, his cheeks, cupped his face with her hands. "Let it rain," San Custodio said, mistaking the cool of her skin for a sudden shower. As he drifted back to sleep, Teresa understood how he had loved the monsoon, the silver needle drops which fell gently, and gently falling called forth frogs, weeds, and watermelon vines from the black loam of his home swamps. She could see him as a boy, naked and barefoot, elemental as the rain drenching his shoulders and back.

She walked the dry path of her mission by sunlight and sailed the tumultuous ocean of his fever by night. On the seventh dawn, the heat tide ebbed from his body, leaving him lucid. Teresa, sitting by his bedside, spoke to him then, struggling to hold him fast this side of consciousness. "I'm finished," he said, with such a look of resignation that her heart lurched. In that instant, she fell in love, terribly and irrevocably, and understood that she and the Diablo were twins, two souls isolated by a numbing fear of isolation. San Custodio realized what had happened to her and sly with need, smiling, asked: "You will take care of me, won't you?" Teresa, helpless, nodded. That was how his destiny was averted and her own sealed.

From that moment on, he gave no further heed to his sur-roundings. His nightmares abated, leaving him afloat on a vo-luptuous sea of nothingness where he was laved by the warm currents of his dying. His mind sank into primal infancy. His skin began to acquire a marble sheen and his face took on the indifference of a statue. A sweet odor, ineluctable and delicate, permeated his flesh, and Teresa understood that he would hover thus, eternally, in that strange divide between life and death, never quite reaching either country, beatified for all of time as her own special ikon. The instant she had said yes, he became her trophy and cross. She would have him forever. Steeling herself, she swallowed both grief and lust and turned her passion into relentless fealty, the better to preserve him. It was the perfect fate for an idolater.

When news of the airplane's disappearance reached her, Teresa decided to return to her father. Hector's uncertain fate doubled the danger about her, and while she could weather it because of her gender and her family name, she wasn't sure the Diablos would survive. Thus that night two master carpenters of the town of Ora constructed and finished, literally under the gun, a fragrant pallet of sandalwood. San Custodio was laid out on it in the morning, cushioned by a cotton-stuffed mattress, and covered with a cream linen sheet, an altarcloth actually, heavily fringed and embroidered, smelling of a century of incense. Sent by the Widow, it was said to possess remarkable powers of healing. As the sheet fluttered down on him, San Custodio gave a tiny sigh and settled deeper in sleep.

She expected the Governor, her father, to raise a fuss, but the eerie sight of the undead San Custodio riding between the shoulders of the three Diablos and one helicopter pilot must have unnerved him. He only suggested that the injured man be placed in a tobacco warehouse, in the hope that the pungent aroma of drying leaves would revive him. It was useless. San Custodio slept on, a hand half-curled under his right cheek. Forty-eight hours later, Teresa lost her patience and had him transferred to her old bedroom. The Governor was scandalized.

"I'll sleep in your study room," she said to him.

"It'll be bad luck on the house," he said.

"That came when I was born," she answered, unable to hide her grief and bitterness.

He had five mayors billeted in the capital, said the Governor, awaiting her return and eager to join the Basbas crusade. "Of course, that's all changed now," he said, as his official car brought the two of them to the only tolerable restaurant in the area. News of the disaster had reached the mayors first; "otherwise, I would've kept it a secret and told them—well—later, when it's definite."

Teresa sucked in her breath and held it, the better to fight down the inchoate rage filling her. There was no denying the look of pity on her father's face, the sound of it in his voice. She was done for, he was saying—obliquely, as truth was said in the archipelago. She would have to return to the province. She crossed her arms, holding herself tightly, as the car stopped and the sounds of a celebration reached them. Disaster or no disaster, the mayors were enjoying to the hilt their stay in the provincial capital.

By the time she took her seat among them, she already knew what to say. "Sheer bad luck, gentlemen," she said, signaling a Diablo to shut down the benighted jukebox. "We can't anticipate everything."

They made appropriate noises of sympathy. "He would have been a great president," said one, raising a beer mug in salute.

Like hell. Teresa bit her underlip, allowed the mayors a moment to guzzle their beer. "However, we of the north must learn to take a long-term view," she said, deftly cutting off her father, who'd inhaled deeply, preparatory to launching into oratory. "The point is moot, granted, and that makes the gesture easier. Sign the petition."

Dead silence. The mayors looked at her askance.

"She has heatstroke," her father muttered.

She kicked him under the table. "An expression of sympathy to the family," she went on, suppressing the quaver that threatened her voice. "The Gloriosas will not forget."

Well, now . . . The mayors and even her father shifted in their seats. No telling how Blackie would take that, considering he was the only contender in the arena. Two mayors shook their heads in protest.

"Tell Blackie—and note, gentlemen, he's not one to kick a person who's down—that it's a noble but useless gesture. A sop. *Consuelo de bobo* to the Gloriosas." She stressed the name. "They are still wealthy, and who knows what could happen in the future? They have money; they have a son."

Uneasy silence, the beginning of doubt. She saw, felt, her advantage. Victory, she admonished herself, went to the determined. "No doubt Blackie himself will be properly sympathetic.

He'll be at the funeral himself. Come, come; we're not un-civilized. He'll understand. It's all academic. And the Gloriosas will be grateful."

The mayors glanced surreptitiously at the Governor, who mea-sured Teresa with his eyes. She saw he was trying to gauge whether she knew something he did not. After a while, he shrugged and said reluctantly, "Well, it's not bad reasoning." Teresa nodded slightly to a Diablo, who stepped forward and placed a petition before her father. He shrugged again. "The Gloriosas have been around for a long, long time. I expect they'll be around longer." He looked at the mayors, searching for a signal, but they were as mystified by Teresa's offensive. He signed finally, though without a flourish.

It was bitter but it was a victory, as Teresa told the sleeping San Custodio. She got them all. And two-thirds of the region along with them. "Mission accomplished," she said, letting the words fall like benediction upon his head. He half-smiled, shifted and left on the pillow his beard's remnants, a half-dozen curly black hairs. Sudden hope flared in Teresa's heart that he would awaken any moment now. Awaken, get to his feet, strap a gun belt with two .38s about his naked hip, and ask her to dance— which was how she'd always wanted to dance: held and led by a man nude from head to toe, so she had to be very careful with her spike heels, as she pivoted, slid forward, cut the air with her right shoulder, left shoulder, face in profile like a new flower. And at the end of it, he—her terrible enforcer—would whirl to face the crowd, her hand light on his hand, and say: "Obey her."

Alas, it was not to be. He slept through the day and the night, slept through the distribution of the remaining cash-stuffed shop-ping bags, through the special mass which the Governor, her father, had a priest celebrate at the cathedral, and slept through the move back to the helicopter. "Watch out for turbulence," the radio crackled as they went aloft, the air suddenly moist and

sweet inside the aircraft. Teresa glanced at San Custodio propped
up and belted on a backseat. Eyes closed, his head rested on his
right shoulder—which was how he would be, Teresa saw, until
the day, oh how far into the future, the day a torrent of people,
crashing through the doors of her home, found him, still asleep,
still young, but half aware, as his suddenly upright member
showed, of the tremendous excitement boiling in the streets, in
the house, outside the door of his vestal room; the crowd, not
knowing what to make of this zombie and mistaking him for an
inanimate instrument of perversion, consigned him to a bonfire
of portraits, memos, cushions, and tables in the yard, where he
awoke and died at the same instant. But in between, through
the years . . . Teresa took her eyes away from the premonition
and considered the sky, which was slowly darkening from blue
to gray, as roils of agitated air began to attack the helicopter.

Only the tail end of the typhoon had struck Manila—but that
had been enough. A mildew smell overhung the city, where, on
uncemented strips of land, the grass shook itself free of water to
thrust green blades upward once again, as birds returned to electric wires and posts to contemplate their reflection in the shim-
mering puddles on the streets. Teresa and the Diablos deposited
San Custodio at the Hospital de Santa Perpetua, where he would
stay for ninety days, until Armand grew bored with the recurrent
bills of his care and summarily ordered Teresa to "get rid of that
thing." She would then convey San Custodio in the dark of
night, unknown to his wife and children, to a long-prepared
room in her house. She took the trouble of easing the semi-
widow's pains, though, by sending her a monthly check.

In the meantime, repairs had to be ordered on the Basbas
house. Patches of damp stained the walls and floor, the jasmine
vines had fallen in the garden, and a litter of leaves and branches
blocked the driveway. Everyone present was subdued, including
Epee, whose hysterics had ebbed to a sniffle. Even Katerina was

calm over the phone when she asked Teresa to inquire about the weather. She wanted to return to the city as soon as possible, but de Naval was panicking about atmospheric turbulence and would not budge.

Unable to locate Armand, Teresa had to attend to it all. First, the government weather station declared that air travel could resume in a day's time—which news Katerina accepted with relief, not even mentioning the disaster to the meteorologist. Next, Teresa summoned the *mayordoma* and charged her with setting the house to order, as "Herself would not take kindly to coming home to chaos." She was having a cup of cocoa in the living room and mentally steeling herself for the confrontation with Epee when the girl came downstairs herself, face swollen and eyes red from her marathon weeping. When Teresa put down cup and saucer and opened her arms, the girl folded herself into manageable size and entered the embrace, asking in a hoarse and inexplicably aged voice how it could be possible, it wasn't possible, was it, that there would be no news, no news at all, and an object as hard, as big, as *commanding* as an airplane would disappear.

"He can't just disappear," Epee said, wetting Teresa's left shoulder with a fresh shower of tears. "He promised me . . ."

Teresa caressed the girl's hair. Promised what? A movie, a shopping spree. "I'll take care of it," Teresa said. "Just tell me what he promised."

Happiness, the unhappy girl whispered. Happiness.

And Teresa had to admit grimly that that was what Hector Basbas was all about: a promise of fulfillment, a null point beyond which further effort was neither possible nor necessary.

Poor Epee, she murmured as she stroked the child's damp hair.

"He promised me a house," the child went on, "where I could

be Mother. My own house. What will happen to me now? And to my child?"

Oh. Teresa's embrace loosened and Epee slid off her lap to huddle on the floor, face veiled by her hair, as she said, oh yes, that part was true enough, she and uncle had been doing it, yes, Tita Te, it, it, since she was ten, starting early enough to make certain of the clarity, the purity, Tita Te, of the lineage they were founding, oh, what was she to do now. . . . Like an unripe sheaf of grain scythed too soon, there lay Epee, the terror-child, wondering what was coming next and terrified most of all of what Katerina would, could do, while Teresa had risen, wondering as well what else was in store for them, hearing the honking of Armand's Mercedes-Benz outside the gates and knowing, even as she was replying to the girl's heartbroken query, that "of course, we'll adapt all your bastards, won't we," that this was indeed what would happen, there was no evading that fate, one-two-three pairs of eyes looking at her across the gulf of years, three pairs, all Epee's kids supposedly by various men but all by her uncle-father, all Teresa's legal adoptees, her children by law and her masters by fate and fact, looking exactly as Katerina's three looked now, pride and pain of the house, past and future confused, creations monstrous and banal at once. Despite herself, she could not help taking the vision for a guarantee of Hector's survival, wherever he might be at that moment, in whatever condition, the devil take him.

When Armand walked in, disheveled, eyes rolling in his head and feeling quite, quite mad, he found the two weeping on each other's shoulder. He flung himself into an armchair, confirmed that there was no news, no news at all, and abruptly began to cry himself. Teresa had to divide her efforts between the two of them, now comforting one and now the other. The strange thing was, she thought quite irrelevantly, neither the child nor the man made a move for each other.

11

Please *understand* that Hector was no monster—so Katerina said, as soon as she'd changed and gulped down a cup of tamarind broth to settle her stomach from the flight from the southernmost island to Manila during which she and de Naval became convinced that Teresa had set out to murder them with her claim that the weather station had said it would be all right, out to murder them in a seemingly accidental plane crash, yet another one, for the aircraft had roiled, bumped, leaped, and bounced, sending the Diablos retching, and only she, Katerina, had had the iron nerve to withstand that roller-coaster flight, breaking three of her acrylic fingernails against the padded seat arms and finally summoning the strength to sing, sing, all of you, goddammit, sing, exorting the men at the top of her voice, belting out the words: *to know, know, know him/is to love, love, love him*, over and over again, with the Diablos hiccuping into vomit bags and her own stomach going up and down, up and down, with each word, beating time to the melody, tears coursing down her cheeks as she thought of her brother, Hector Basbas, who should have been a Tercero, the III, but wasn't. What the hell.

She blew her nose, using tissue paper from a box—a plain cardboard box bought from some highway store, Teresa noted, and not disguised in the elaborate marble sleeves of which the bathrooms had plenty. For once, Katerina was ignoring appearances. Her pompadour had loosened, the flesh on her arms had loosened, and even her belly sagged beneath the iridescent blue-green cloth of her dress. Her eyelids, without makeup and mascara, were swollen, but her lips were hard with both tension and determination. She'd had barely enough strength, she said, left over from that godawful flight to fend off a gaggle of reporters who'd somehow caught wind of the plane's arrival and were waiting at the airport with cameras, flashbulbs, and video lights to boot, waving copies of Blackie's statement to the effect that everything was being done to locate the missing aircraft of his rival because after all, when one came down to the bottom line, "he was one of us, gentlemen."

Like hell. But she was too well trained, Hector-trained, to forgo the chance to score a few points, and thus, unsmiling, with as much dignity as she could muster despite her wrinkled clothing and the faint sour scent of airsickness clinging to her nostrils, she'd faced the cameras, said she was grateful for the President's help and hoped that everything was in truth being done; that she was calling on all of Hector's supporters to pray and on those who lived in the area where the plane was last spotted to search, please search, with all the fervor of the loyal, because time was of the essence. And here her voice had splintered into a tiny sob.

And would she, supposing that, you know, things were really hopeless, would she take her brother's place? It was the question of the moment, asked by a radio newsman.

A heartbeat. Her pulse tapping out a ziggurat. And then calmly: it was too soon to think of such things, but—and she'd shrugged daintily—why not? She couldn't let her brother's dreams for the nation evaporate just like that, could she? "This was never a matter of personal victory," she added. "He had plans, great plans, for this country."

There. Before entering the limousine which Teresa had sent to the airport, she'd hissed into de Naval's ear that shit, he wasn't coming with her to the house. He was to round up all the Diablos and get whatever was needed to search for Hector's plane, hang the cost, and a shopping bag of cash to the man who first laid eyes on the accursed airplane. Only then did she see Armand inside the limousine, huddled at the far corner, his face as desolate as a century-old shipwreck. She'd nearly lost her temper but biting her tongue had smiled sweetly and climbed aboard, extending her right hand so he could help her. At the first street corner away from the reporters, she'd kicked him out, telling him to hie off to the Church of the Mystic Limb for help, the idiot.

All in all, she could pride herself on behaving well and of managing even to give Blackie something to worry about, that old fart saying Hector was one of *them*. Like hell. Hector wasn't; never was, never could be, she said tiredly. She and he were alike in many ways, but not even she was in the same category. "No one's like Hector, no one quite like him," she said to Teresa, who felt the living room's air congeal with the cold fire of Katerina's rage. The windows were all shut and shrouded with the curtains, as a shield against unfriendly eyes, for Katerina had assumed at once that the house was under a state of siege. She had the servants close the gates, close the front door, the back door, every possible entrance/exit into and from the house; close all the windows, lock and cover them top to bottom. With a broadsword stroke of a glance, she had sent the children scampering to their rooms, the little beasts dumbstruck because of the power shift in the family. With just a glance, mark that, Teresa, she had stilled their clamoring and clamped a lid, as it were, on their distress and grief.

"Understand he's not a monster, but there's no one quite like him." She sighed. Sprawled on the sofa, with Teresa at her feet, she looked old and drained, a V-shaped furrow having settled between her eyebrows.

Freeze-frame. Chunks of time lived through but never savored. The claim that the dying saw their lives was false, Teresa thought.

It was the survivors who saw the lives of the dead and the dying, who watched helplessly as scenes with the departed unwound like a bad film before their eyes. Hector lost was Hector remembered. She saw him as she had first seen him, the afternoon sunlight an elusive cape about his shoulders, climbing one step, two, three, four, up the house's white marble front stairs, the black limousine from which he'd emerged parked in the driveway. Forehead held high, shoulders back, and each footfall a deliberate, concise move. Her breath had caught as she waited for him to notice Katerina in the shadow of the left front door panel, one hand flat on its edge, the other holding the knob, ready to shove the door shut in case of an ill wind, for this was the day the two women had returned from their year-long peregrination through the archipelago.

He saw her and stopped. An incredible light washed over his face, filling up its hollows, smoothing out his frown, so that he looked instantly ten years younger. Not moving, he waited, while Katerina was drawn from her shelter reluctantly, hands clasped before her breasts. With no more than a look, he pulled her towards him. And when she was close enough, he folded his hands over hers. There they stood, the twins who were not twins, one man, one woman, her hands imprisoned in his. He held her that way for a long time before she dropped her head to his left shoulder. He, on the other hand, glanced backwards, over his right, down at the limousine, and jerked his chin up. The chauffeur must have been watching, for the vehicle revved up its engine and departed, though not before Teresa had seen a woman's face suddenly clear in the window: Katerina's face, younger, rested, and made-up.

For a long time, Teresa thought she had seen a mirage created by Hector's longing for his twin; that he'd managed, by the sheer intensity of his missing her, to call forth a succubus out of sunlight and color and to shape and mold it into Katerina's likeness. The

131

explanation was simpler, as it turned out. The flesh-and-blood woman had been discovered among the ramshackle brothels of Culi-culi by the Diablo Emil Emilio, who'd seen beneath grime and dirt and sour smell to her priceless quality. With eyebrow pencil, lipstick, and rouge, with the appropriate wigs, and lastly with a generous spray of Katerina's favorite Nina Ricci perfume, the Diablo had completed the woman's transformation. Properly dressed, she looked, sounded, and smelled like Katerina Gloriosa, though she nearly wrecked her presentation to Hector by abruptly turning around and asking him to unzip her. The idea, Emil Emilio said, in the beginning, was merely to cover up the scandal of Katerina's disappearance—but the instant Hector's eyes fell upon her, in the third month of his sister's absence, he was restored to such an equanimity and so abruptly that the Diablos understood they had answered a need their boss couldn't acknowledge. The story had not diminished Hector in Teresa's eyes. Instead, she took the lesson to heart: there was no beggaring the absolute nature of the twins' affinity. To someone alone for most of her life, it was a virtual fairy tale.

When Teresa confessed this to Katerina, one late afternoon when they were snacking on slices of green mangoes dipped in salt, Herself had nodded and said she had reached the same illumination through her marriage to Armand. When news of her betrothal hit the newspapers, along with fabricated intimate details of a romance which allegedly had bloomed in the discordant years of World War II (totally imaginary, Teresa; I never even knew there was such a son-of-a-goat as Armand Gloriosa), Hector had suddenly appeared at the Montelibano plantation one night of the full moon, completely and staggeringly drunk. He'd traveled nonstop all that day, sipping continuously from a gallon jug of sugar wine cradled on his lap as he'd sat in the passenger seat of a decrepit truck, which was all the transportation he could commandeer on such short notice. Traveled and drunk

and peed occasionally by the road, not even bothering to halt
for meals, because he'd understood from the very first word of
that news report what this was all about: to split the two of them
as irrevocably as one halved Siamese twins, without a by-your-
leave and with no consideration for their health, limbs, and life,
perdition take them all.

Tossing the jug into a patch of cogon grass, he'd bellowed for
the guards to open the gates, even as he was already unsheathing
a brand-new machete. Once inside, he'd proceeded to decapitate
the roses, the ferns, the orchids of Aunt Doña Perfidia's pleasure,
hollering all the while that done for though he might be, he'd
take them all on nevertheless, the entire hydra of a clan which
had cheated him in the first place of his heritage and in the
second place of the true value of his chest of jewels for which
he'd scrounged like a rabid dog throughout WWII, God help
them all. . . .

For when it had come to turning his capital of gold and gems
into cash, Katerina said to Teresa, Hector had discovered how
profound indeed was the clan's control on all manner of com-
merce in the province. The Chinese buy-and-sell merchants,
whom hitherto he'd thought of as independent traders, could
offer Hector only one price—a pittance, a joke of a price, an
insult of a price—and there was no budging them, no matter
how many times he held up to sunshine the stunning green of
emeralds and the uncompromised luminiscence of pearls. When
a month passed without his having disposed of a single piece of
jewelry, his uncle had sat him down at the parlor and made him
an offer: in exchange for the jewels, he would see Hector through
law school and provide him with a small capital after graduation
to open an office where he could hang up his shingle. It was
totally unfair, of course, his uncle had admitted, but that was
how life was. After all, Christ never promised happiness on earth.

Hector understood then that his uncle held the purse strings of the Chinese merchants and more likely than not held their lifeline as well. With a bitter chuckle, he'd agreed—with one proviso. That Katerina be cared for while he was unable to assume that responsibility. Uncle had consented readily. After all, this was what the family intended to do; he confessed himself insulted by Hector's even bothering to bring this up, since it was a foregone conclusion and all that, smiling evilly all the while, for young and not having mastered guile as yet, Hector had revealed his one spot of vulnerability. Hector did manage to upset him, though, by looking straight into his eyes (the impolite uncouth; no young man should look his elder in the eye) and saying, as they shook hands on the deal, that this was on his uncle's head, he'd better believe it.

Katerina had been memorizing the chronology of her supposed romance with Armand—he saw her at the beginning of the Japanese occupation but she was too young and he too aware of his tenuous future as a guerrilla commander (what rot, Teresa; he spent four years in total debauchery, having been freed of his father's tyranny by an obliging Japanese soldier who'd lopped off the old man's head for some venal transgression) to pursue the matter; they'd seen each other again many years later, quite fortuitously, when he'd passed through the Montelibano village at the same moment she'd sallied forth one afternoon to purchase the illicit pleasure of a bowl of sweet *tajo* and gelatin from an itinerant vendor, at which he'd jumped out of his car forthwith and noting how grown-up she was by then, made her stand back to back with him, just to make sure their heights were equal and she wasn't taller (more rot, Teresa; I'm allergic to *tajo* and would've broken out in hives; also I am half an inch taller than Armand! But there's no helping the Matriarch's tawdry imagination)—in any case, all this was running through her head when Matrimonia came rushing into her tiny room, shouting she had to go outside to quell the wrath of her twin brother

Hector, who was now hemmed in by a circle of a dozen security guards, wildly swinging at them with his machete, though they forebore from drawing their guns and shooting him dead, because, well, after all, once upon a time, they had known him to be a relative of the overlords. So there was Katerina, hair spilling to her waist, dressed only in a white cotton batiste nightgown and with hemp slippers on her feet, running to the front yard screaming Hector's name above the loud male voices, women's screams, and the barking of Dobermans.

He couldn't hack her to pieces, of course, and took the easy way out by fainting in her arms. He was carried by the guards to her room and left spread-eagled on her bed, his hands roped as a precaution to the bedposts. She had to minister to him, wiping the stain-stench of vomit and sweet fumes of fermented sugar wine off his face and chest, herself weeping as though God himself had died and wondering what was to become of them, the twins who had been orphaned so young and could thus be bartered and traded without a by-your-leave. Although, truth to tell, this was all high drama, because she knew that while Hector professed aloud his helplessness in the clan's hands, he'd taken the precaution of lying about the contents of the second wicker chest, saying it had nothing but clothes and shoes and war memorabilia, which in fact it had, along with raw nuggets of gold, loose diamonds, emeralds, and rubies, and some really delicious items of jewelry—all of which he'd buried in a series of small holes during clandestine wanderings in the hills beyond the plantation.

The following morning, with Hector still tied to the bed, Uncle came in to deliver a tongue-lashing, saying he had it in his mind to strop the foolish youth; what was there to object to in the marriage, after all? Armand Gloriosa had tendered a decent, not much, but still decent bride price: brand-new furniture for the entire M-B ancestral house and a piece of vacant lot in Malate good for a modest-sized house—which, of course, would accrue to the Montelibano-Basbas clan as payment for expenses incurred in the nurturing and education of Hector's sister.

"You sold her," Hector shouted, sending the blood to Katerina's face, because, truth to tell, she'd never thought of it that way, having accepted marriage as a normal part of a woman's life.

One could choose to look at it that way, said the uncle, but on the other hand, she would be allied to a very rich, very prestigious husband and would never want for anything in her life ever again. Hector would be relieved of the burden of having to care for his twin and could live his life as he saw fit.

Hector had sighed, lifted his head to look at Katerina, and ordered her to loose his hands. He would not go berserk anymore, he said; the time for that was past. He asked his uncle to allow him two things: first, a horse so he could roam the back hills of the plantation to commune with himself; second, a visit to Armand's house, so at least the man would realize that Katerina was not entirely without protection.

"That's the civilized way, man," Uncle said. "You're learning."

It was done. Hector spent a week in the Gloriosa manor, and, having seduced Armand completely, could return to smirk into his uncle's face that henceforth no one would ever take anything from him. He was as good as his word, for from that point on, everything he touched was his, though he never got over the bitterness of his sister being taken over by another man, of being owned by another. Still, he and Armand became such good friends that Katerina had to run away to test her brother's fealty, run away clasping to her chest the monstrous discovery that her husband was one of those who liked it sweet and swollen up his backside: enemas, made-in-Taiwan porcelain dildoes, cucumbers and summer squashes, whip handles, chairlegs, not to mention the real thing, as huge, as brown, as hot as he could get it.

No, Hector was never quite the monster others had been or were—not to say he didn't try to live up to their standards. He was actually a simple man, an ordinary man, one who could love very deeply, without compromise; indeed, that was the stuff of his personal tragedy, because he lived in a country of compromise. The more he was forced to bend, to alter, to adjust, the angrier he became and the blacker the vengeance he swore to extract when the proper moment came. Unfortunately, there never was such a moment, and he was altered so much he became what he swore to be avenged upon.

What he did not notice—and here Katerina wept so violently Teresa had to run for a glass of water to calm her down—was that having been altered and having changed himself, he contaminated his twin, herself, Katerina. So that they became not two people but one, dividing between them the polarities which should have been the possession of one individual and which kept a person balanced and in moderation. Where he was strong, he was relentless because she could be soft and vacillating; where he could take, she had to throw away; whatever he was indifferent to, she became addicted to; and where he was cold-blooded, she had to be sickeningly sentimental. Each of them, having nothing to check their excesses, was just much too much of whatever quality it was that they absorbed and expressed. This was the twins' secret, Teresa. And also the reason why though Hector couldn't care less what others thought, so long as he got what he wanted, Katerina found herself with an incessant hunger for applause, adulation, and flattery. "One of us has to have the love the other swore to go without," she said, exhausted by so many truths. She was afraid, oh how afraid, of the transmutation which his absence would require—her changing again. "It will warp me again," she said, wiping her cheeks with tissue paper. "But do not pay attention to me. I've been crying nonstop since I heard the news. I'm now in a lucid instant, but tomorrow I will forget."

Katerina slid to the floor beside Teresa and, playfully almost, rested her chin on her drawn-up knees. The twins' years, she said, in their uncle's plantation had been difficult, but what had fortified them against the misery was a taste of untrammeled happiness for Hector, beginning with that fine morning their father, Basbas Segundo, had dropped like an emptied sack to the garage floor, between his cot and the twins' bed, instantly and irrevocably dead from cerebral aneurysm. "Think of what the media could do with that," Katerina said, "if they knew." That their father was done for the two had realized at the same time, but it was Hector who felt immediately the danger they were in. It was he who decided to keep the death a secret as long as possible. At his urging, they had pushed, shoved, hauled Basbas Segundo to the cot, slipped a pillow under his head, and drawn a linen bedsheet over his body, up to his chin, so he would appear to be sleeping.

They lived with the dead for three days and two nights—an intensely happy time. Hector made Katerina climb into their own bed, after she'd gone into hysterics when the corpse had repulsed her hugs with relentless indifference. Obeying her brother, she'd drawn the covers over her head and announced her intention not to leave the bed ever again. Hector took charge. He warmed the water for their father's wash each daybreak and nightfall, lovingly laving his feet and face, combing his hair, and once even trying to shave the dead man. With a bouquet of kitchen rags, he mopped up the fetid dark liquid that started to bubble from Basbas Segundo's nose and mouth, whispering reassurances all the while to the corpse, telling it not to worry; all the twins needed was just time enough to grow up and run away.

At night, he lighted a single candle and read to both Katerina and the corpse out of his grade-school textbooks.

For money, Hector used the garage's stock of empty beer bottles in pine cases, concluding that since each was marked with the words *return for deposit*, a living could be made off them. He would take a dozen or so to the corner store, retrieve the ten-centavo payment for each bottle, and purchase food, soap, candles for the house. He was sure, he told Katerina, there were enough empty bottles to see them through a decade at least of growing up, by which time he'd be old enough to work. Buoyed by success, Hector forgot they were still children and were supposed to be in school. And that was how Katerina's music teacher walked into the situation one afternoon and alerted the authorities with her screams.

In the years to come, weird as that moment of their life had been, an odd compound of innocence and conspiracy, Hector would tell Katerina it was the best time of his life. He could take care of his father, who'd never been one to accept a child's ministrations, and take care of Katerina as well. "For once, we were a real family," he'd say, negating the years when he hadn't been in charge.

Since nobody actually needed Hector at the Montelibano-Basbas plantation, life there had been a trial for Hector, and, as he would tell Katerina, were it not for her, he would have run away. The M-Bs were too quick to respond with blows and slaps—and Hector never got used to that. What loveliness he had as a child was perpetually obscured by bruises and swellings. He looked like a thug in constant trouble. Once he promised to bring a Coke from the kitchen to a cousin and then forgot because of a hundred other commands. The cousin complained to his father, their uncle, and Hector was dreadfully whopped about his thighs and the backs of his knees with the leather belt. That was how he learned to keep his promises.

"You can always tell when he means it," Katerina said. "He would look you in the eye and his own pupils would become like twin pinpoints of black light. He would shake your hand firmly. Once he does that, he'll do everything, possibly even die, in the fulfillment of his promise. But very, very few have seen him that way. I don't think even you have."

Teresa drew out another tissue from the box and blew her own nose. "He makes a lot of promises in his speeches."

"Oh, he never means any of that," Katerina said. "Sometimes he even promises the opposite of what he intends to do. He learned that trick from the older politicians. He's a simple man, really. One way of making a vow; one manner of loving; one overriding fear . . ." She giggled. "Fear of public humiliation. Which he acquired because our uncle made him go a whole day minus pants. As punishment. Naturally, all the servants and the cousins thought that a great joke. They made all kinds of remarks about his little thing."

"Does he fear death?"

"Only because it's humiliating." She smiled.

And with those words, the two women reminded each other of Hector's disappearance and probable demise—a thought so bitter that both covered their faces with their hands and began keening like peasant women in grief. Teresa, hearing her wails echoed by Katerina's voice, was overwhelmed by the inconvenience of it all, what with San Custodio in her house and her heart turned into custard by love, but wasn't that just like a man, to do what fate decreed him to do without a by-your-leave from his women, Satan take them all; how would she be able to shield herself from her own predatory relatives if Hector wasn't there as talisman and threat?

"Life is shit," Katerina said after a while. Eyelids pregnant with tears, Teresa had to agree.

12

A scream—*screaming!*—zigzagged within Armand's skull and he hardly felt the cold-wet-slime of sodden grass up to his ankles, ruining his black deerskin shoes and hundred-percent-cotton socks, as he saw again AND AGAIN the stage roof, that stage for the inaugural ceremonies, hauled aloft by steel lines running from its four corners to a center knot threaded by a crane's massive hook, rising, slowly rising, to the iron-gray skies, as men scampered on the decapitated stage itself, holding up their arms as though to catch the massive weight. Armand was already congratulating himself on his brilliant idea, meant to negate the destruction wrought by the typhoon, whose winds had not only severed the roof off its pillars but slewed it leftward to the earth so one edge was buried in mud and grass, when oh WHEN there was a resounding crack—CRACK!—and the stupid crane fell forward with a hoarse shriek, stubbing its nose as it were, a yellow rocking horse fallen forward and still shrieking though this time in several voices and different pitches and everyone was running, shouting, cursing, the noise petrifying Armand, who could only cover his face with his hands because the screaming was so godawfully, oh Lord, human. Human.

Eight men crushed; six still alive while two were irrevocably dead, sacrificed for the fulfillment of Hector Basbas's destiny. Armand heard the workers' teeth chattering and the heat lightning of the foreman's voice calling out the names of those pinned under the roof: *Beltrán! Tonio! Pepe! Doming!* Answers and no-answers. Through the fence of his fingers came the tiny click of a camera shutter. He dropped his hands but it was too late. Tomorrow, there would be a front-page photo of himself overwhelmed, shielding his eyes from that vision of destruction. Head hanging, he turned and walked away, one step at a time, ignoring the cries of *sir, over here, sir, Señor Gloriosa* and the contemptuous *They always walk away; always, always, always . . .*

His dejection kept others at bay. He reached the seawall without interference and climbed to its flat top, there to balance himself against the wind and to scan the boiling waves for sanctuary. He could jump in, he supposed, but the typhoon as usual had overwhelmed the city's drainage system and raw sewage coated the shoreline rocks, uggh; an epidemic of cholera and typhoid fever would follow pretty soon. No ships, no boats. Just gray water and gray skies. Nothing to hold his eyes, which caromed back and forth, banging against one segment of the horizon to another, while at his back, in the distance, the keening of ambulance sirens began. He took one deep breath, two . . . and found tears streaming beside his nose as his spine curved forward, his shoulders hunched towards his chest, and he had to draw on all his willpower to keep from curling up like a fetus, vision blocked by knees, hearing stopped by hands.

A most terrible feeling, he confessed to Teresa, who was, as could be expected, the first to turn up, hitching a ride in an ambulance as soon as she caught the news over radio. She seized his elbow and guided him back to the area of the ruined stage, now roped off by the police, and only after the initial volley of flashbulbs did she fend off the media. "A little decorum, gentlemen," she said firmly. "Mr. Gloriosa is devastated. As you can see." Indeed, he was, trying to cover his face again; tears were falling nonstop down his cheeks. It was shock, nothing but shock, he muttered, but she shushed him quickly, waved a paramedic closer, and asked that Armand be given a Valium or two. As he sat ineffectual and weeping in the backseat of his car, she was mapping out strategies to contain the damage, checking with the foreman so he would tell the right story, fending off reporters who threatened to swamp Armand, calling the Diablo head-quarters by walkie-talkie so the men could hustle up another crane. She made Armand stay until the last body had been wriggled out of the wreckage into an ambulance. And only then, a good five hours later, did she marshal him towards the lim-ousine Katerina had sent, though not before instructing one of the men to drive Armand's car to the house. It was efficiently done. Nothing of what she thought showed until they were well on the road, midway home, when with her right hand she sud-denly clipped him on the back of the head in exasperation.

"Who told you to mess around with the stage?" Having de-livered herself of her anger, she leaned back against the leather upholstery and let her face sag in exhaustion.

Armand burst into fresh tears. He ducked his head and dove into Teresa's arms, sobbing out how terrible it all was, had been, terrible, since news of Hector's disappearance. "Feeling so aban-doned," he said, between hiccups, "so alone. So helpless." He'd gone to the Church of the Mystic Limb, where Bishop Andy had taken him to the basement, past the freezer room where the corpse of the founder lay in state in its archbishop's cape, into a smaller alcove whose walls were covered by banks of radio equipment. The operator, Bishop Andy said, was calling the sect's chapels in the area where the light airplane had been last reported. Even as they stood there, teams of the Mystic Limb's followers, fortified by the archbishop's promise of an absolute and irre-ducible redemption, were braving the floods in their boats, rafts, dugouts, on foot and horseback, to search for the missing plane while their wives were busy slaughtering chickens, hacking off their white-feathered wings, and stringing these into perverse wind chimes in a magical gesture meant to keep the plane aloft, whether in air or on water. "As you can see," Bishop Andy had said, "we're doing all that can be done. Beyond this . . ." And he'd shrugged.

Shrugged!? They said their farewells friendly-like, but Armand understood that the archbishop, who wasn't available at the moment, was already in quiet negotiations with Blackie in an effort to save the day. Accommodating though Bishop Andy might have been, he couldn't quite mask—indeed made no effort to hide—the cool indifference of his impeccably proper manner and tone of voice. Armand read the message the young bishop was taking pains to telegraph: for the moment, the Basbas-Gloriosa family was without allies. And he thought he was a "wise man" and had a destiny of his own!

It was a bitter pill to take, Teresa. From their very first handshake, Hector and he had worked indefatigably to surround the family with allies, so many guard-crocodiles in a protective moat circling the Basbas tower, as it were, pardon him for being romantic. It had taken their combined guile to keep the crocodiles content so they would patrol instead of attack the vulnerable perimeters of the family's power. They'd worked their fingers to the bone, in expectation of that day when such work would be unnecessary, when the family was impregnable, unassailable, and no longer need worry about pleasing anyone. With Hector's candidacy and victory, the day had seemed well-nigh at hand, and the two had allowed themselves the luxury of a half-sigh of relief. Then this. How could something as whimsical as an off-season typhoon undo the work of decades? "The gods conspire against us," Armand said.

Depressed beyond words, Armand had driven to the downtown park to console himself with a look at the unfinished stage, as truncated as Hector's career would be if he did not survive this new challenge—only to be greeted by the horror of the roof on the ground, the pillars naked, and bamboo and wood beams scattered among the hedges and on the well-trimmed grass drowning in rainwater. His scalp had jumped at the sight. How could one life hold so many disappointments?

The public works men were already there, assessing the damage. Armand, wishing to have one thing at least finished on schedule in this benighted presidential campaign where everything that could go wrong had gone wrong, had inserted himself in the discussion. His idea—to lift the roof and settle it as it was on the naked posts—was so monstrously simple the men were taken aback. They had hemmed and hawed, saying well, now, we don't know; the pillars could've been weakened, the stage foundations could've been thrown out of kilter, the crane might not be strong enough, you know—their hands, palms down, dipping back and forth, in that unmistakeable gesture of doubt. Oh, it had been maddening, this sudden hesitance where there had been none before—more proof that the family's power was being eroded minute by minute. Though these were government men, none had demurred when Armand had called on them to begin the construction. The department head had readily gathered men, supplies, and machines despite President Domínguez y García's warcries. All he'd asked was that Armand remember in the years to come how cooperative the department had been. Now, this? The stronger the men's reluctance, the more saddened Armand became.

In his melancholia, he had blustered and threatened and insisted on having *his* way. That was how it was, Teresa. All he got for his good intentions was the promise of a recurrent nightmare of a crescendo of screams, tenor, baritone, alto, soprano, singing out his indictment, perdition take this land.

Teresa sighed, patted the top of his head, handed him a box of tissue paper. "Fix your face," she said. "Katerina's already in a bad way." She had banked on a decent interval before rats started jumping, but . . . She gathered herself up, as though to draw herself from misery. "It's not over yet. He's only missing. Not confirmed dead."

Armand groaned. "I have a mole on my left shoulder," he said, "right where my neck muscles slope to the joint. I am accursed." He blew his nose. "My nanny used to say it was a sign I was unfortunate. I have the mark of the Crucifixion. I could expect to live my life being crucified."

He'd shown Hector the mole at once, he told Teresa, minutes into their first meeting, that impossible October of his betrothal when a stripling of a man had entered the Gloriosa ancestral manor with precise heel clicks on the fossil-embossed polished granite of the living-room floor. At first, Armand had thought he was a peasant come to sell the secret location of a primary forest in the vicinity—for, Teresa, the family guild had constant need for good wood and it was getting harder to find the proper kind on which the master craftsmen could exercise their skills to the Gloriosas' profit. But the sound of those footsteps, which the young man did not bother to muffle, made him think again. Having been forewarned by the Montelibanos, he realized who his visitor probably was, though he was somewhat surprised that Katerina's brother would come alone, without fanfare, and with such a furnace of anger in his eyes. Without preamble, the visitor had said his name: Hector Basbas. Just like that. No titles, no elucidation. At which Armand had picked up a silver bell off a sidetable and given it a discreet shake or two, to call in witnesses just in case, for Hector was fumbling in his jacket's pocket and who knew what weapon was concealed there? But it was a knotted kerchief which appeared on the man's palm, and ignoring Armand's panicky offers of beer, coffee, wine, tea, while two plump and dusky peasant girls stood at the doorway awaiting the gentlemen's pleasure, Hector proceeded to untie the cloth to reveal matching pieces of a ruby-encrusted ivory high comb, earrings, necklace, and a ring. Armand saw that by their material alone, they already constituted a minor fortune; as art and antiques, they were priceless.

"Katerina will wear these at the wedding," Hector said. "Then they go to your family vaults." He laid the kerchief, with its seeds of jewels, on the table before Armand. "She will not enter your house in poverty."

Understand, Teresa, that when the possibility of this marriage was first broached, Armand was a singularly unhappy man, approaching middle age and barely recovered from a four-year binge occasioned by the anarchy of the Japanese occupation. His own father's death coinciding with a total breakdown of the order of things—"Life as we knew it was over," he said, "you're too young to know what that means"—had conferred upon Armand an incredible latitude, one he'd never expected even in his wildest dreams. Government had disappeared, on the national and provincial level; the parish priest had disappeared; high society had disappeared; and even gossip, that guardian of private morals, had disappeared. All nodal points of social control unraveled and survival became the primary objective and principal virtue. He'd expected things to settle down after a while, for some kind of administration to grow in place of what had vanished, but constant clashes between the Japanese garrison and pockets of USAFFE-linked and communist-inspired guerrillas made anarchy desirable and convenient.

They came and went, the guerrillas and the soldiers, marching between and among the trees of the Gloriosa estate, now and then knocking on his door for "contributions." Armand had enough supplies of sugar wine and palm wine, for there were palms galore for miles about the house, and had the means to make more. He still had tenants at the time and land to grow his own food, excepting rice, for which he bartered liquor with the garrison commander, whoever and whichever nationality he was. In the process, he managed to forestall a complete expropriation of the estate's produce. Unknown to the Japanese, the guerrillas also camped out in the Gloriosa backyard and drew from its warehouses what was needed to augment infrequent supply drops by U.S. submarines. "I did what I could for the cause," Armand said.

Apart from that, there was nothing much else to do. The two forces had free run of the whole area, without a by-your-leave from anyone. Though that had ensured Armand's survival, it had shaken his self-confidence, so used was he to being respected and giving orders. Those accustomed to ruling, Teresa, had trouble coping with the extremes of freedom, precisely because their own freedom was based on the control of others. Because there was no one to control, Armand lost his self-control and drowned himself in indulgence, partaking liberally of the sugar and palm wine in the company of six boys recruited as servants from the outlying villages. His little ducks, as he called them, decided to opt for survival forever and created a vegetable garden and fish-pond for the estate, stocking the latter with a strange new variety of fish which had arrived in the wake of the invasion, a voracious African fish the Japanese preferred for teriyaki. Once loose in the rivers of the archipelago, though, the fish decimated all other stock, turning out to be the worst kind of cannibal.

Gradually, by whose decision no one knew, the pond began to double as a swimming hole where Armand and the six boys cavorted naked, day in and day out, perfecting their knowledge and practice of underwater romance and submarine intercourse, and singing at the top of their voices to drown out the staccato of gunfire deep among the estate's trees. For Armand, helpless and inutile as only a total breakdown of peace and order could render him, had allowed the guerrillas and the soldiers to use the plantation as a kind of execution grounds, the first bringing in their enemies in the dark of night, bashing in the back of their skulls with two-by-fours, and burying them in the embrace of coconut tree roots; the second ceremoniously marching their captives to the house's front yard, to decapitate them—swish, swash!—with their swords as they knelt beside the dry Italian stone fountain, and then burying them, one to each bush in the front yard, while chuckling to Armand that he would have the most wonderful garden in the whole archipelago. One Japanese soldier even spent time landscaping that cemetery, bringing in white pebbles, varicolored rocks, chrysanthemums, ferns, and roses and creating geometric patterns of colors and textures to contrast, he said, with the stateliness of the mansion's facade.

He'd awakened from all that to realize, when liberation came, that he owned the world's largest cemetery. Who knew how many bodies *exactly* fed the vegetation and the trees, and fueled the giggle of leaves and branches in the wind? Hardly anyone, of course, with the exception of the silly peasants (to whom no one listened anyway), talked about the estate's other use and identity, since both the defeated and the victorious suspected that Armand had enough on both sides to let rip the biggest scandal ever in the nation. On the other hand, those on the winning side felt it wasn't fair for him to get off scot-free—and thus made free with nibbling at his property, prying off this piece of land, that share of stocks, tempting this or that tenant village to switch allegiance. Armand had to tolerate all that because, stupid man that he was, he had not linked (couldn't, Teresa) himself to any man of power, unlike two or three leftover families of the Spanish empire in the Pacific who'd attached themselves with dispatch to a returning archangel by the name of Douglas MacArthur.

This was the way things were when a matchmaker arrived with the offer of Katerina's hand from the Montelibano patriarch. Armand was three days into his "drying-out," his hands still shaking from delirium tremens and colored spots floating before his eyes, but he gathered his remnant intellect to consider the proposition. A young girl, of an impeccable name, properly educated and, judging by the sepia photo in the matchmaker's hands, quite lovely . . . one did not come by such treasures on the roadside, so to speak. But the matchmaker hurriedly assured him that the bride price would not be a matter of contention, that no scandal was whispered in connection with the said lady's name, that the Montelibanos were prepared to arrange for the couple to have a senator, a provincial governor, and an army general as matrimonial godfathers. It was a sweetheart of a deal. Though he questioned the woman repeatedly and even dangled a bribe, Armand couldn't ferret out the secret agenda behind the offer. He gave his tentative agreement, pending, he said, his own investigation into the prospective bride's background and pending furthermore a meeting with her, for the matchmaker knew full well it was easy to fix photographs. She could be suffering some deformity, like a withered leg, for instance, which her voluminous skirt would hide. Or maybe she had three breasts?

"She's healthy," the matchmaker said. "Wide-hipped. She'll give you children to continue your illustrous line."

She had the grace to lower her eyes at his sneer.

"Very well, very well," Armand said. "It's done for the moment, give or take a week or two for my final word. I'm cash-poor, so we can't discuss the cost of the ceremony itself . . ."

"Oh, but the Montelibanos are prepared to spend for the wedding," the old woman said quickly. Now, that was unprecedented, for since time immemorial, the groom's family paid for the ritual. "They want the marriage over and done with and the young lady taken off their hands."

With that, he understood that the evil of the proposed wedding wasn't directed against him but against the woman. He chuckled then, pleased by this sudden turn of fortune which would find him wed to a woman outlawed by clan rules. The matchmaker, mistaking the meaning of his laughter, hastily assured him that the woman's honor was untouched, her body pristine, and she

wasn't about to bring to the Gloriosa manor a bastard load. He'd
dismissed her with the rather surprising comment that he didn't
really care, it would be to his advantage as a matter of fact if she
were . . . let it all be done.

And now here was the young man Hector Basbas, eyes taking
in the disaster that had become the Gloriosa ancestral manor—
dried and crusted wine spills on the floor, dust on the furniture,
gray curtains half ripped off their metal rods; nose taking in the
pervasive odor of fermentation, saying: "This place is not good
enough for my sister." The eyes swung around to Armand to take
in the dark hollows of his cheeks, the uncontrollable shaking of
his hands. "And you're not good enough for her either," Hector
Basbas said in the voice of a God rendering judgment. Armand,
his bladder suddenly a petrified stone in his groin, nodded. "Yes,"
he said. "No good. Unfortunate. I have a mole on my shoulder."
He tugged at the left collar of his half-buttoned shirt to bare the
mark, much as a whore would unveil coyly part of her charms. An
acrid stench surprised him, and he looked with confusion at a
spreading discoloration on his pants front. He'd peed on himself,
Teresa, which was by way of acknowledging how much of a coward he was, for he had had a split-second glimpse of an army of the
plantation dead crowding in through the door behind Hector,
bending the empty sockets that served them for eyes upon this
scene which would bring them retribution at last. Armand thought
of how stupid he was, so stupid he hadn't even asked whether the
woman had any siblings; he really deserved what was coming to
him. The next instant, his body was folding, his head trying to
touch his knees, and he sagged to the floor in slow motion as his
legs buckled. With relief, he sank into the rising darkness.

How he wished he'd retained that ability to faint with ease,
when the roof had come crashing down on the poles and the
eight tiny figures standing on the stage and the howling had
risen—*aray! araguuuy!*—in tenor, alto, and baritone.

———

13

Katerina *was to be* rudely reminded that women didn't go around stepping on male toes, especially not on male politician toes, not even out of pique and though compelled by a tragic pride. Blackie Garcia, informed that Hector Basbas's twin was considering taking his place in the presidential campaign, guffawed. Wiping the corners of his eyes with a scented handkerchief, he said that, seriously, gentlemen, had he known it would come to this, he, Blackie, would've conceded defeat to Mr. Basbas immediately. At least then, Hector would've gone down in the plane with his ambition fulfilled and without leaving behind the fetid air of his opportunism to torment others, his twin sister included. That was direct enough, but Hector's running mate, the rather colorless but useful Emmanuel Patpatin, handpicked because he was the Jukebox (hand over money and he sang the right tune), suddenly announced that since Domínguez y García had conceded in effect, then it was all official, *he*, fifth son of the fifth Patpatin son, was president in accordance with the constitutional provision that in the event the elected head of state was incapacitated and so on and so forth, the vice-president should take over. By gum, that was him, hallelujah!

This public disloyalty was too much for Katerina. Outraged, without telling anyone her intentions, she ordered her limo readied, jumped into it, had herself driven to the Gold Cup Café, where Patpatin was feeding a small but fervent crowd of hangers-on. She pushed her way through, shoving men and women out

of the way, they falling away from her in stunned silence (for if
truth be told, her expression was terrible to behold, Teresa), until
she faced a table for eight where the silly twerp Manny, the
Jukebox, the ratfink, was holding forth on his vision of national
development. When what blossomed instead in his vision was
Katerina, dazzling as God's wrath, he turned as pale as the ta-
blecloth and half rose from his chair while his mouth and jaws
warred between stretching into a smile and dropping down slack.
He did manage a bleat.

"President? You?" Katerina's shriek vibrated against the café's
bay windows. "Over your dead body!"

And drawing back her right fist, she unleashed a punch that
caught him at the point of his chin and lifted him up and away
from the table in an arching movement which was stopped by
the wall banging on the back of his skull. His chair toppled over
as he slid down to the floor. "A real professional KO blow" was
how an eyewitness described it later on television. Not bothering
to look back, not caring if the Jukebox still breathed, the hell
with him, Katerina stormed out of the café, drawing in her wake
the man's friends, who tried to appease her and wash their hands
of culpability at the same time, saying *ma'am, it was just talk,
he wasn't serious at all, ma'am, we thought he was just trying
to get Blackie's goat . . .*" She shook them off and returned home,
nose in the air, hands folded on her lap demurely. The blow
had eased her anger, and though her right hand throbbed and
pulsed, she was rational enough once again to consider reper-
cussions.

She didn't tell Teresa about the incident and dismissed inquiries about the elastic bandage on her hand, saying she'd hit
it against a wall, some wall. She thought the Jukebox would keep
quiet about the incident. But of course, nothing could remain
hidden in this land, perdition take it, she should've known better
than to even try, for there on the late news was the ridiculous

Jukebox, flanked by two eyewitnesses, with an oversized turban of white bandages and with a blue-and-purple chin, saying this was too much, after all he'd done for the twins, and while on the one hand he could understand Mrs. Gloriosa's frame of mind, what with the demise of . . . well, surmised demise of—here he grinned broadly, pleased by his wit—still and all, he couldn't forgive her for assailing the dignity of a man like him, a man who had graduated with honors from the Ateneo Law School, who had served as justice of the Court of First Instance . . . And the Jukebox unfolded and proceeded to read from his vitae every single item thereon, including awards and publications.

He was definitely filing assault and battery charges against the woman, not for the money mind you but for the principle involved.

"Did you really do that?" Epee asked, awed.

"He was insufferable," Katerina said in confirmation.

To her surprise, Epee rose from her chair and gave her an awkward embrace. She patted her daughter's arm, saying don't worry, one twin usually sufficed to take on the world; the children shouldn't worry.

"But you've never done it by yourself," the child whispered, folding herself once more into her fears.

Katerina smiled and waved her away. When she and Teresa were alone, they considered the fear Epee had expressed; the twins might be a match for the world, but only one of them? "I have done things by myself," Katerina said, as they settled down on the sofa and waited—oh, this interminable waiting by the phone for news, as for a lover's call. Though the two men, Armand and Hector (how double-blessed indeed Katerina was, having two heads for the household), would never admit it, there had been a time when she had been alone, by herself, fending for herself. Oh, they'd worked it out between themselves; they'd agreed and because they'd said that this was the way it was—she was their dependent—they'd simply forgotten that not everything every time had gone their way. Not exactly, because from time to time, she had refused to behave as expected. They forgot now, for instance, how her marriage to Armand had been delayed five months because she had run away, just like that, as soon as her brother had left for the Gloriosa manor, following his drunken protest, and just as soon as he'd handed her a few items of jewelry, saying it would be unseemly for her to be without a trousseau. She'd hocked the jewels, but instead of going shopping, she'd packed her meager belongings and run away to the city of Manila.

"I didn't exactly thumb a ride," she said, half smiling at the memory. She'd gone by train, third-class, spending a few coins at lunchtime on the syrupy red-orange water peddled by barefoot children who clambered without fear into the coaches and dropped off at the next stop. The intrepid waifs, mobile as fish all day long, going up and down the railroad tracks, confirmed her decision. If they could survive despite the most terrible of odds, there was no reason she couldn't.

From her store of information, accumulated little by little and almost half-consciously from the constant gossip in the Women's School, she retrieved the name and location of a cheap board-inghouse in the Echague district. By paying a few pesos, she joined the thousands of anonymous bedspacers—poor students, mostly—who rented half of a double-deck bed (four in each of the three bedrooms, two in the hallway) and a third of a closet. Here, before the other spacers returned, she sat on her lower bunk, head bent to accommodate her height, and took stock of her situation. By eating only twice a day—a heavy breakfast of *mami* noodles and steamed buns at the Ma Mon Luk Restaurant; a dinner of one meat-and-vegetable dish and rice at a foodstall in the open market under the Quiapo Bridge—she could stretch her finances to cover many, many days. For a peso, the landlady pressed the three decent dresses she'd brought and hung them on wire hangers, which Katerina then hooked to a large nail sticking out of the wall behind the bedroom door.

In those times, she told Teresa, jobs weren't offered in newspapers. One found them through contacts—a person here, a friend there, a cousin elsewhere. She riffled through memories of conversation in her uncle's parlor and came up with a list of ten businesses whose president/managers would be likely to know the Montelibano-Basbas clan. She was efficient then, and this involved her survival. It took her two days to find the ten's addresses, checking phone books and newspapers. The hardest part was maintaining her patience, keeping still until she had the complete information. The temptation to knock on this or that door and proceed with the adventure was overwhelming. But on her fourth city day, as she came to call this time of her life, she shucked her everyday clothes, showered, put on one of her three decent dresses, thrust her feet into high-heeled shoes, and made up her face. Patent-leather bag on her arm, she sallied forth, clutching the pieces of paper on which her roommates, landlady, and assorted busybodies had written directions to her targets.

As she expected, her uncle's name opened three out of four doors she knocked on, the phrase "niece of the Montelibano-Basbases" ushering her right past secretaries and clerks to the executive office of the president/general manager. The deferential treatment did not faze her, indeed gave her courage. She came right to the point: she needed a job—and said that as though it were the silliest thing in the world, thereby conveying the impression she didn't really need one, was only looking for something to while away her time until her real destiny came along. For she knew very well, Teresa, that in this our world, the best way of obtaining something was to pretend one didn't need it, that it was totally unnecessary to one's existence. The response was heartwarming though amazingly the same; the executives would be pleased to have a Basbas join the company, though unfortunately this wasn't something which could be decided at once. Could they call her in a week's time and so forth? Not having a phone, that rattled her somewhat, but she frowned sweetly, saying that might be difficult because she came and went so much, could she call herself, say around midweek next week?

Thus, truly joyous, she trotted from one company to another, crossing off names from her list. What she did not realize until much later and should have anticipated was that the managers would contact her uncle. That was the end of that. When she called as agreed, every single one of them was unavailable, at a meeting or conference, out of town, and so on and so forth. How people survived this phase of growing up she would never understand, Teresa, for by the third evasive reply, she felt like an absolute zero, totally unwanted, without value and absolutely helpless. If they'd said well, see here, your training's shoddy and inadequate, you've got no skills—why, she would've understood and taken it in stride. But how did one deal with this answer which was no answer at all, only rejection complete and indifferent?

Broken-hearted, though not for the first time, she sat down at a table of the diner whose phone she was using—twenty-five centavos per call, please—and hid her face in her hands, not minding that her elbows were nestled on grease and soap streaks. She didn't cry, couldn't cry, but only shivered, long cold shudders running up her spine to her shoulders. That was how Aurelio Aureus found her, he of the beds in the hallway, because, as the landlady explained, although she was modern enough, she wasn't as progressive as to allow men and women to sleep in the same room, no matter how badly she needed money. Thus, the hallway spacers were four males, one being this young man training for the movies, training to be a *stuntman* in the movies.

"If it's that bad," he said as he sat down on the other side of the table, "you should try a novena to Saint Jude."

He was two inches shorter—his only drawback. He was kind, gentle, and good-mannered, with a not-displeasing face, and being pure Malay, had skin like burnished copper. Later, Katerina would wonder occasionally whether he would pale with old age, like those seventeenth-century church doors bleached by time, or whether his skin would darken, like good wood regularly waxed. At that moment, though, all she could think of was her desperate state and the prospect of returning to the M-B plantation. Completely forgetting her elders' admonition never to disclose to strangers one's vulnerabilities, she blurted out how she hated looking for a job, especially looking not for the fun of it, but simply because she needed one. She couldn't help it; his had been the first concerned voice she'd heard in a long, long time.

"Can you play the piano?" he asked solemnly.

"Only 'Claire de Lune' and 'Chopsticks.' " She arched her hands over the table edge. "You don't believe me?"

He did and took her to a music store on Pasay Road, which in those times, Teresa, was flanked by genteel shops servicing the needs of the old Manila *ilustrados* who hadn't completed their decay into a quarrelsome bunch of city intellectuals. The music store offered guitars, violins, accordions, Steinway pianos (white, mahogany, and red-brown, baby and grand), and one secondhand harp. After looking her up and down, listening to her do "Chopsticks" and "Claire de Lune," the manager hired her at a pittance above the minimum wage because, as he said, she looked *mestiza*. Since this was before the age of transistor radios, stereos, and quadraphonics, Katerina did brisk business. There was no lack of mothers who, taking one look at the elegant tall woman with her music scores (props only, as she couldn't read notes), imagined their own daughters showing off on a white, brown, or black piano, doing variations on the two tunes that Katerina had mastered in one of three suitable keys. Truth to tell, after two months of that, she could play "Chopsticks" backwards.

After paying her rent and buying a few items of clothing, Katerina calculated she could keep ten percent of her wages in a passbook account. Had she been willing to spend more, she could have had an easier time of it, perhaps a whole room to herself in the boardinghouse, but she thought of her twin every so often with sadness and with the aching wish that she could tell him to come, there was a place for the two of them where they could forget the L-Bs, M-Bs, and all the incestuous tangle of the clans. She knew, however, that to persuade him to abandon his feverish and secret war with them she would have to have something to offer. Which was why she was determined to build up capital as quickly as possible, as humanly quickly as possible, so she could purchase a piece of land where they could settle, far away from everyone. Property, she told herself severely whenever she grew impatient with the long wait in front of the common bath-and-toilet, or was awakened in the middle of the night by a late-arriving spacer, was the key to wealth and freedom. She could not, however, avoid one expense: a treat for Aurelio Aureus, who'd brought her luck.

He refused the dinner she offered. Instead, because he was a religious man, he insisted that she go through a nine-Thursday novena to Saint Jude, Patron of the Hopeless. And to make sure she did not renege on her promise, he collected her at the music store once a week at closing time and brought her to the saint's church in the San Miguel district, quite near the presidential palace, if that wasn't irony. There, in the thunderous recital of the litany to the saint, amidst the crush of desperate bodies smelling of sweat and burned diesel oil, and in the heady fog of incense and tinkle of silver bells, they fell in love. The nine weeks became an indefinite ritual.

Katerina forgot her brother, her name, her past. As in no other time of her life, Teresa, did she savor that kind of recklessness brought only by complete anonymity—the absence of worry as to what might, could, would be said by others; the total indifference to past and future; the sense of the eternal lived day by day. Time passing in the company of Aurelio Aureus—an hour or two, twice a week; a few seconds in the boardinghouse corridor, just long enough to trade secret smiles—brought her a sense of forever.

Stolen kisses in the hallway. Breathless gropings in the darkness of a moviehouse balcony. Aurelio Aureus's chest, hard as a cement wall, pressed against her breasts in the bower of shadows at alley mouths. His hands, the texture of packed sand from the rope-climbings and wall-scalings of his avocation, caressing the delicate skin of her neck. Bruises on her shins from the heavy boots he wore to his training classes. Such were the elements of this romance—fragmented memories of touch, smell, and sound—for it remained unconsummated, Aurelio being, as had been said, a deeply religious man, a devotee of the saint of the impossible, who once each week confessed to a German priest his venal "transgressions of the flesh" and who, therefore, would never even dream of having sex without a wedding ceremony, the silly goose.

As in no other time before and after would Katerina open herself up as much to her surroundings. She was surprised to discover that the city itself seemed to have entered the same miraculous stage of liberation, raising itself like a green sprout from the rubble of the war and sniffing at the sun and sea air from which the odor of scorched aircraft and exploded ships was slowly fading. For lack of wherewithal to buy entertainment, Aurelio and Katerina spent Sundays strolling down streets and looking into bazaars while he relieved himself of the burden of his dreams. Aurelio's growing mastery of the stuntman trade was not exactly what he wanted; what he really wanted, for which he besieged the saint of the impossible relentlessly, was to be a radio advice dispenser, a wise man of the airwaves picking his way through the labyrinthine problems mailed in by desperate, weary, and lonely listeners, an ambition which would be realized years later in the sympathetic voice of Johnny Bulalakaw, whose fans were legion, and who closed his weekly Thursday-evening program of reading selected letters and pondering the problems they contained in between Frank Sinatra and Vic Damone songs with the mysterious but tender admonition for precious, precious Katerina to "sleep well." Never "be happy" but simply sleep well.

Aurelio bought mooncakes for the two of them, and the taste of sweet purple beans and flaky crust was a subtle accompaniment to their contentment. Nothing could mar their peaceable imaginings, not even the rumble of trucks, the shrill calls of bus conductors hailing passengers, or the zigzag path they had to follow among and between the makeshift stalls of roast-corn vendors, banana-cue vendors, and plastic-toy vendors. Such were the city's sights and sounds that Katerina could be forgiven for not having noticed Aurelio Aureus's unease until the day he broke her hold on his hand and streaked away, cursing quietly under his breath. When she reached him again, totally bewildered, on the other side of the street, he was darting shark-glances at the crowd.

A man, he said, had been following them for three weeks now.

Though she protested she knew no one in the city, that those she knew didn't know where she was, Aurelio Aureus remained suspicious. He reduced her to tears with a barrage of questions, fearful that she was, as he said, conjugally compromised. She was naive enough to believe he meant a sin so repulsive it could only be alluded to, not named. Sobbing, hiding her face from him while she clutched at his hand, she confessed to having loved one other person. Her brother, her twin. Aurelio Aureus misunderstood completely and was relieved. The scriptures didn't forbid loving one's relatives, he said, and gave her paper napkins to wipe away her tears. There, there, there.

"Hush now," he said. "People are looking at us."

For they had sought sanctuary at a diner to resolve this problem, and Aurelio had ordered two cups of instant coffee.

"It could be him," he added thoughtfully. "But why doesn't he talk to me? My intentions are honorable."

"It can't be him," Katerina said. "He doesn't know where I am."

"What's his name?" he asked before Katerina could prevent him.

"Hector," she said, and the name rang through her mind like a bell. "Hector." And at last, finally: "Hector."

It was the end. Hector named was Hector conjured; there he was, one Friday afternoon, outside the music store, leaner and darker than she recalled, waiting with his precise eyes. Katerina, he said, as she came out of the double doors, which the manager was already locking. She couldn't rush inside for sanctuary; besides which, think of the scandal if she had run to the manager in hysterics. Katerina. One word. She froze and the world went on without her, the jeeps and trucks and buses rattling past, pedestrians walking away, the sun sliding towards the horizon, clouds fleeing overhead. She was dead, she thought. Katerina. Even her tear ducts had petrified and she couldn't weep for the lost Aurelio.

He accompanied her to the boardinghouse, helped her pack her things, waited as she said goodbye to the landlady. Though she spoke, she felt as though she'd gone mute, unable to say what she wanted to say, only repeating over and over again that her brother had come to take her home and hoping, in despair and in anguish, that the information would reach Aurelio Aureus somehow and ease his pain.

"He struck it lucky right after I left," she told Teresa. "A radio station hired Aurelio, and for five years, six months, and two weeks—one hour every Thursday at nine o'clock when household chores were over but it was too early to sleep—a good ten million people listened to his voice. He had more devotees than Saint Jude himself." The gulf between his and her world was a virtual chasm by then; no one linked Johnny Bulalakaw's lovelorn and love-weary closing message with the sister of the rising political star Hector Basbas. "We have two countries in this country," Katerina said. "But I knew who he was, and because he said so, I slept well once a week."

Once a week as well, she recognized herself, her story, in the final letter that Johnny Bulalakaw ostensibly chose to read from among thousands. Katerina saw herself in the heroine of simplicity assaulted forever by a host of villains: the overbearing stepbrother who connived with the banker to steal the family fortune; the autocratic landowner who demanded the whole harvest and her love as payment for land use; the corrupt politician who besieged the fort of her secretary desk; the corner thug who conspired to sell her to a white slaver . . . Aurelio Aureus was not only a great radio personality; he turned out to be a good writer, to boot. In the desperate pleas of this letter (and variations thereof) which ended every show, Katerina heard her own voice, her yearning for escape, the sweeter, the more intense, for the knowledge of its impossibility. But beneath this desperation, she heard as well the extravagance, the self-indulgence in the letter writer's piteous cries for help and was forced to acknowledge the evil that Johnny Bulalakaw delicately hinted at, this desire to be used, to be imposed upon, to be burdened and aggrieved and thus escape responsibility for one's life. Bulalakaw's measured words of advice, on the other hand, both masked and revealed Aurelio's frantic search for a solution, for words of such undeniable luminance they would enable her instantly to know how, where, and when to save herself. Thus would come the end of suffering, not only for her, but for all of Johnny Bulalakaw's ten million fans.

It was an epic struggle—Aurelio's wrestling with Katerina's dark angel—and it was all fought in metaphor. Amazing.

It ended abruptly, as all epic struggles did. Hector Basbas purchased the radio station and closed down the show, and not even the veritable deluge of protesting letters (a thousand every day for a whole year) could change his mind. As a matter of fact, Johnny Bulalakaw's popularity made him go further; he called the owners of other radio stations, told them about the letters, and convinced them it was dangerous to allow such power to accumulate in one man's hands. "What if he advised everyone to revolt?" Hector asked.

That was that.

Aurelio Aureus disappeared. Abroad, some said, to relieve himself of boredom; to his grave, said others, in despair over his unfinished lifework; to a monastery, said the charitable, to pray for world salvation. Thus, Katerina never received whatever solution Aurelio had contemplated for the two of them. All she got from that episode was the discovery that Armand and Hector had been running an illegal and secret gold mine in the back hills of the Montelibano-Basbas plantation. That was how Hector could buy a radio station without quibbling over its price.

14

For all the furor surrounding (His Excellency to-be) Hector Basbas's disappearance, the family itself treaded still waters and breathed in the charged but calm air of the storm's eye, leaving only Teresa to keep track of gossip swirling in a city recovering from a typhoon. Jukeboxes were beginning to clear their throats; beer gardens shook droplets off their awnings and reopened; buses, jeeps, and cars ventured back into the streets as kuchi-kuchi girls picked up their interrupted song-and-dance in the cocktail lounges and in that maddening manner of stylized rock choreography inched their right hip, left hip forward, arms akimbo, to be followed by the left shoulder, right shoulder, faces held in profile as instantly created lyrics about this terrible tragedy oozed their oily way past larynx and throat and from mouth to mouth. The accursed country sang about everything, including Hector Basbas's disappearance and the magnificent uppercut de-livered by his twin to a perfidious partner.

Rumors surfaced intermittently, sometimes over radio and tele-vision, mostly about what could have happened and what could happen—and Teresa, noting the phenomenon, understood that all over the archipelago an ugly speculation was working its way out. No doubt it was without basis, but who could stop men clustered over chessboards and checkerboards, over coffee and rice wine, from tossing out theories at one another? The thing was, as she told Armand, to take advantage of it. A conviction was growing that the aircraft carrying His Excellency (to-be) Hector Basbas and his aides (no longer bodyguards nor security) had been sabotaged, and the finger of guilt was pointing—surreptitiously, true, but pointing nevertheless—at Blackie. It could be put to good use, she said. Armand was amused. "Who, Blackie?" He laughed. "He's old-school." And what did he mean by that? Teresa demanded. "Old-school means only followers are damaged; never the leaders." Teresa lost her patience and shooed him out of her office.

COMELEC decided to postpone the hearings on Blackie's petitions until the Honorable Hector Basbas, senate president, was found, dead or alive. The senate and house followed suit, carefully hiding their watchful treachery by announcing that the tragedy of their colleague's disappearance had made them unable to deal with the question of presidency.

At least, Teresa told everyone, they would not have to worry about the hearings and could concentrate on the search. In truth, she was disturbed by how the Basbas family was lapsing into secretive silence, with house doors locked and windows curtained. In the fake twilight within, the children glided like sleepwalkers, always underfoot but never obstrusive, marking the rites of their own game. From an upstairs window, through a gap in the lace curtains, she saw Epee one afternoon on her knees in the backyard—whether digging a hole or filling it up, she couldn't tell. When she taxed the girl about it, Epee mumbled something about a dead cricket and shied away. Later, Teresa came upon Marmol squeezing out from between piano and wall in the living room. He froze when he saw her, then grinned uncertainly before streaking away, running on tiptoe. Inè she found in the kitchen, poking into closets under the counter. When she asked what she was looking for, Inè smiled and slithered away. Mystified, Teresa took the precaution of checking the storeroom where Crate #2 had been stashed. But the padlocks were intact and the door bore no signs of tampering.

She was puzzling out the children's behavior when the phone rang in the living room. She picked it up, heard de Naval's voice at the other end, and heard, as well, the extension phone in the study being lifted. De Naval, his voice reduced by fatigue to a rasp, could barely offer consolation. Most low-lying areas of the Great Plains were no more than a slick sheen, broken by a bedraggled tree or two. Roads were nonexistent, and mayors of submerged towns, panicked by the loss of their territories, kept flagging down the amphibian vehicles the Diablos had commandeered, trying to divert them towards rescue work. "It's a weird scene here," the ex-captain said. "People, birds, and snakes perched on the same tree, not even noticing one another." The family couldn't see it, but the whites of his eyes were gone, his pupils floating on two pools of blood. "I've got to sleep sometime," he said.

"Dead or alive," Katerina cut in over the extension line. "Not before you find him. Dead or alive. And remember it's a shopping bag—hell, two shopping bags. Whoever sees him first. And my undying gratitude, to boot."

De Naval cleared his throat. Better economize, he said; if worse came to worst, Katerina would need all the resources she could get.

Her thin shriek cut him off. Before Teresa could intervene, Katerina had launched into a furious and hysterical tirade, alternately cursing out and pleading with the man. Teresa slammed down the phone receiver and dashed to the study room, where Katerina stood hunched near the desk, knuckles white about the phone, her shoulders shuddering, a vein on her neck swollen. The three children had risen to their feet from the settee and were staring at their mother, hands clenched and faces twisted in a parody of her hysteria. Teresa's appearance broke the spell. Katerina threw one aghast glance over her right shoulder and quieted down. "Do what you can," she said. "Please." She began weeping quietly. "It doesn't matter what happens after. I—we—need him found. Dead or alive." The children sighed and, putting their heads together, began whispering to one another.

The tableau broke as suddenly as it had formed. The children turned wide eyes at Teresa, innocence so obvious it was fake. How furtive they had become, the children, slinking through the house almost on tiptoe, widening their eyes when addressed directly as though to deny any culpability. Now they gave her a strained smile apiece, separated, circled the room once, twice, and then exited, one after another. She was too familar with them not to know their movements had purpose. Frowning, she considered following the children, but first . . . oh, Katerina came first, always first. Teresa shivered in the deathly chill of the study room. The twins' propensity for freezing their environment doubled during moments of extreme emotions.

Having closed the conversation, Katerina set herself down in Hector's chair, her palms coming up to press against her face. But she was dry-eyed and calm when she lifted her face toward Teresa, who noted how they'd all fallen prey to useless gestures. She caught herself nervously sliding her left palm over the back of her right hand and remembered how Armand would walk to a window as though mesmerized and stare, looking out at nothing. They had to pull themselves together, she thought desperately.

"De Naval says Blackie's lying," Katerina said. "He saw nothing by way of rescue."

"Should we call the palace?"

Katerina grimaced in distaste. "What's the use? He'll say help has to be apportioned. The Central Plains are devastated. No, we're all alone with this."

"Armand's still pressing the Mystic Limb."

"Fine. Meanwhile, we have to start preparing." She sighed again. "It has to be done. We have too many enemies."

Teresa's eyebrows lifted. This was becoming a constant refrain: the existence of many, many enemies. They'd even forgotten how to be, pardon the pun, politic, and with the house a cloister, Teresa alone had had the foresight to have mugs of coffee taken to the clump of media people outside the gate who were on what they called the Death Watch. Seething, wishing she could bawl them out like a fishmonger's wife, Teresa oversaw the distribution of coffee and cookies, joking as lightly as she could that Hector might disappoint them and turn up as alive as one could wish. Midmorning and midafternoon, the garden boys wheeled out a tray of goodies to warm the media's stomachs—galling generosity on the house's part, Teresa thought, but it was cheaper than handing out envelopes.

For Katerina to say that preparations had to be made was an affront. She, Teresa, had gathered as much of what she thought would be needed without alerting the Death Watch. Three doctors on call; the library recreated into a surgery room; medicines and sterile instruments; oxygen tanks and tents . . . what else would be needed?

"Public pressure to cancel the election results and to have myself declared a candidate in the new one," Katerina said calmly. "Not that I like the idea—but there's no helping it." She picked up a pencil, drew a sheetpad close, and began scribbling. "How many signatures do you think we'll need?"

"That would be very costly."

"We have the other crate. Don't make a face; you become uglier. I'd like nothing better than to run away with the money and disappear. But I've thought and thought and thought again. There's just no helping it: one of us has to be president."

"But—"

"Everything falls apart if that bridge isn't crossed." She fell silent. "A million, two million, signatures perhaps . . . and opinion-makers. Columnists, radio broadcasters."

"You can't run."

"Why not?"

The reasons ticked off her immobilized tongue. Because you're a woman, because it's only been a week since the plane disappeared, because you're inexperienced, because you're mad . . . A pause. Katerina, talking as much to herself as to Teresa, went on writing. A sumptuous wake—sixty days at the senate, all flags at half-mast, hour-on-the-hour spot coverage by the media; Armand would have to check with the Mystic Limb how they kept their founder unspoiled . . . "That way Hector will draw sympathy throughout the campaign," she said, her lip corners crinkling, "for me." She had to use him, she said, should not hesitate to use even his corpse, "just as he used me. That's the Basbas strength, Teresa. We do not spare one another. Now, please call Emil and have the Diablos who can be spared gather here tonight."

On the way to the living room, Teresa chanced upon Epee hugging a biscuit tin to her chest. The child backed away, a tiny whine escaping her lips—and that was enough to rouse her suspicion. She beckoned, if a little imperiously—what the hell for was she hanging around in the midst of this disaster if she could not do this?—and the girl approached with reluctance. Without a word, Teresa took the can. It was light but something rattled inside. She wrenched the cap off and saw an assortment of medals, cufflinks, bracelets, and a gold pen—all Hector's.

"What the—?"

"I'm—we're—putting things away, Tita Te. Don't tell Mama. Inè, Marmol, and myself. We're hiding things, his things, our things. So they can't be found."

"Hiding—from whom?"

"Enemies. I take care of Uncle's things, Inè takes care of Mama's, and Marmol hides Papa's. That way, when they break in, they'll find nothing. Don't worry. We keep track of all the secret places. In code." The girl snatched the can back and hurried away. "Keep doors and windows locked," she said in parting. "And don't worry. We'll hide everything. And we'll deny and deny and deny. Nothing will ever be found out."

The children, Teresa realized, were acting out Hector's last words to his family. They would do so over the years, today and forever, folding secrets into secrets like elaborate origami constructs, until they themselves lost the ability to tell truth from falsehood. She shuddered. Hector's disappearance was affecting them all in different monstrous ways. Where would it all end?

A bray of laughter was Emil Emilio's response to news of Katerina's intentions. "The men will never buy it," he said, "and neither will the financiers."

"Convince your men and I'll take care of the others," Teresa said, dutifully affronted. "Mediawise, it'll make a great story— the insignificant housewife called by a higher destiny, against all odds, despite all obstacles and all that. Every widow who's run in her husband's place has won."

"But she's not his widow."

"Same banana," she said, cutting off further arguments. "Better even, because she's a Gloriosa. Prepare the men and I'll alert Armand." She sounded, she thought, far more convinced than she really was.

To her surprise, Armand took the news calmly. He'd expected it, he said; anyone who knew the Basbas twins would have realized what could, would, happen. Polls were already underway, as a matter of fact, on the popularity of the bereft twin. And the betting was pretty heavy in favor of Katerina's running. "We could use the poll results when we make the announcement. Hope they come down on our side." He sighed. "I just hope we find him before his body's damaged too much. If she plans to display him, a mutilated corpse won't draw as much sympathy as a nice-looking one."

"Don't be morbid."

"Am not. Just practical." He made a sound which made Teresa's ears perk up.

"Are you crying, Armand?"

"A little," he admitted. "I owed him—uh, everything. Only the twins knew that." He sighed. "Someday, I'll tell you about it. Someone has to keep accounts, after all." A pause. "Ask her what can be used against her."

Why, nothing, of course—so said Katerina, enthroned on the white-and-gold stool of her vanity table, as Valero the couturier dabbed her cheeks with one rouge tint after another, dipping elegant brushes into the cosmetic pots on the dresser. Herself had led a life pawned to another's dream—a Christian ideal, no? "What can be said against me?" Four of Valero's seamstresses were working on a black shirtwaist spread out on the bed. Pale, muttered Valero, very pale; the perfect makeup to go with the mourning clothes. "Fragility with determination," he added. "That's what we're aiming for." Then he shook his head and said he had to give her credit; considering what had happened, he wouldn't have blamed her if she'd gone totally to pieces.

Katerina nearly fell apart then, moaning, "Oh, Jesus, Jesus . . ." Teresa had to threaten Valero with a hairbrush to calm everyone down.

Herself had decided that a test run of her candidacy was in order. The best opportunity was that evening, at the campaign headquarters where the staff had taken to gathering for dinner and to say a rosary for Hector's safety—that is, for as long as the campaign budget allowed them to remain on the job. If she couldn't sway the staff, Katerina said, she might as well give up; after all, their jobs depended on a Basbas victory.

It was a good choice: a ready-made audience, a willing-to-believe one, with religious hysteria prowling at its edges. Already, two or three women were claiming to have dreams about Hector.

He wasn't dead; he was alive though in suspended animation on some mountaintop; his magical amulet—a lead triangle with cabalistic markings—had thrown him into deep sleep while it renewed its animus. Or something to that effect. Defeat, fear, powerlessness—the proper mix to engender fanaticism. Teresa had to acknowledge that if Katerina pushed the right button, she could have the beginnings of a crusade.

Hmmmm. Teresa entered Hector's bedroom, the only place where she could be undisturbed in the house. Locking herself in, she worked on a four-page statement until three in the afternoon. With the proper coaxing, Katerina could read it well— few polysyllabic words, short sentences, a fluid cadence, and "compassion" repeated maybe thirty-two times. That was one great word, Teresa told Herself; suggestive and vague, general and yet with seeming specificity. It would be the keyword of Katerina's campaign. The speech itself worked around the figure of the avenging female; no threats, no accusations, but heavy with intimations of foul play and retribution. "We've got nothing stronger in our myths," she said. "This reaches in deep. Deep into the psyche."

Herself nodded, motioned her away, and was secluded with Valero over the next two hours. When the door opened again, she was ready, fully made-up in muted colors, wearing the black dress and black high heels ("This is the one time to stress your height, darling," Valero said. "Don't slouch"), and with a light black veil over her head. Even Teresa's breath caught and she had to marvel once again at how lovely Katerina was, what a malleable face she had. She looked—ooooh, regal, and yes, admit it, powerful.

The conference room where the staff—about a hundred all in all, augmented by twenty Diablos shepherded by Emil Emilio—exploded into a roar of approval when Katerina entered. She had dismissed Valero and was flanked only by the three children, somberly dressed. Two maids in white uniforms and Teresa in a Franciscan-brown skirt and blouse brought up the rear. Valero had decided that only Katerina should be in mourning, to firmly fix public attention upon her person. She moved like a burdened woman toward the front of the room, near the blackboards, where a microphone and lectern had been set up for the rosary leader. But when she turned to confront her audience, she straightened her shoulders back and with the tips of her right fingers drew one wing of the veil to reveal half her face. She gave them the full impact of her beauty by hiding half of it. The sounds of weeping seeped through the room quietly. Teresa threw a look at the maids, signaling they should keep a firm grip on the children, afraid that they would do something to destroy the moment. It was unnecessary; the three never moved at all, merely kept their eyes fixed on their mother. At such moments, the children could be so admirably disciplined.

Now, Katerina's right arm was slowly rising, palm down, over the heads of the people gathered in the room.

"Hector," she said, the hoarse whisper filling the room. Then, volume rising: Hector. And yet again: Hector.

HECTOR! the room thundered back. Hector, Hector, Hector. A chant, an invocation, a calling forth of the spirit. Hector, a woman screamed, beating her chest with her right fist in a *mea culpa* gesture. Hector, a man cried out, slapping the air overhead with both his hands. Hector, the Diablos roared, snapping their hands against their thighs in one synchronized slap.

Without casting her eyes on the text she held, Katerina said something. It was lost in the applause. Teresa allowed herself the luxury of a smile by then. Herself was speaking—smoothly, without hesitancy—words approximating what Teresa had written. But the crowd wasn't listening. Words didn't matter here. Katerina's appearance was reassurance enough, and Teresa understood that the staff had arrived independently at the obvious:

the twins were one and the same. In the absence of Hector, Katerina would take on his persona. It was all over except for the counting.

By the time Katerina signaled the white-frocked priest to begin the rosary, there wasn't a dry eye in the room. But to the last instant, Herself remained vigilant. She looked at no one, merely moved towards the door as Teresa, the children, and the maids discreetly stood at the crowd's edge, waiting for her to reach them. She maintained an inviolate air, surrounded by cleared space, as even the Diablos fell to their knees when the priest intoned the opening prayer.

Once in the limo, though, Katerina pulled the veil off her head, folded it carefully, and handed it to Teresa. "Send a box of Swiss chocolate bonbons to Valero," she said, her eyes fixed upon an internal landscape. "From me. Personal. You've got to give it to the faggot. No one's better at staging theatrics."

15

One had to hand it to the twins. No one quite like them
around, Armand said. Or rather, quite like Hector, who could
take the raw stuff of a human being and mold it into a marvel
of a weapon. Hector was a walking miracle, so exceptional in
his being ordinary, "an aggregate of all our biases and fears,
certainties and doubts, and every contradictory quality one could
think of," that he became instant confirmation of the beholder's
faith in his own self. When Hector roared about the need for
peace and order in the archipelago, every businessman—from
the shopkeeper threatened by day-to-day robbery to industrialists
threatened by strikes—fell to his knees in rapturous agreement.
When he proclaimed himself the leader of a new revolution, this
one from the top, the poor and the dispossessed hailed him as
messiah, for sparing them the need to wage war and struggle on
their own. When he called for the restoration of traditional val-
ues, the churches, every single one of them, concurred. When
he said universities should be bastions of independent thought
and in the next breath proclaimed that the duty of students was
to study and prepare for careers, he swept a majority of that crowd
and their parents to his side. He offered everyone the path of
least resistance, said Armand; he told them all they could be
what they were at the moment and still become what they wanted
to be. Because he, Hector Basbas, fulfiller of myths, would take
on all responsibility. He freed everyone from being answerable
for his life. He was everyone's supreme patriarch, matinee idol,

patron, and dedicated servant. "He had discovered long ago," Armand told Sunday Smith, "that ninety percent of humanity preferred to be told what to do. That way, if anything went wrong, they could always blame, not themselves, but someone else. God, the devil, the politician, the leader—whoever or whatever they chose to believe in. They could complain then that this trust was betrayed, this faith misplaced. They forget how they and not anyone else, they themselves, chose to believe. If truth be told, this whole procedure is simply a process of hoodwinking themselves." Of course, Armand thought but did not add, while Hector volunteered to take over all responsibility, he also took on all power and privilege. That was how the equation worked.

The 'Kano wasn't particularly interested in this exposition but had to listen, since he'd come to Armand's office in the disguise of a foreign correspondent, a journalist. Oh, his credentials were real enough to some extent, he assured Armand later, for from time to time he did file stories with an international news agency, which fed them back to the country's provincial newspapers, from which, in turn, they were picked up by Manila periodicals. It was a cumbersome machinery, somewhat slow, but until such time as all publications could be brought under a single but seemingly disparate ownership, this was the only way it could be done with a degree of verisimilitude. "How do you think those stories about Blackie's corruption get into the press?" Meanwhile, since Armand's secretary was hovering nearby, busily arranging biscuits and coffee mugs, he had to listen to Armand reminisce about the vanished Hector because he'd claimed he'd come to get the family's views about the mystery.

But what he was interested in really was WHAT ABOUT ALL THAT MONEY? The question shimmered in the office cold air as soon as the door closed on the secretary's back.

Armand gave him a puzzled look. "Bad investment, of course. Win some, lose some."

The man looked so ill ("We're talking millions," he said in a hoarse voice) Armand was disappointed. What did the guy expect, Armand raged to Teresa, this modern-day buccaneer who'd swum into Manila Harbor in the wake of General Douglas MacArthur's returning armada, this post-WWII carpetbagger who one day, he was dead sure, they would find enthroned as an archipelago expert in some public relations office in New York or in a Boston academia, parlaying his familiarity with the islands as capital and making a good living off it, what did he expect? "That we should return the money, pay it all off? I thought him more intelligent than that."

And what really offended Armand was that the man should do this even before there was confirmation either way. Hector hadn't been categorically classified as dead or alive, merely missing, but here was the son-of-a-goat knocking on the door and asking about money. "Thoroughly without a sense of timing," Armand grumbled. "No *delicadeza*. Why ever did we associate with such a creature?" He just had to get rid of the creature, Teresa; and so promised him that as soon as Hector was found dead—mind you, not breathing, *corpus delicti* and all that—he would render Mr. Smith an accounting and return the unused money. "Imagine having to account for political donations! Who ever heard of such a thing?"

It had upset him so much he couldn't even enjoy the report that the tender trap had finally worked, after everyone had given up on it, including the blond Valkyrie herself. When Hector's plane had gone down, she'd collected her final "allowance" from Emil Emilio, bought herself a decent blouse and skirt—startlingly modest, considering the décolletés and red spike heels she'd been wearing all along—and decided to have a calm afternoon tea at a French pastry shop in the Makati district, all by herself, enjoying the peace and quiet after the turmoil of chasing Blackie's campaign manager from one cocktail lounge after another, when . . .

Oh, too late this turnabout of events, but nevertheless, there he was, having cappuccino and a slice of Black Forest cake, also alone, his eyeglasses clouding up from the air conditioning, which was something the German blonde couldn't understand, meaning why in this place where the cool season meant ninety degrees in the shade, interiors were always kept at an arctic forty, perhaps to enable the men to wear dark blue suits as in Wall Street—no?—never mind. . . . There he was and he caught the glance she inadvertently aimed his way and smiled and she smiled back and before you knew it, they were head-to-head, so to speak, sharing her table while she played coy in keeping with her modest clothes and while he tried very hard to impress her with his importance, his bank accounts, his cars, his swimming pool, and his forthcoming appointment as head of the public works department, the most lucrative position in the whole government, where a man could and did become a multimillionaire overnight. When she demurred (actually being bored to the death), refused to say she believed him, all this time pressing her (unpainted) full lips on his rather small mouth, for the two of them had somehow moved from the patisserie to a dim bar and were downing gin and tonic, all this time, in between his words and her casual "Uh, I don't care if you're poor or whatnot, I like you, you see," she was sucking at his tongue, caressing the bones of his knees, patting his pectorals, and sighing, sighing, sighing that it was her fate to meet *an unknown* in this far-flung country. By luck she had discovered that nothing drove the men of the country wilder than to be thought a nonentity. Irritated beyond belief, assaulted by both lust and humiliation, he'd taken her to a cousin's house in the hills of Alabang—lost hills, alas, they'd been flattened to accommodate the instant antique colonial houses of the very rich—where . . .

Blackie's men had been using the house as secret headquarters, he said while she rumbled innocently, "Who's Blackie?" No one knew about the place, and it had a good-sized safe in the study where campaign cash and sensitive documents could be hidden until needed. The man opened the safe and showed her the neat stacks of hundred-peso bills, all newly printed and in bundles of ten thousand, but she pointed a long red fingernail at big brown envelopes on a lower shelf and asked, "What are those?" The man laughed, said they were something to blow the Basbas campaign sky-high ("Who's Basbas?" she asked, convulsing him with laughter), slammed the safe door shut, and pushed her toward the desk, where she had to bend over, rear end up, while he rolled her skirt over her hips and up her back and ripped her panties down because, as he muttered, he'd always liked doing it like this, just like this, knowing it would be so good, oh, so good, considering how dogs stayed linked for hours on end after having done it just this way, but that stubborn wife of his had consulted a Jesuit who'd said this was a sin, a major sin, a *cardinal* sin, yeeeees! wasn't it, HMMMMM . . . SO GOOD! while she tried to read an upside-down letter on which her nose rested. He paid her well, offered her a job as his private secretary just as soon as his appointment was confirmed, tried to do it again but couldn't ("His physique leaves much to be desired," she told Emil), and then tried to persuade her to stay the night. She declined, of course, because what she really wanted, if Armand wished to know, was enough capital to buy a small house where she could live to the end of her life with an unremarkable husband and five children.

Armand paid her well, too, though he didn't know if there was any use to the information. He called Emil and told him to hop on it; go raid the place. After all, if Katerina was running, they might as well begin with a clean slate.

A very clean slate. He'd never forgotten Hector Basbas's words the morning Armand came out of his faint to find himself naked and clean in his bed, his cloth slippers side by side on the floor and his silk robe folded on a night table. It was eerie to open one's eyes to familiar surroundings and yet be certain, for some reason, that one was a stranger. He considered staying in bed, not moving at all, but remembered his visitor and understood that the problem of Hector and Katerina Basbas would not unknot itself. There was no helping it; he had to attend to unfinished business despite his knocking knees and shaking hands. So willy-nilly, he donned his robe, thrust bony feet into the slippers, caught a glimpse of his ruined self in the dresser mirror (did his jowls really sag that much, his belly precede him by that much?), and inched his way to the staircase, calling out the names of his two attendants at every step. Abysmal silence. Then a rustling and a ripping, a low laugh, thuds on the floor—it was Hector, having the time of his life jumping onto sofa and chair backs and leaping again for the ceiling-to-floor curtains shrouding all the windows, swinging on them like an inebriated orangutan and riding their slow collapse as the cloth tore and shook loose from curtain rods, only to collect himself from the swirl of dust that marked the curtains' demise and to do it again. Sunlight cavorted through half of the room, dust motes dancing in the yellow rays, when Armand poked his head in and was jolted out of his lethargy. WHAT THE HELL DO YOU THINK YOU'RE DOING?

Hector swiveled at the sound, laughed, said today was the day for starting with a clean slate, and drew a, Lord, revolver from his pants waist. Armand was dead. He knew it as he flung himself toward the dining room, through the kitchen, and out the back door, his soft slippers crunching the earth of the never-planted vegetable and herb rows of the rear garden, slipping on the gravel of the Japanese front garden, and finally getting themselves stuck in the mud around the fishpond. Three times around the house Hector chased him until he collapsed on the terrace, heart hammering and lungs wheezing, his nose resting on the dim outlines of a fossil fern on a granite slab. He could only close his eyes and wait for oblivion. "Kill me," he gasped out, "but don't make me run again."

Hector merely pulled a wrought-iron chair close to Armand and sat down. Good, he said; good. The run should've stoked Armand's blood; he could have his breakfast now; it had been prepared by the women who were at that moment in the tenant village recruiting servants for the Gloriosa manor.

"I have to forgo the pleasure of killing you," Hector added. "So we're starting on a clean slate."

Armand was so grateful at being allowed to live—he had no doubt that Hector would have enjoyed his death—that in the week the young man stayed at the manor, he obeyed him without complaint. Each morning, Hector had him run for exercise three, four, five times about the house, and IT WORKED! By the fifth day, his body was remembering how good it was to be lithe, slim, firm, to be a good-looking Gloriosa, and the acrid fumes of rice-sugar-coconut fermented wine which had tainted his sweat had become no more than a relic scent lining the odor of dried roses. He was sure it would soon be gone, for Armand didn't dare have a drink, no, not even beer, because Hector was just waiting for the slightest excuse to inflict upon the other's body the most heinous of tortures. Meanwhile, a battalion of men and women descended on the house, gave it a thorough scrub and rinse for the first time in five years, fixed the various gardens, even let loose some astonishing goldfish in the pond and cleaned and washed and sewed and repaired until the manor looked as though the power of the Gloriosas had been restored. When Armand inquired diffidently where the money was coming from, since "I'm cash-poor, at the moment," Hector told him that the next three crops of the coconut plantation surrounding the manor had been sold. Armand nearly choked; they'd been grossly underpriced.

But Armand couldn't complain, not really, since Hector kept reminding him that he himself had had to forgo a supreme pleasure. That was the way Hector was, Teresa. He traded with whatever magical spirits he believed in, swearing with terrible oaths to undergo this or that repulsive experience in exchange for something he desired; or vowing to give up a pleasure— drinking, smoking, eating for three, four days—for something he wanted. Despite catechism classes, he could not bring himself to believe that the universal order dispensed victories for free. How he had come upon this barbaric belief in a barbaric god who traded favors for pain he never told Armand. He simply met fate's just demand for balance by punishing himself first.

On the sixth night, the eve of his departure, he sealed his alliance with Armand, leading him at midnight through the coconut fields to a clearing deep in the plantation. Here, in a patch of half-buried boulders fringed by wild bougainvilleas, Hector made him swear the most frightful oaths of fealty, calling on the ancient crocodile, the lightning, the mammoth bird, and other creatures of the pre-Hispanic underworld as witness. "And may the river siren who spreads out the silver net of her hair once a year to catch herself a fisherman for tribute come after me if I break my oath." So spoke Armand on Hector's orders. The words did not seem ridiculous to him.

Using a silver-bladed knife which he sterilized over a lighted candle, Hector pierced Armand's thumb, allowed the blood to run into a cup filled with a dark fluid, did the same to himself, and ordered Armand to drink. Terrified but seduced, Armand obeyed. It was Coca-Cola. Hector finished off the drink, wiped his mouth, and then . . .

Oh, and then. The true seal of the bargain. Oh and oh, as

Armand was laid open to the air and to himself, and he experienced such a love, such an affection, as complete as he could ever imagine. Later, he would explain away the ecstasy as the effect of drugs dissolved in the Coca-Cola, some hallucinogen, powdered mushrooms or the pollen of certain flowers, perhaps the angel's trumpet, known to tribes in the Cordilleras, but that night he understood he was and would forever be Hector's. That night had been the end of his state as orphan. Hector Basbas had adopted him.

And because he did not spare himself from the oath, binding himself as he bound Armand with sweet finality, Hector could be sure that his newfound disciple was his unto death.

It was no surprise then that though Hector left by morning, Armand kept the rules which had been established, so that by the time the wedding date rolled around, he was—allow him the immodesty—a very handsome lord bridegroom, strong enough to survive the week-long festivities both at the Montelibano house and the Gloriosa manor, which glittered with so much light it looked like God's castle. Not a few women fainted each time he appeared among the guests in his raw silk tuxedo, and for the first time in such a long time, Armand had that hard edge of arrogance which was his by birthright. He couldn't drink, of course, not scotch, brandy, rum, or beer—for Hector had warned him, with appropriate threats.

It was no surprise, as well, that Armand immediately agreed when, upon passing the bar exams, Hector asked him to arrange for Hector's appointment as defense secretary. By then the Gloriosa fortunes had recovered somewhat, and with a hefty contribution to the campaign war chest of the then president, Armand secured the post for Hector. Not out of the goodness of his heart but out of the need, so detailedly explained by Hector, for a cover by which they could arrange a secret and illegal mining operation in the hills behind the Montelibano plantation. Hector's wanderings among those hills as a child had revealed to him the existence of a gold vein which, properly assayed, wasn't rich enough for commercial mining. But with minimal expenditures in overhead and labor, it could yield a minor fortune.

The labor-intensive, no-machines, just-pickax-and-wheelbar-row enterprise was inaugurated under cover of a military plan to train an all-Muslim contingent for the invasion of Sabah in North Borneo. Hector had successfully parlayed the idea that the country should press its claims to the Malaysian region, notwithstanding perturbations in Asia's balance-of-power situation. With the connivance of several southern sultans who had reached the limits of wealth in their own territories and among their own people, the idea of wresting control of the area from Malaysia was born. Sabah had timber, mangrove and arable land, and possibly oil—temptations galore for everyone with the exception of Hector and Armand, who knew full well the impossibility of that dream. Thus, a boot camp was set up behind the Monte-libano plantation, the area secured with barbed and concertina wire and sentries, and not even the powerful M-Bs would pierce through that secrecy.

The labor recruits were mostly from the south, Muslim in belief, and both they and the soldiers were given to understand that the mine's yield would go to financing the invasion and the restoration of their sultans' patrimony. The gold ores were smelted and purified and fashioned into gold bars, 99.9 percent pure, and carried by army trucks to a makeshift dock, from which they were shipped to Hong Kong. De Naval, still with the military and newly returned from a CIA adventure in the Congo to which he'd been assigned after flying shotgun and dropping supplies for Indonesian generals, was named officer-in-charge. He drove both workers and soldiers hard but softened their evenings by regaling them with his life in Africa, where he'd piloted a fighter plane and spent afternoons strafing, as he said, the *nog-nog*, naming the black people he saw scurrying from the spatter of bullets from his machine guns after the husked, curly-haired brown coconuts of his own country. All was going so well no one noticed how the workers were digging deeper and deeper into the hills, with only the flimsiest of bamboo scaffoldings to hold the earth from collapsing—which it did, after a week-long fall of the monsoon, water-sodden dirt suddenly just filling in every nook and cranny, every crevice, every inch of empty space including agape mouths, in those honeycombed hills, stiffling screams, movement, and life so abruptly that the soldiers didn't even realize what had happened until nightfall when no worker returned to the barracks. By then de Naval had instituted his own creative accounting of food, clothing, and equipment supplies, stealing everything he could lay his hands on. The enraged soldiers, grieving for their Muslim brothers, broke into a stupendous rage, assaulted the officers' barracks, and killed half a dozen before they were sub-dued. De Naval claimed ignorance of the situation, promised an investigation, marched the men to the waterfront, and ordered them aboard a rickety ship which he claimed would take them to a southern pier where an armada waited, ready for the invasion. Once on the high seas, though, the booby-trapped ship imploded before falling apart and all three hundred soldiers disappeared under the waves, save for maybe a dozen who, minus a leg or an arm or with gaping wounds, managed to swim to this or that island—which explained, Teresa, the origin of this sullen anger which greeted Hector each time he made a foray to the southern Muslim areas and which was why he sent Katerina there.

By this time, Hector had given up drinking himself, only taking spring mineral water ordered by the gallon from France. It made him constipated, but that was part of the divine exchange, he said, and he suffered in silence. When the cave-in happened, he couldn't bear to eat meat anymore, claiming to smell blood from even the most well-cooked, shriveled piece, and when the ship went down, well, that was the end of eating fish as well, for Hector was terrified he would cut open a broiled *bangus* and find an accusing finger in its guts.

But he could still allay Armand's fears, assuring him that whatever was due for this tragedy was his, Hector's, alone to pay. When that wouldn't suffice, he had de Naval swear before Armand that on his officer's head be the retribution for it. De Naval was retired from the military in the ensuing scandal and by that much paid for all the deaths, though he was richer by almost a million pesos and had a new sinecure to boot as Hector's organizer of the Diablo Brotherhood. If truth be told, it was mostly Hector who paid, having had to give up drinking, meat and fish and sweets, and dancing, contenting himself with watching Armand amuse himself on the dance floor, Katerina munch on rare goodies, the children suckle, and so on. . . . This had all been done, he would say, for the purpose of enjoying the earth and life; he'd taken on all the dues for it so Armand, Katerina, and the children would not have to deprive themselves of anything, and it was quite all right, for any pleasure that accrued to them accrued to him as well, for they were one. The three of them—Katerina, Armand, and himself—were one, and with the children, were one still, more one in the children than in anything else, these children who were of the Basbas blood and of the Gloriosa lineage.

They were one. That was, had been, preordained—so said Hector, who knew more about the workings of destiny than the Church of the Mystic Limb, which had irritated him by naming this callow grandson of the founder bishop instead of Armand. There would be a reckoning about this someday, not now, but someday. Still and all, Hector being the fountainhead of everything in their lives, Armand could be forgiven for being so elated as to kiss Bishop Andy full on the mouth when the young elect told him that sometime in the previous night, a radio message had come in from a sect member in a pimple of a settlement on Mount Arayat—a message which said that the missing airplane had been spotted, lying on its belly in the middle of a flooded stretch of ricefields, still unreachable because of the current and down-floating debris, and though there had been no signs of life, still that was good news, wasn't it? And oh yes, Teresa, the young bishop tasted of fermented sugar juice—tart sweet-and-sour, like *escabeche*.

16

$\mathbf{T}$*he die cast*, so to speak, there was greater need for that clean slate, as Armand kept repeating to Teresa and Katerina. He'd shaken off the laziness of sorrow, abandoned stupefied grief, and now bent his back to the new work, listing down dos and don'ts, and three or four items which, he admonished his wife, had to be rectified. He had the wisdom to declare that contrary to traditional norms of conduct, it would not do for him to hover about Katerina. She'd have to go it alone—press flesh, give speeches, and so forth—with the rest of them in the background, not to blur the image of Woman Bereft which they wanted etched in the public mind. "I *am* a woman bereft!" Katerina snapped, but Teresa laid a cautioning hand on her arm, warning her against just such outbursts. "You no longer own yourself," Teresa said. "You're a public figure now."

Those words made her eyes glitter. Though closer, so to speak, than lips and teeth the twins were, Hector had never given her an intimation of how it felt, how it was to be in the quiet of a storm's eye, cocooned in absolute stillness while holding the skeins of action in one's hands. A twitch—and movement rippled through the Universe. Her will was Done. So this, Teresa, was what it was all about, the men's obsession: to cause commotion while one remained immobile. The fullness, the certainty, the completion—never before had she felt as satiated even as she hungered for more, wanted more, and was sure there was more, that this was an inexhaustible sensation.

And because she wanted more, she would be pliable for the moment, Teresa, and fulfill her duties, fully recognizing that sometimes it was necessary to be what one didn't want to be in order to become what one wanted to be. There would come a time when she alone would define her duties, define her days, define even the hours, telling the sun even when it was time to rise and to set, the moon to be full. She would set the clock for everyone, but for the moment . . .

She cast a discreet eye over her shoulder, checking if the staff, her staff now, six women in deep blue, were behind her, carrying cellophane-wrapped fruit baskets of mangosteen and rambutan, the most exotic in the market for the season, down the hospital corridor to the ward where a problem had to be attended to. She cringed inwardly at the chemical odors, assailed by memories of her pain with her three children; she hated hospitals and avoided them as much as possible, but there was no helping it. The six survivors of the stage collapse were billeted here, and she had to weave between and among cots of pregnant women mewing quietly, bellies heaving beneath threadbare cotton sheets three inches too short or too narrow for their function. What meager amount was budgeted for the City General Hospital, where the injured and diseased poor gathered for treatment, was further reduced by theft and kickbacks. So said the hospital director when she inquired about the situation. She would correct this, she swore to him, once she was, uh, in power. Better still, she'd build a new hospital—bigger, more impressive, named with her own name and thus assured of her patronage forever; a hospital for the public, no, for women and children, no, for children only, as it would not do to help the sin-ridden and only with children could one be sure, a hospital so beautiful, with beds shaped like toy cars, with playrooms and libraries, everything scaled down for children, so marvelous that strangers from far and wide would come to gape and know the grandeur of her generosity. Perhaps, if the director could help form her Doctors for KBG, he would also head the new hospital, no?

She crooked a finger, was gratified to hear the campaign secretary bustle forward on short legs. "Make a note of it," she said, raising her voice. "This situation will have to be corrected. We will build a new hospital." And she wove the dream with words, plucking names from her memory—the best architect, the best interior decorator, the best doctors, the best child psychologists, the handsomest nurses, pass that on, as she passed down the corridor, dragging all of them in her wake. She waved, patted a nearby sheet-shrouded limb, shook a hand, two, three, and was seemingly oblivious to the excitement boiling around her. At the lower end of the ward, nurses were wheeling forward curtain screens to seal off the beds of the construction men.

She accepted a chair within that white recess, noted the bandaged arms, legs, turbaned heads of the six. One man had lost his left leg. She turned to him, knowing he would be the most difficult, leaned toward him while tears welled in her eyes. She could weep this way, easily, without meaning.

They'd both suffered a loss, she whispered and let her head dip toward him, so the nimbus of her hair's perfume could touch and overwhelm his senses. She promised him, them, everything: lifetime care, her influence and prestige behind their demand for justice; compensation, full medical coverage, full pension, and for the man no longer nimble enough to scamper up and down scaffoldings, a desk job. It wasn't right, she said, for government to stint on safety requirements; it was niggardly of government to have spent for bamboo scaffoldings instead of stout beams and logs; it was terrible of government to have stuck them in this place, without adequate care. She spoke and deftly restored the blame where it belonged: to Blackie's camp, exonerating Armand, though she cursed him for his stupidity. But it was what one would expect of a Gloriosa—the sudden panic, the sudden effort to turn things around, the inevitable overreaching and consequent disaster.

She noted with approval, from the corner of an eye, how the women, her staff, smiling like houris, were distributing quitclaim forms and gold-filled Cross ballpoint pens to the injured men. So overwhelmed by her presence were these simple carpenters that their eyes filled with tears. They signed, with no hesitancy, trusting their lives to her promises. That was the way it was in the archipelago. Laws were suspect, contracts unenforceable, and the only true protection came from the rich and the powerful. She sighed, smoothed down the folds of her skirt, and told them they could keep the pens. There remained only the problem of disengaging herself gracefully. A photographer thrust himself, to the staff's outraged disapproval, between the curtains and proceeded to fire his camera: five, seven, nine flashes. When he finished, she turned to him with a frown, remonstrating at this impolite intrusion. He grinned.

Then, sirens preceding her white limousine, she was headed for the Jukebox's campaign office, a rather sorry-looking building next to the impeccable Basbas headquarters. With a weary clanking of chains, the dark elevator carried her, four women, and the Diablo bodyguard to the fourth floor, where the Jukebox had his personal quarters. She had to smile, Teresa; so obvious was Hector's disdain for the man, this man who'd agreed to be his running mate in the expectation that money would flow into his hands, that no space had been allotted for him in the campaign's nerve center. But he was kept just this side of paradise to whet his appetites.

This was even simpler than the hospital. She swept in, already stoking her anger, demanding why such a man was treated this way, a loyal Basbas follower, it was shameful . . . and so on and so forth. She signaled to the Diablo to place the hefty briefcase on the Jukebox's desk, not letting it go just yet, of course, while she talked on and on. Everything would be rectified, she promised the vice-president-elect; the two of them would go on. This was much more than winning now; it was a holy crusade. They had to join, merge, forces to crush the evil which was threatening the Grand Alliance, their political party.

"Does that mean I'll be your running mate?" the man asked.

She smiled. It was too late to dump him. "Only if we come to an understanding."

He signed. The quitclaim form and the receipt for a hundred thousand pesos. She pushed the papers toward her secretary; they were of no importance, 'pañero, but would he do her a favor?

"Anything."

"Take that bandage off," she hissed. "You look like a sheik."

Now for the hardest part, she told herself as her caravan moved again, borne on siren wails, messing up traffic in a movable three-mile radius. The one nice thing about a military escort, Teresa, was one didn't have to suffer traffic jams because one caused them. Too bad she wasn't here, Miss Tikloptuhod, to witness how magnificently she was performing, but the girl—she still thought of her companion as a girl—had her hands full dealing with the media, her impatient father, and the restive Diablos. This was the last stop anyway, the Forbes Park mansion of the Montelibano-Basbas, where least-liked cousin Matrimonia reigned over twenty-two servants and probably forty-four tons of inconsequential memorabilia.

They were served weak *kalamansi* juice in eight cloudy glasses, no distinction made between Herself and the entourage. Bad sign. Having grown up in the M-B house, Katerina knew enough about subtle signals. Once, Katerina had gotten into an argument with Matrimonia over Christmas gifts and had received a cursory lesson in social interaction. The biggest, most expensive ones were reserved for those who didn't need them in the hope they would take notice and confer grace and favor. Less fortunate relatives got the smallest boxes and cheapest gifts. There was no need to placate them and their gratitude was a certainty, anyway, for having been remembered at all. Ditto with the service: the most elegant dishes and silver were trotted out for fancy guests; plastic and paper napkins for the poor who wouldn't know the difference anyway.

The glasses—ordinary, not even cheap crystal—were a bad sign. Katerina considered leaving, as her cousin was driving home the point by making her wait.

She controlled herself at Matrimonia's appearance, pressed her right cheek, left cheek, to the other woman's rouged face, sniffed at the sandalwood perfume the Montelibanos preferred, lamented their common tragedy, and asked, with due humility, how her *prima* was, well she hoped and bearing up. Matrimonia giggled and said an astonishing thing had happened just that morning, would you believe, a bill arrived from the couturier Valero for an astronomical amount, surely a mistake, but a call to the presumptuous dressmaker had brought the explanation that this was on Katerina's instructions and included the cost of her gowns and those of, uh, what's the name of that little dark twerp she kept as social secretary, Teresa something-something, never mind, imagine that?

"It was a mistake, wasn't it?" Matrimonia asked, smiling. "Not that I wouldn't pay, if you were that hard up, but I'm sure he misunderstood . . ."

"Don't worry about it," Katerina said, brushing aside what promised to be a major embarrassment. She had forgotten all about that. "Think no more about it." What was important, she went on, was this matter of who would run, now that Hector was—well, absent.

YOU?

The woman laughed. With many excuse-mes and so-sorrys. With many attempts to stifle her amusement: swallowing her lips, pressing her hands to her mouth, coughing . . . but laughed nevertheless. Katerina swept her staff with a glance. Outside! They slunk away. Matrimonia's eyes darted toward the silver bell which would call her servants; she considered it briefly but forbore. Katerina was glad she could still frighten her cousin.

"But you can't," she bleated at last. "You're a woman."

Katerina was relieved. This was familiar ground. Briskly, she laid out her arguments: her knowledge of Hector's political philosophy, her understanding of his goals, the similarity between his and her styles of campaign, the sympathy votes she would get on top of those already committed to him. "And it's about time women took a leading role in this country," she added, shrewd enough to realize how this would sound to her cousin. "We already manage so much, don't we?"

Matrimonia hesitated. She motioned towards the terrace, inviting Katerina to follow. The air of the side garden was cool, moistened by a slight mist hissed out by hidden water sprayers. The woman contemplated her garden for a moment, perhaps to restore her equanimity.

"Why come to me?" she asked, after a while.

Because, Katerina nearly blurted out, if her own clan didn't support her, there was no convincing others. She shuddered, laid a tremulous hand on Matrimonia's shoulder, and said instead: "Because I knew you'd be the first to understand." Flattery. "Because you're that admirable combination of tradition and the modern; you'd know it's shameful how we women have hidden ourselves in the political closet." Lay it on; make it difficult for her to disagree. "Because you're my closest relative and should be the first to know and to judge." A lie. "Because you're invaluable to what we hope to do." True enough, that one. "Because I couldn't go on with this without the strength that only a clan matriarch could give." Bull. "And because you know all of them." Aha. She stopped.

Matrimonia's nose rose. "That's all very well, Kate, but I've never been consulted before. Why should I be now?"

Katerina gritted her teeth. She hated the nickname, and Matrimonia knew it. Kate, do this; Kate, do that; Kate, clean this mess; Kate, wipe my nose, wipe my ass . . . She'd sworn she'd never be called that again and had succeeded so far by ignoring anyone who used the nickname, perdition take them all. "Oh, but you still remember our childhood names," she said, forcing the words out between her teeth. "I haven't heard that for a long time." She clasped her cousin's hands in hers and beamed. "I'd thought all along that Hector—ah, say no more. I am ashamed. I was under the impression that you were an important part of the campaign; Hector said something to that effect and I—I believed him, of course. Ah, I am dismayed. This is such a . . ."

Matrimonia laughed. "He's taught you well at least," she said, shaking off Katerina's hands. "What I say or do won't make any difference. The whole family, every single one, says that. That's all we talk about at family reunions. Though no one bedrudges you twins your success. Tooth, fang, and claw—you made straight for the top." She strode back into the house, muttering to herself. "Silly, silly us. One day, all this will catch up with every one of us." She waved to Katerina to follow and led the way to the library, a huge chamber of book-lined walls. Books old and new, with an occasional framed sixteenth-century map glinting in the sunlight.

All business now, Matrimonia walked to her desk, opened a drawer, and took out a sheaf of papers. "There," she said, handing it over to Katerina. "Names, addresses, and phone numbers of the entire clan, to the sixth degree of consanguinity. Marital alliances, business partnerships, and so forth. I knew it would come in handy someday, so I kept track. I keep track, Kate, and

that's all I do. You'll have to do your own pleading. If I did, for
you, then I'd be throwing the prestige of my own house behind
your decision. I can't do that. It's all I have, not having a family
of my own. If I lose—we lose—I'm done for." Matrimonia bowed
her head.

The blood rose so abruptly to her head that her vision dimmed.
"You're refusing," she blurted out.

"Not refusing, not condoning. Staying neutral. And even for
that, I'll have my reward. It's time you twins paid your dues."

"Haven't we? Haven't we?"

"Not to me. For that"—Matrimonia tapped the sheets in Katerina's hands—"I want an appointment for myself, some work
to take me out of this house, give me a name of my own. A
cabinet position, perhaps."

"A what?"

"Social welfare. Secretary of health and social welfare. I'm
very good with socials, anyway." Matrimonia lifted her eyebrows.
"We have our understanding. Now, go, go. Don't say thanks or
anything. This is between relatives, after all."

Was one to laugh or cry, Teresa, at such effrontery—which
was not a surprise, the M-Bs being known for their ruthlessness
when they espied an advantage. In the car, on the way to the
campaign headquarters, the precious list on the seat beside her,
she swore grimly, and not the first time either, to get every one
of them, starting with Matrimonia, when the proper time came.
Timing, Hector used to say, was all. The perfect timing, for
which one prepared nevertheless. So Teresa would please draw
up a list of M-B property, estates, businesses, and whatnot, in
preparation for their complete ruination.

"I'll ruin them," she shouted in the suddenly frigid confines
of the limousine, the temperature dropping abruptly even as sweat
spurted on her forehead. She dabbed at her face with a fistful of

tissue paper. The driver rolled down the glass screen and apologized in a meek voice: the air conditioner was on the blink again, brand-new as it was.

"Never mind," she said.

With two blue-uniformed women, she worked the telephones, calling up the names on the list, liberally sprinkling her spiel with Matrimonia's name—which was useless. She and the other party knew the cousin would be on the phone herself, were she backing this decision. There would be more phone calls, Matrimonia would be chatting with the clan members, saying, oh, dear, I couldn't disappoint her outright, you know, she's one of us, after all; but I did tell her I'd remain neutral, oh, did she use my name, oh, the gall of these twins, but they've always been like that, you and I know, remember that time when . . . By bedtime, the woman would be so full, so satisfied with all the gossip and gossiping, she'd fall asleep instantly. Katerina had been taken.

"I'll ruin them!" Katerina shouted, smashing her palm flat on the desk, startling her aides. She shook her head, waved them back to work. "Never mind."

Politics were so much talk or nothing but talk. Talk, talk, talk on the phone. There were fifty-three names on the list. Twenty-four were unreachable, or so it was claimed, being out of town, overseas, in conference, ill, or perhaps, she said to herself, far more likely, insane. Half of the rest refused to come to the phone and had their maids say they'd call back. She wrote them off. The rest listened to her—because this was something to talk about, Herself calling them, imagine that—and hemmed and hawed and promised to think it over, which was no good at all, as both parties knew, for in the archipelago, if the answer wasn't a straight yes, then it was a no, never mind the prevarication, hesitancies, and circumlocution. She'd been set up—which was, if truth be told, a bad comment on Matrimonia's shrewdness. Katerina Basbas Gloriosa would have forgiven a direct refusal; but this—the woman couldn't even begin to dream how Herself would be avenged.

She was mulling over fitting punishment for all those sons-of-a-goat when a commotion outside roused her. The door opened and two old women—Sister Mary Rose and Sister Ludi—entered, bawling loudly. They'd taken up station at the conference hall, where nightly prayers for Hector were said, and did brisk business with healing by the laying on of hands and offering undecipherable messages from the absent hero. Sister Mary Rose accused Sister Ludi of being a Blackie spy, an evil spirit who was hexing everything and everyone in the place. Sister Ludi accused Sister Mary Rose of being in league with the devil and of the essence of a succubus. Both were incoherent in their denial; both vehement in their protestations of loyalty to the Basbas twins; both threatened each other with bodily harm, curses, and hauntings. Their superstitions stirred, the campaign people didn't dare get in between the two—which was how they'd managed to reach Katerina's private office undeterred.

"Go away," Katerina screamed. "One to the conference room; one to the front room. If I hear a peep out of you again, *I'll* curse you. Your skin will boil away, your hair fall off, and your joints disassemble! Go ahead. Make me angry."

The two crossed themselves rapidly but did not budge. Katerina rose to her feet and bared her teeth. That was how, Teresa, all this talk about her being a *mangkukulam*, a witch for all witches, a supreme chanter of curses, began—for to her and the staff's surprise, the two women turned as pale as dawn and visibly trembled. Sister Ludi threw herself to her knees and wept no, please no, all she wanted was to warn the *señora* that a man was coming who'd bring ambivalent luck, good and bad at the same time; in her vision, it was a white man, but this other woman, this fake healer, had protested as soon as she heard of the premonition that it was a dark, dark man.

"I didn't want you to get the wrong warning," Sister Ludi finished.

She shooed them off, feeling her luck turning sour indeed, understanding for the first time as she glanced at the list in her hands and while the two women were being hustled off, while the crowd before the office door trickled away, that she, Armand, and the children, but most especially she, Herself, had no allies, no friends, no support, that the Basbas nuclear family was alone and on its own. Which wasn't a nice state to be in, particularly if one had terrible secrets to guard. She was thinking about all this when she glanced up, more to demand why the door had remained open, and saw, coming down from the far end of the corridor, where the elevators were, this man in a white shirt and white pants, carrying an awkward brown suitcase banging against the side of his left leg with every step, and though he was still in the shadows and still far away, Katerina recognized him immediately.

Aurelio Aureus. Drawn by the news of Hector's possible death from whatever rathole he'd hidden himself these many years. In the scuffed and battered suitcase he carried everywhere were the accumulation of all those letters in which he'd written down, under various guises and signed by an extraordinary variety of names, Katerina Basbas Gloriosa's tale and problem—3,443 letters in all, written whether he had or didn't have his radio program, because as he took pains to explain to her, this was the only way he could bend his mind to its resolution. He'd lost two upper front teeth and was burned nearly black by the sun of his travels. "I came to offer my condolences," he said, saliva spraying the top of Katerina's desk.

Katerina was nonplussed. She covered her open mouth with

her elegant right hand, inspected Aurelio from head to foot, saw him as he was and saw him again as he had been, and felt such a sense of waste and regret—a form of passion, Teresa, such as hadn't touched her since the time of their own journey—but she waved away the Diablos who'd come running, shaking her head no for they were unholstering their .45s and .32s.

She had to clear her throat twice before she could ask: "And did you ever find the solution?" Not that it mattered now, Teresa, so much time having passed. She was not prepared for the sudden gratitude in Aurelio's face. "You understood," he said. He bowed his head and wept. After a while, he shook his head no. There was no solution to Katerina's problem.

She drew closer and whispered, "Why not?"

"Because you like it, Katerina." The words sounded like a condemnation. Katerina's heart withered.

But what to do with this husk of a memory of a man? A clean slate, Hector had said; and if Aurelio Aureus were to appear now, surfacing with the tale of his hounding by one of the twins, it would be a disaster indeed. She motioned to Emil to come close, whispered to his bent head, and then turned a brilliant smile at the stranger.

"Follow him," she said to Aurelio. "And take that"—she pointed to the suitcase—"with you."

So, Emil bought the suitcase of letters, Teresa, for an immodest sum and advised Aurelio never to interrupt his traveling. "Go to Bhutan or search for God" were the words Katerina had entrusted to the Diablo for Aurelio's ears. The minute she'd laid eyes on her old love, Katerina had understood at once the old women's vision. Nothing, she told Teresa, would bring Hector faster from wherever he was, even the grave, than this dark man in white turning up, ambivalent luck it truly was that he brought, and she hoped she'd acted quickly enough to avert it. She was saying this in the dining room where they were having dinner that evening—Herself, the three children, and Teresa, Armand having disappeared God knew where—and even as she was reaching the moral of her story, to the effect that the loss of a man was his woman's grief and liberation at the same time (were Hector alive, would she be a candidate?), the central telephone with all its extensions began to ring, *riiiinnnng!* and she was saying yes, yes indeed, he was a double-bladed luck like most men, Aurelio Aureus was, *riiiiing!* Teresa rose and answered and turned to her with the news already legible on her face: the plane wreck had been sighted, though the rescuers were still too far to see if anyone was alive.

"I told you" was all Katerina said.

17

DOWN. *Going down.* Space below, space above, and a long black tunnel of sound. A roar. A crackling. A humming. Together, all at once. He was going down. They were going down. He pulled in his head, drew up his knees, clasped himself with his arms, and imagined, wished, himself a turtle withdrawing into his carapace as the plane bucked, swayed forward, backward, rumbled, and then dropped, for God's sake, IT WASN'T SUPPOSED TO DO THAT, falling like a yo-yo with cut strings, straight down, plunk, kerplunk, a fall which ended in a terrific crunch and more CRUNCH, while bags and cushions came tumbling down, something yowling zipped past his head and there was a blow on his right shoulder and he was jerked forward, the seat belt cutting into his belly and there he was, right in the center of a magnificent THUD. Silence. Tiny metal screechings and creakings and the sighing of water. There was a sword slash of lightning, a growl of thunder at its heels, and the air was sulfurous of a sudden— by which time, Hector Basbas, Esq., senate president, president-elect, His Excellency (to-be), was certain the plane had done what it wasn't supposed to do, meaning Fall-Straight-Down. He became so enraged he hollered for *'Bastian! Sebastian!* who was his chief aide of the moment. Nothing. A hollow groan from up front. He called again, and the same wordless sound answered him. Get me out of here, he demanded, cutting through the groaning and his own coughing. When nothing happened, he began calling out the Diablos' names over and over again, and then simply shrieked until his throat's lining was raw, his vocal cords threatened to snap, and he was reduced to a helpless mewling. His teeth chattered; his knees bumped against each other; his muscles slithered fitfully against his bones. He wrapped his arms about his bowed head, seeking warmth against a deathly chill which shrouded his shoulders. Stop, he said, he had to stop lest shock killed him, because he was otherwise unharmed, as far as he could tell, save for a knot of pain in the middle of his back and assorted pricklings and throbbings all over his body, nothing major—or so he thought as he turned his eyes inward and checked himself: legs okay, arms okay, belly okay . . . But he did not dare consider what was out there in the dark, and he balled himself about his heart's yammering while his teeth clacked and clicked against one another and his jawbones clenched and gritted.

How long he remained that way, senseless in the clutch of a terror so profound his body nearly disassembled itself with trembling, he couldn't tell. When he opened his eyes, the pale glow of daylight—dawn?—filled the port windows and defined a jumble of objects inside the aircraft. Reaching out with his left hand, taking care not to uncurl because he didn't dare, he wiped the port glass with the cuff of his shirt sleeve. Nothing but raindrops and streaks. The plane rocked like a gently stirred cradle. He groaned aloud, heavily, thinking he could move whoever was alive in the plane with pity. Silence.

After a while, he summoned the courage to unbuckle the seat belt, to move aside a cushion which had tumbled over his shoulder, and ducking below a panel full of wires which had come loose from the ceiling, he inched his way forward, past the five—count them—men lying helter-skelter among dislodged seats and tumbled luggage, among carbines and Garands, some with snapped barrels, among a settled confetti of paper money, five men some with heads at an impossible angle, two or three staring with mouths open as he made a triple sign of the cross over himself. The cockpit doorway had crumpled, but he could see in the eerie glow the pilot and copilot pinned by the control panel, which had slid to their laps, the pilot's wheel pressed against the man's face, barely giving him space to move his mouth for a groan, for it was he who was groaning softly, but over the next hours, he would groan louder and louder, more and more frequently, before the sound petered out again to leave His Excellency (to-be), sir, alone, in silence. Hector considered calling to him but he couldn't remember the man's name.

He became aware of an octane odor and backed away, picking his path through the debris and twisted metal, to the emergency exits, one on each side of the plane, only to find them jammed by the crash's impact. He could thank Fate it had contented itself with taking the lives of his men and, for sure, the two pilots as well, and spared him—but it wasn't over yet, he told himself, what with that smell growing stronger and water seeping in, he could still end up barbecued or drowned. Or maybe, because he was Hector Basbas, both: drowned first and then roasted. Wouldn't his enemies like that? He clucked his tongue at the thought and was jarred by the pain radiating from the roots of his teeth. Christ, he was going to be a toothless, bare-gummed His Excellency (to-be). He forced himself to forage, saying excuse me as he patted down the dead, ferreting in the plane's small cupboards, opening leather bags and pulling out clothes by the fistful. He found two chocolate bars, one of which he thrust nearly whole into his mouth, suddenly conscious of hunger and thirst. In the shirt pocket of a Diablo he found a handful of rock candy, neatly wrapped in cellophane; on the floor was a twelve-inch butterfly knife. He could use it to pry the exit doors open, but what if the touch of metal on metal created sparks and ignited the fuel-slicked floodwaters now rising to his ankles? There had to be a better way out.

He made his way back to his seat, calculating that it had kept him safe so far. In the seat behind was a Diablo sprawled upside down; no telling how the man got to be that way, with one leg flung across the backrest and his head somewhere there in the shadows of the floor. But what was important was that a denim jacket hung from his upraised foot, hooked there as though draped by a careful hand. Hector took the jacket, cleared his seat of debris, salvaged four or five cushions from nearby seats, made a nest, and curled himself up again. The jacket he spread over his chest, thinking that if he could keep warm, chances were he would survive.

It was sabotage, he told himself, stoking his anger against the mangy dog of despair skulking at the rim of his consciousness. He'd get them one by one, starting with Blackie Domínguez y García, so help him. His muttered threats were a roll of drums beneath visions of his family, of how Katerina would take the news, of his enemies popping champagne bottles, of the entire Basbas clan saying to one another, breathlessly, scarcely able to conceal their glee, *can you imagine that*, the devil take them all, while his family, spirit broken, hung their heads. He'd see to each and every one, see their knees buckle and their water pass uncontrolled from their bladders, even as he imagined himself raising the faithful, those who remained loyal to him, to a kind of heaven. How could he have allowed himself to be overtaken by fate in this manner?

And because he was Hector Basbas, he set up a weighing scale in his mind and began stacking to one side what could be bartered for his survival. All his leftover little pleasures: the momentary women, the hand-tailored clothes, the tenderly hand-sewn shoes, the garden's flower scents, a sunny day, the silver glint of the monsoon rains, the riot of colors that was sunset in this country. He vowed to give up each and all, feverishly praying that would be enough. He would live a life to shame the most ascetic monk in the most spartan monastery. The capacity for grief and joy, satisfaction and discontent, tenderness and lust—those, too, he would give away. Pleasures of the eyes, nose, ears, mouth, touch, he would dispense with. No spices, no salt; no meat, no drink save water; no tobacco; no film nor theater; no music and dancing; no velvet nor silk, even, just cotton—for he was a true child of the archipelago and knew that survival had to be paid for. His enemies' discomfiture he would even refuse to enjoy.

"I am Hector Basbas," he said to the silence. "I am president-elect." The words were chased by a sniggering *this can't be happening to me* and a taunting *oh, yes, it is.* He felt the offended dead of his life hover closer to the airplane, and his heart shriveled in his breast. He knew who they were, though no one else did. Gossip, rumor, and biographies did not include these, his true enemies. He had not been held accountable for them; not a single one of the dead known to be his responsibility was among them. Neither the dead of the mines nor the dead of the sea nor the occasional rival dispatched by his command—men who had been foolish enough either to merge or lock their fates with his. They had deserved their dying.

No, these ones now drawing closer to the planes with an insidious hum of hunger had the faces of sixteen- and seventeen-year-olds, pitiless in their youth, merciless in their mourning for a life unlived: his classmates once upon a time (oh, words of fable) at the military school, the select among the children of the clans who had been sent to the academy to learn discipline preparatory to their assuming their family's powers. Seventy-five of them in Hector Basbas's class, with whom he had spent two years of common sleeping quarters, study room, and mess hall. Very nice kids, he told himself wryly, also stupid.

They'd been left behind by the older cadets, on the theory that the invading army wouldn't harm them. That had been true enough. On the other hand, the Japanese captain refused to let them leave and set them to menial work in his camp, tending vegetable plots, cleaning the barracks, doing the laundry. At night he had them returned under guard to their school dorm. With a dusk-to-dawn curfew, checkpoints and sentries everywhere, and the routine of evening roll call, it was impossible to escape.

If Hector had been miserable before in the academy, he was in a worse state this time, suffering day and night, his soul's center of gravity pierced by the thought of Katerina alone and helpless during a state of war. Though he was surrounded by young cadets in various degrees of homesickness and worry, Hector believed his pain to be without equal. He cast his contemptuous eyes upon his classmates, condemning them as fools for trying to match his agony with theirs. He wriggled and writhed about the delicate shaft of his pain like a pinned butterfly. Katerina, he thought; the name trailed him like the tick-tock of a clock as he washed floors, clothes, plates and saluted the alien soldiers. He had to get away, to get back to her.

Because he was Hector Basbas, he couldn't stop searching for what could be traded for his freedom. Searched and spied and pried and found nothing. After a while, he was driven to understand that he would have to create the circumstances of barter himself. Recalling all this, time and again through the years, he liked to think he hesitated, but if the truth be told, because he was Hector Basbas, the instant the plan was born at the center of his pain, he had gone to work immediately. He convinced all of them, seventy-five boy-men; wore them down with irrefutable arguments in the corridors, shower stalls, the dark of their sleeping halls, in the garden. He convinced them because if he had any virtue at all, it was the ability to convince. One moonless night then, the seventy-five, armed with knives, hoes, and pick-axes, crawled past the school fence towards the building occupied by Japanese soldiers and met their death.

Hector Basbas had traded them and their plans for a military pass. Seventy-five not yet fully grown about-to-be men, whose lives were forfeited; seventy-five bodies bleeding; seventy-five hearts stopped—so he could make his way safely past checkpoint and sentry towards Katerina, his twin. But before the Japanese captain handed him the document of his safety, he had the grace to force Hector Basbas to look upon his comrades, stripped of shoes, socks, and valuables, piled atop one another next to an open and fresh trench.

It took all of four years to reach Katerina, for the dead pursued Hector. In his innocence, he had believed he could shake them off by taking a zigzag path. They clung to him, though, giggling in the dark when he settled in some secret place to count his earnings. They leaned over to suck sleep from his eyes and nose, driving him mad with fatigue, forcing him into hallucinations. After a while, he thought of them as ghouls—pale and lanky, their hair matted and stiff, their nostrils and eyelids lined phosphorescent green. He began to proffer tribute, hoping he could satisfy them and therefore keep them at bay: a woman's innocence, a boy's life, a family's ruin . . .

They ate what he offered but returned just when he was beginning to feel he had escaped. They were a greedy lot, his ghouls, never satiated, stripping off and stuffing themselves with pieces of his life. He felt them close now, pressing in against the plane, which rocked to the left, rocked to the right; trying to get in so they could touch him. He shrieked at them in terror; they should not touch the aircraft. It could explode; it could slide into the sea . . . and here he turned cunning and said, if that happened, where would they all be, the game would end and the fun would be over. Slyly, he offered them the remnant joys of his life, saying what about this and this and this . . .

But because he was Hector Basbas, he knew he was hedging, knew even as he shied away from the mocking thought that he hedged, keeping back what really gave him pleasure, his strongest passion. He resisted the ghouls' teasing, claiming he had nothing left to give, but the pressure was too strong, and after a while, he said yes, yes, he would give that up too: the joy of contempt, that hot contempt with which he viewed each and every one, the world, humanity, the universe, knowing everything sentient for the fool that it truly was. Fool! he said aloud, trying to brush away the thought that went skittering through his mind that there was more, one more offering which he prized even beyond survival, that which the ghouls were after, had been after, all these years.

He tried prayer then, terrorized beyond barter by the ghouls' importunings. But the god that met him was a god of indifference and boredom, and Hector Basbas understood that for men like him, there was no salvation. All right, he said wearily; so be it. And on the scales of justice, he placed his Katerina as a counterweight to his guilt. Have her, he said to the ghouls, who laughed without sound. Effortlessly, almost as though he were in the best of beds, he slept—a deep, luxurious sleep without dreams.

When he next opened his eyes, it was dark again. Hunger and thirst stoked his mind to full awareness. Unknotting his body, letting his feet drop to the floor, he discovered that the water had risen and now gripped his shins with cold fingers. He bent down, scooped up a handful, and brought it close to his nose. It had a strange odor, a mix of mud and chemicals. He dampened his lips, hoping that rescue was on the way, that it reached him before he died of starvation and thirst in the aircraft that was as sealed as a tomb. He unwrapped a rock candy and popped it into his mouth, felt his tongue blossom with the taste of mint, and was amused momentarily by the thought that at least he would have lovely breath when he was found.

Rolling up his trousers, the legs wet now, he wondered if he should force himself to move, to walk through the plane. This was such a joke, he told himself, a terrible one. Gingerly, not trusting the dark, feeling with his hands for seatbacks, he made his way forward, his eyes getting used to darker shadows within shadows. Nothing had changed, except for the silence in the cockpit, where the pilots were both dead now, he was certain of that. To make sure, he called out: "Hey, there!" There was no response. They were dead and he was alive—but there was no relief in that; he could still die. What a joke that would be; to have survived the crash and then to die because he couldn't open a door, any door. He groped his way toward one of the emergency exits, felt for the lever that was supposed to open it, and pushed. Pushed. Pushed. It turned. It turned. But the door itself would not budge. It was jammed. Or perhaps blocked. Disheartened, he made his way back to his seat, his hands brushing the dead along the way. "Poor fools," he told them, "you certainly bought it." Why couldn't one have survived to keep him company? After a while, he thought it was better they were all dead. No one would witness how he would eat human flesh—a slice off a leg calf, a strip off a rib—to survive. Because he had to survive, being Hector Basbas. Angrily, overtaken by another need, he unzipped his pants and peed into the water underfoot, taking care to aim away from the direction of his seat.

The indignity of it all, having to drink what he peed into. He grumbled to himself as he returned to his nest, curling his body and legs, covering himself with cushions and assorted jackets. When he made it back, he told himself, he would see to it that everybody paid. Everybody. He would play a joke on the entire country, north to south, east to west; on each and every one of the fools of this archipelago, on all those who walked on their knees every Wednesday, Thursday, and Sunday from church door to altar in an endless cycle of novenas; on those who whipped themselves and had themselves whipped with pliant and thorned branches of young bamboo every January 9 as the monstrous

Black Nazarene on its wheeled platform crushed its way through entranced and sweating bodies; on those who danced barefoot on the path of jagged stones in tribute to Saint Claire; on those who spent sleepless nights of vigil at the foot of the Antipolo Virgin who blasted her worshipers' eyes with the glint of her gold crown and the coruscating lights of her jewels; oh yes, on all of them who prayed and begged and tried to appease the gods for all their minor miseries while he, Hector Basbas, was shivering with cold, hunger, and thirst within the maw of a dead plane. He would make them pay, given the chance; he, Hector Basbas, given the chance, would play such a joke that it would never be forgotten; a joke so good it would last a whole history.

He would stop time in the archipelago, he vowed quietly. There would be no time before and after the Year of the Twins. It would be the Age of the Gemini year after year, forever and ever more. He would never leave the palace; he would never be anything else but president. No, more than that; he would be everything to the people of this accursed land—their burden and salvation. They would raise their children without knowledge of anything else but the worship of the twins. He would force them to set Himself and Herself in the altar of their minds. Never since and never before would they have anyone quite like Hector Basbas and his sister. The twins would occupy all space, breathe in all the air, drink all the water, eat all the food, and sit like merciless birds of prey upon the shoulders of the living. Let them deal with the twins.

He cursed aloud in his rage, but the echo of his voice so frightened him he looked up the aisle. Up front, he could see the shadow of a dead man's elbow still resting on a seat arm. What if the elbow moved—did it move? What if they stood up, these dead men, and confronted him with their eyes? He whimpered, cowered in his seat again, drawing the jacket over his head. Snatches of prayers in Spanish, English, and Latin floated in his brain, the chanting finally calming him to sleep.

It felt like noon when he stirred again, his joints protesting. The plane's interior was steaming, the air sweltering. Bad luck for him. It meant the Central Plains were flooded and roads were reverting to primeval mud or riverbed. Help would have trouble reaching the wreck. A sudden groan from the cockpit shattered his equanimity. He shrieked. Clapped his hands to his head and cowered. Another groan. He listened intently. It was the pilot, still alive. Hector drew a deep breath and yelled at the man to stop; there was no helping it; they simply had to wait for help. "I'm not going up there," he shouted. Meantime, he was unwrapping his last chocolate bar and measuring how much he would eat. The pilot groaned again. Hector chewed lovingly, carefully, on the chocolate. The pilot moaned, a little softer this time. Hector cocked his head; perhaps he was dying. Silence as he waited. He jerked, nearly dropping the chocolate bar when the pilot groaned once more. He yelled at the man to shut up, and when he wouldn't, traded screams for groans, yelling that the man should die and leave him in peace in this unbelievable country which, every rainy season, lost contact with bits and pieces of itself, not knowing who was born or who died, who was alive and who ill, never mind that rockets were already streaking to the moon and satellites garlanded the globe, perdition take the entire archipelago.

He shuddered to a stop, exhausted, and wracked by a terrific thirst and the need to pee at the same time. He rose from the seat, bent over like an old man, not daring to remove his shoes and peel off his socks, no telling what lay beneath the fetid water, unzipped his pants and uncovered his miserable worm of a penis, and urinated, not caring that he was sploshing the seat across the aisle. Then he waded forward, stuck his head into the cockpit doorway, and rasped at the pilot to kindly keep quiet as there was a crisis here, goddammit, and did he know where drinking water was hidden. When the man failed to answer, merely muttering incoherently, Hector walked back, shoes sloshing in the water, licking the taste of chocolate off his lip corners, and wondering, as his eyes fell on a Diablo, whether he should work on preserving some of the, uh, meat available, just in case, for the dead were turning an unsavory dark blue, flesh swelling and straining their clothes.

He'd never been as alone, Hector thought as the pilot began a new round of moans. He settled himself in his seat again, threw the denim jacket over his head, and broke into tears, pitying himself, managing to ignore the terrible noise of the dying man in the cockpit. Let rescue come, he prayed silently to the ghouls and on the weighing scale of his mind, he placed Armand first and then the children, holding on to Epee last, simply because he had hoped to extend his dynasty through her. But finally, he surrendered them all, saying their lives were forfeit for his. And if fate did not ruin them, he promised, well, then he would do so himself, given the chance.

The pilot must have died that night, as his moans died out. Hector did not know when exactly; all he knew was this silence in the morning and the thought that at least he could be sure which was the freshest meat in the plane. Time passed for him in alternating light and dark, the change from one to the other so abrupt it didn't even occur to him that he'd been trapped, was trapped for four days running, dehydrated and bruised blue all over, the hair on his chin busy growing. He ate the remaining chocolate and all the candy, and when hunger and thirst grew as sharp as knife thrusts into his belly and throat, eyed the upthrust leg of the Diablo behind his seat but lost his appetite as he became aware of a new smell, an insidious sweetish smell insinuating itself into the octane and mud odor cloud within the plane. He did drag himself to the cockpit once, the butterfly knife with naked blade in his right hand, driven by visions of steak and *sate babi*. But the dead pilot's eye pierced him with a look and he lost his courage. To be surrounded thus by water he couldn't drink, by meat he couldn't eat, was the kind of special irony reserved for the mighty. After a while, it didn't matter so much; he was so weakened all thought had disappeared and he was barely conscious. He tried to call out, but his throat was so parched, so dry, and besides which there was a racking pain in his rib, something sharp there, scraping against his inner muscles, heaven help him. Two more days of light and dark, of silence, the odor of death now overpowering even the smell of octane, but try as he could, Hector couldn't imagine himself dead, lying in state in the Senate assembly hall. Death, his mind told him, happened to others, not to the Basbas twins.

He was so weak he couldn't move when the voices came, a deep male one halloing, a higher female one almost singing a wordless hail. He thought they were a hallucination and wondered why angels or devils should be calling out thus—which question recalled him to himself. A spasm of joy wracked his body at the realization that he was found. The Lost had been FOUND. And he considered how, in what attitude, he should be found, the better to turn the mishap into capital, hell, he was a true child of the archipelago and knew that every opportunity should be used to one's benefit. But despite the voices and thumps against the plane, he could not move. The fear possessed him then that in truth, he had died and was in rigor mortis, his joints and limbs locked, while the knocking on metal persevered, to be followed by scrapings and more thumps, while the voices cheered and hollered. He realized he'd been found by ignorant peasants intent on cannibalizing the plane and who, in that instant, were using an ax, a crowbar, something of metal, against the plane's skin, whoever was the son-of-a-bitch doing it had better stop before the clash of metal against metal drew sparks and blew them all to kingdom come, the living and the dead alike, AAAAH!

That was how he was found: Hector Basbas, Esq., curled in his seat like a fetus prematurely expelled and paralyzed from head to foot by fright. The man who found him, a peasant adherent of the Church of the Mystic Limb, closely examined the dead one after another, felt in their pockets, gathered the loose leaf of paper money strewn all over the plane and floating on the water, lifted the denim jacket off Hector's face, and had to place two fingers against the neck of His Excellency (to-be) before breaking out with his apologies, excuse me, sir, begging your pardon, and sliding his arms underneath Hector's body, not even minding the stains and stench of the sudden outpouring of presidential fright (for Hector had shitted and peed on himself), to bear him like a gift of the gods out of the ruined aircraft. He laid the burden tenderly on a dry spot near his dugout's prow and took up his oar again while his wife covered Hector with a plastic sheet. Throughout the ride, she fought the pull of the swift flood currents with incantations, jiggling a severed white hen's wing in repeated passes over the boat's load, now and then shrieking aloud to keep away evil spirits. In great excitement though terrified, the two reached the last standing stilt-hut in the area. Here they heaved Hector into the hut before the man climbed to the roof to raise the prearranged victory signal per the sect's radioed and chapel-disseminated instructions: the Mystic Limb's pennant—a white satin cloth painted with a hacked-off tree branch with a single leaf which all sect members were required to purchase, in cash or twelve monthly installments according to their capacity to pay. After that, it was only a matter of waiting to see who reached them first: the Diablos, who of course had learned the secret church signal, or sect officials, to whom the possession of Hector's body, dead or alive, would have meant leverage unsurpassed. The couple, worn out by what had seemed an endless floating on the treacherous flood, ate a *pan de sal* bun each and shared a smidgen of gin. Being peasants, they did not bother Hector after dumping him in a corner of the hut. It sufficed that he was not being rained upon, that he was breathing. He was too mighty for them, too different, for them to consider his comfort. They settled on the bamboo slat floor, sitting on their haunches, and seemed to disappear into the stolid patience of river boulders. They stirred only when they heard voices hailing them from outside, at which point the woman vaguely regretted not having wetted Hector's lips with the sting of gin, as he was undoubtedly more of value alive than dead. But it was too late, and judging from the plastic-shrouded mound's immobility, it was likely that His Excellency had not survived his travail after all.

18

The *Diablo raised* the barrel of his Garand and fired, not bothering to take aim. With a dull *whomp*, the transformer behind the chicken-wire fence, metal gray in the snare of three floodlamps, exploded. A blue-white flash arced to the ground, spitting and hissing, and just as abruptly, disappeared in instant darkness. The three Diablos, not stirring from their army jeep, watched night spread downward from the Marikina Ledge towards the city, as the starpoints of street and house lights winked out almost instantly. After a while, the jeep engine came to life and moved away.

That was how they brought the love of her life back, Teresa. Aboard an old van, its side panels bearing a painted popsicle and the words *Magnolia Ice Cream—Delicious*, traveling at midnight under cover of a power outage inspired by a transformer exploding. The Basbas mansion had been forewarned. The van had no trouble slipping through the rear service gates, which now stood open, to halt before the kitchen back door. Had a stranger or reporter been watching, he would have surmised that a midnight delivery was being made and dismissed that as some eccentricity of the rich. But no one noticed, not even the Death Watch group huddled outside the locked front gates.

He was still a frozen oversized embryo under the stretcher's blanket when he was unloaded from the van. Two Diablos in worker denims took up his weight. They spoke in monosyllables, preferring hand signals. With a measure of tenderness, as Katerina tottered beside them, they carried His Excellency (to-be) Hector Basbas to her upstairs chamber. Here he was unveiled, unwrapped, and transferred to her bed.

Oh, look at him, she whispered as she wrung her hands. He was pale as pale could be, ashen, a ghost of his former self, with bristles on his chin and above his upper lip, the black nimbus of spikes that was hair about his head making him look like a demented rock star. His clothes, oh his clothes—he who'd always been impeccable—were torn, soiled, and reeking of dismal exudations. The back of his shirt had a pattern of rust-colored splotches ranging in size from a baby's hand on his shoulder to a tiny button-stain on the shirt hem, dried blood from . . . oh, you know, the Diablos had to take care of the peasant couple who'd seen and therefore could testify, though gossip was the more likely, about His Excellency (to-be) Hector Basbas's condition.

They scissored the clothes off him, straightening his limbs in the process, before turning him over to an orderly in white who proceeded to give him a sponge bath. Another Diablo pair had fetched two doctors, they assured Katerina, and would arrive any minute now. As far as they could tell, based on their paramedic's training, nothing major was wrong with His Excellency (to-be), except that, as one could see, freed of restraint, his limbs returned to their old position: hands curled beneath his chin, knees drawn up. Whether this vegetative state was reversible—that was the question. Which was why, Teresa, he was brought in this way, de Naval being thorough if excessive.

When the doctors arrived, rumpled from having been pulled out of their beds, everyone retired to the living room. Katerina could be thankful the children were asleep. Frightened maids wheeled in silver food carts and began dispensing coffee, cognac and liqueur, and pastries. Katerina, surprised to see de Naval, realized he had been the van driver. Such loyalty made her eyes water. She watched him tenderly as he poured brandy into a glass, downed it in a single gulp, and sighed audibly before settling into an armchair, signaling a maid for coffee. His pants were stained to the knees with mud and he smelled sour. When he glanced up at Katerina, she saw his eyes were so bloodshot he could be mistaken for the devil.

They waited, de Naval making them wait as he spooned sugar, poured milk into his coffee, and sipped. Only then did the terse words crackle from his mouth, describing his band's adventure through the turgid waters of the flood and telling how he had himself spotted the pennant through binoculars almost at the same instant that the chug-chug-chug of a sect helicopter had resounded overhead. It became a race then between Hector's allies and Hector's employees, with the latter almost losing out, for all they had was this WWII amphibian which could only go this fast and no more. In his frustration, de Naval had fired a burst from his submachine gun and shouted for his men to level their weapons at the aircraft, the devil take it. For a minute or two, the sect members seemed prepared to be martyred, for have no doubt about it, they would've been massacred had they landed. De Naval, being an astute Diablo, had grasped immediately what was at stake here, Hector's safety aside. It was the family's independence of movement, freedom of decision, and the right to care for nothing more than their own self-interest which Hector had worked for and valued all his life. Firing thus, de Naval had risked the possibility of the helicopter dropping a grenade on the stilt-hut and blowing everyone to kingdom come.

Such a look of hatred stabbed him from Katerina that the Diablo faltered. Armand soothed her quickly, saying hush now, everything ended well enough, but they weren't out of it yet, Hector's traumatic—and his eyes widened at the word—experience having reduced him to a senseless lump of flesh. Teresa finally understood the double bind they were in. Once Hector's condition was known, COMELEC would call for new elections, in which case Katerina couldn't run because *he* was back and no woman could usurp the role of family head. On the other hand, there was no guarantee Hector would rise to the occasion. Perhaps Armand could run? She dismissed the idea with regret. Too much could be unearthed about him, including his collaboration with the nation's invaders during WWII, and no telling how the Church of the Mystic Limb would react. Armand seemed to have followed her trend of thought, for he cleared his throat, rubbed his hands together, and said out loud: "What the hell, we've still got one horse left."

That was the Jukebox, oh Lord. The family could bankroll and thus bind him. The Diablos nodded with reluctance. Katerina said brightly that de Naval should be assigned as the man's security.

"That should keep him in line," she said. "Blow his brains out at the first sign of hedging."

De Naval went uh, uh, that wasn't much of a pleasure, and laughed.

Meanwhile, Teresa said, cutting through the merriment, just in case Hector did recover in time, they would have to think about the correct manner of, uh, *presentation*. Her mind was working furiously, lurching from the inaugural ball—oh, shall we stop the dancing to allow Herself to slide-step, slide-step down the beautifully curved staircase accompanied by a fanfaronade —to how to manage news about Hector's survival. She was certain they'd weathered the worst, were merely a step away from their destiny, come air crash, typhoon, thunder, and flood. The mere thought of it made her breathless.

"Public sympathy," Armand was saying, as he swirled the brandy in his glass gently, mesmerizing the group with the lazy motion of light in the liquid.

"Yes," Katerina said. "Maybe a plaster cast on his leg and arm; a turban . . ."

"Tut-tut," Armand interjected. "Nothing exaggerated. One plaster cast. Light bandaging. But not about his head. That might cause speculation about brain damage. Maybe a sling about the arm, ha? Not bad. Broken leg, sprained wrist or elbow. Battered but not damaged. A hero."

The word was a sun in the room. Katerina snuffled a little, dabbing at her nose with a tissue. In the silence, they heard footsteps on the stairs. The doctors were finished. The group rose as one to its feet. The shorter doctor came forward and proceeded to rap out the words: exhaustion, exposure, and dehydration. They'd bandaged his ribs because of a yellowing bruise; they'd hooked him to intravenous dextrose. No overt indications of concussion, but . . . And the two shifted their torsos uneasily. Perhaps he should be taken to a hospital.

"No!" That was from Katerina.

"He's not responding."

"Blackie will find out!"

"But he could—uh—"

"Die?"

"No," the other doctor said with reluctance. "He could get worse. Lose his chance to heal. We need to examine him completely. X-rays, CAT scan, things like that."

"Bring the machines here!"

"Impossible."

"Bring them. De Naval!"

"Hold it." That was Armand, intervening, for the agitated Diablos were responding in the only way they knew how: drawing their guns. "Calm down, everyone. Let's think."

"We won't be responsible . . ." the shorter doctor began.

"Shut up, darling," Armand told him. "Or I won't be responsible."

"Don't let them do it," Katerina shouted, making a grab for Armand. "We'll be finished. Done for!"

"You, too. Shut up." He dug hands into his pants pockets, studied the floor for a minute. "I think we might compromise," he said after a while. To the doctors: "One question. What would you do different if he were there?"

The two exchanged glances. "Examine him . . ." The shorter man nodded.

"By way of treatment?"

"Offhand, nothing, unless the tests . . ."

"In other words, nothing different for a few days."

The doctors looked at each other and then nodded.

"Okay. Let him stay here then for a week . . . no? Five days, okay?—and if nothing changes, we'll bring him in."

"Armand!"

He shushed Katerina, swiveled to face the doctors, and raised his eyebrows. "We've got a registered nurse, and an orderly, and you're both only a phone call and car ride away. Is it a deal?"

They hesitated but agreed finally. Armand exhaled audibly and nodded at Teresa's whisper he'd saved the day. "You watch Herself," he whispered back fiercely. The tableau broke up when de Naval signaled two Diablos to take the doctors out. Katerina excused herself, but not before whispering to Teresa about the two shopping bags for de Naval; his shark eyes had focused on her as soon as the doctors had turned their backs. Good job, boys, she called out, standing on the fourth step of the staircase. She considered clapping her hands but thought the better of it. He was home, at least, and if she couldn't pull back his wandering mind, then nothing on earth could do it.

The bed linen had been changed, the room cleaned and restored to its fresh scent, bloodied clothes and muddy tracks all gone. Only Hector himself, curled like a newborn between the peach silk sheets, remained as relic of the unpleasant experience.

She laid a hand on his brow, ran her fingers through his hair, shampooed and blown-dry now, and smelling of musk. No one had questioned, dared question, why he was brought to her room, this flesh of her flesh, blood of her blood, her twin. Deftly avoiding the plastic tube that snaked down to the bed and to his left thigh, she eased herself beside him, half reclining, half sitting, and cradled his head in her arms.

To her surprise and delight, he croaked. She was off the bed immediately. Dipping two fingers into a glass of orange juice on the night table, she wet his lips. They opened a crack, but her fingernails were too long, they snagged against his tongue. She walked to the vanity, scattered tubes of lipsticks, eyebrow pencils, and whatnot, barely remembering in time that she could peel the fake nails off. With a quick twist, she broke off the nails of her index and middle fingers. Then she returned to the bedside, dipped her fingers into the juice again, and thrust them into his mouth. Warmth flushed through her body as she felt his lips and tongue working on her fingers.

"I'll keep them short," she whispered, "until you recover."

Fall straight down.

That was what he said. Fall-straight-down. She understood at once, seeing him terrified and terrorized within the plane. She settled beside him again and brought her lips close to his right ear. Hush, she said. Not ever again. Never again to fall. Never. But always, instead, to rise—like a moon over this geography of sorrow that had been their life together, the twins' life. She promised to build him an eagle's nest . . . but why stop at one? A dozen eagle's nests: houses perched on cliff edges, accessible only to helicopters, guarded by ack-acks or whatever one called those weapons, so that no one and nothing, not even God, could bring them down from the heights. They would never be brought back to the pit again, that cold, gray-walled room through which echoed the heavy footfall of their relatives stirring in the rooms above; that time was long gone, brother, and there was no other way but to *go-straight-up*.

Teresa handled the "presentation" skillfully. Through a surrogate spokesperson, one of Armand's elegant young men, the world was informed via radio, newspaper, and television that His Excellency (to-be) had been found. BASBAS LIVES! screamed the headlines, but only with photos of the wrecked airplane and the dead Diablos. The story's text itself was muted, quoting an unnamed family spokesman to the effect that the not-yet-sworn-in presidential winner was in the care of his physicians. Guarded announcements followed, with Teresa herself handing press releases to the covey of media people at the gate: Hector had minor injuries. He was recuperating, true, but slowly. De Naval spiced this up by leaking stories from "reliable sources" to the effect that the senate president was despondent over the death of his men and pilots, whom he'd heroically tried to save.

Later, as Katerina expected, the stories would grow monstrous. Not that she was displeased, but, as she demanded of Teresa, how was it that José Domínguez y García was simply Blackie or President Blackie, while Hector was always Mr. Basbas or Senator Basbas? "He's known the press longer" was Teresa's explanation, a totally inadequate one, they both knew, because Hector had had dealings with the media for years. But Teresa didn't dare tell her the truth (oh, so many truths to tell), that the twins were moving farther and farther from the common human pale. They were losing their first names, would soon lose their second names, and in years to come would be referred to obliquely by a hundred and one half-mocking, half-fearful titles: Herself, the *Persledi*, Mother of the Country; the President, Sir, His Excellency, and both of them, the twice-blessed.

The separateness, their being apart from everyone, was what allowed amazing stories to grow about them. The Virgin Mary, so went the gossip, had appeared when the aircraft's engines had stalled. With an imperious forefinger, the Madonna had caused a gigantic winged lion to materialize in a sky racked by wind, lightning, and thunder, amidst the black clouds of the typhoon. Said lion then took the aircraft's weight on its back and bore it gently to earth, thereby sparing the senate president and never mind that four men's necks snapped and four others' spines splintered, what the hell, it was a great story. It went over big, thanks to Sister Mary Rose and Sister Ludi, who swore mightily they'd been "vouchsafed" the same vision on the same night. Two persons dreaming the same dream was statistically impossible, no? Only truth came in such dreams. Katerina, inwardly chuckling, made two appearances on television, wearing a white chiffon gown and languidly waving a white lace handkerchief. Discovery of the president-elect alive, of course, altered her own plans; she didn't mind because her intentions had always been a furtherance of his plans—whatever that meant. "But we have to see what happens. He's not out of danger yet, you know." In her exuberance, she promised that the Basbas family would reward everyone who'd prayed for her brother and who'd helped in the search. "Kindly just knock on our door," she said and smiled such a smile of happiness the cameraman was compelled to zoom out.

That brought an irate call from Matrimonia, who screamed that she was being besieged by an army of men and women claiming to have swum the Central Plains flood. "Please tell that woman," Matrimonia shrieked at Teresa who took the call, "to make clear which Basbas she and her brother are!"

"Bitch," Katerina murmured. "You're done for."

Teresa giggled, saying oh, come now, Katerina did know that the *Sunday Times Magazine* had a spread on the Forbes Park Basbas mansion the past weekend. Armand laughed, eyes tearing, at the thought of Matrimonia confronted by a sea of beggars. Katerina smiled innocently. Something had to be done about the woman, she said; had Teresa finished that list of the leftover Montelibano-Basbas properties? As a matter of fact, she amended, the same should be done for all the clans, sixty or eighty of them, the most "consequential" ones, so the family would know where the right buttons were, exactly.

Two blind masseuses, their walking canes leaning against the foot of the bed, tenderly kneaded Hector's body back to litheness. Katerina watched them crack his fingers and his toes one by one, massage the palms of his hands, the soles of his feet, rub the muscles of his back and his chest, and pinch and probe biceps and triceps, after which they dusted him with baby talcum powder and drew the covers to his chin. With great deference, they retreated out of the room, duty done and money earned, their canes going tap-tap-tap on the floor. She barely noticed their murmured farewells, for she'd set herself on the bed's edge and captured Hector's hand in her own, noting how warm, soft, and perfumed his skin was.

She waited, knowing that Hector's eyelids would flutter, like wasp wings, and then in a hoarse whisper, the words would fall from his lips: *Fall straight down.* He'd lost his balls back there, she thought, when the plane had dropped like a plywood toy mobile shorn of its support, sucked down by gravity. Hiding his face between her breasts, her chin on the top of his head, she sought to reassure him, saying hush, hush, it was over, no way to go now but Straight Up, like an engorged moon breaking the horizon's thin sheath or the sun ripping the sky apart, and if he didn't have the strength for it, Lord help them, then she would take on Blackie herself (oh, why did she call him by that nickname?), despite Armand's and Teresa's advice, to which end, she kept the frenzy going, having told the Basbas campaign organization to keep up the pressure. "A soft pressure, Hector," she murmured, in a lover's voice, "a soft push, not too strident, so as not to precipitate a sudden decision while we wait for you.

We're waiting for you, digging in our heels and stalling for time."
Which was when, inevitably, the question always came to her:
what for? What was it all for? And she was assailed by this terrible
impulse to take her twin, take him as he was, and flee. They
had enough to live in comfort until death took them together or
parted them. They could fade back into anonymity and breathe
again—a little more freely, perhaps, not with this tension, this
slight catch of the throat and lungs, fearful that some stranger's
eyes, some stranger's ears, would discover their secret, their one
true secret, which wasn't a secret at all but was paraded constantly
on children's feet every hour of the waking day. Truth to tell,
she told Hector, viewed rationally, it wasn't so monstrous at all,
merely pathetic, a case of twin-children so starved of affection
they had had no one to turn to but each other. "Children are
handled so badly in this country," she said, eyes smarting with
dryness because this was one of those times when she couldn't
weep, couldn't afford to weep. Pathetic, bereft little twins. If they
ran now, perhaps they would have the time to reorder their world,
to take control of it, instead of being carried along, helpless, by
the currents of the flood they had themselves loosed upon the
earth. "I'd like to have the time," she said, before the secret's
weight and its shadows muddied up her lucidity again, "to read
the letters that Aurelio Aureus composed."

His eyelids flickered. Opened. He looked straight at her with
aware eyes. Downstairs, at lunch, she told them that, telling
them how his hand had sought her hand so they could steeple
together, two halves of one greeting, one plea for a blessing.
Armand was so embarrassed he kept his eyes on his plate while
Epee hurled herself from her chair and up the stairs. But Katerina
had ordered the nurse to lock the door and not to open it except
at her command. Epee was reduced to thumping her palms on
the door and weeping. Teresa finally persuaded her to take herself
off to the garden, where Inè and Marmol, in high spirits, were

digging up what they had hidden. "Your uncle needs rest," Teresa said firmly, loathing the girl so much it was all she could do not to rain blows upon her head.

"He will recover," Katerina declared.

"In time?" Armand asked.

Katerina would not meet his eyes. She knew COMELEC had scheduled the hearings again, and while the battery of lawyers hired by the Basbas campaign could deal with the commission, sooner or later Hector would have to make an appearance. The longer the delay, the greater the possibility of gossip. But she had no answer. Hector was still meandering in the plane wreck.

She shifted in her seat, telegraphed with her eyes a plea to Teresa—who stirred uneasily.

"Perhaps we should get a therapist for Epee," Teresa said, glancing over her shoulder to make sure the dessert maid was out of hearing. "For all three, as a matter of fact. This must have been a shock to them."

Katerina agreed, grateful for the change in topic. Armand looked dubious and asked how they would deal with the therapists afterwards, in case the children did lay out the family case. At which Katerina paled, swallowed her custard the wrong way, and nearly choked. Stalemate, Teresa thought.

"She only needs to be beautiful," Katerina said after a while. "We should make inquiries . . ."

Teresa nodded. She'd grown used to off-tangent talk within the family. The three would talk about this-that, never quite focusing on any subject—which did not explain how everything else linked to them operated with admirable efficiency.

The Basbas organization had metastasized to pursue contra-dictory goals. A kamikaze air swirled through the uppermost rung, where she and Armand were, as though it were the Basbas family and not Blackie who was being ejected from a last fortress. But two rungs down, among various aides and secretaries, celebratory preparations were in full swing, with the stage construction at a brisk pace, Valero designing gowns furiously even as he oversaw decorators and seamstresses doing curtains, table linen, and whatnots of the inauguration. Basbas lawyers were deep in debate as to the proper course to take with the COM-ELEC hearings, while de Naval's band was busy breaking every law possible, running through their two shopping bags of money.

Five Central Plains mayors were detained, de Naval had said, a gold toothpick dangling from the corner of his mouth, "temporarily—so they can't bother COMELEC." Furthermore, he'd met with Smith and worked out a surprise, which he wasn't prepared to discuss as yet. "But soon," he said. "Soon."

Teresa threw him a glance of deep suspicion. De Naval meeting Smith on his own volition could be disturbing. The Diablo head evaded her questions and simply patted the back of her hand. "After this, Blackie will give up," he said. Doubly perturbed, she went to Katerina, asking what it was that de Naval was planning, but fat with peace at being able to care for her twin, Herself merely shrugged and told her to ask Armand, who also shrugged and said he was too busy to baby-sit de Naval. Anyway, the Diablo knew what he was doing, and Smith was his old comrade. "Those guys understand each other," Armand said. It was no use. Try as she might, Teresa could not discover what de Naval had set up. The tension of being on the alert, waiting for an unwary sentence, waiting to spring into action, was wearing her down when Hector spoke. She heaved a sigh of relief then, trusting that the family luck was turning. It couldn't be coincidence, she thought, that as reported by Katerina, Hector's first coherent words three days after his homecoming were: "We're not going down."

19

They struck at midnight, overrunning the main building of their own camp and setting it on fire, but only after they'd emptied its small armory of weapons and transferred the files on liberals, humanists, communists, stand-up comics, and other assorted subversives to their barracks. Here, asses parked on the edge of their bunks, they broke the seal on folders marked *Confidential* and scanned the contents within idly, all the while smoking fragrant brown *cigarillos*, and while their ringleaders went outside to confront a stupefied assemblage of reporters and junior officers. The leaders—three captains—then announced that this here particular marine unit was on hunger strike until the state of uncertainty obtaining in the country was resolved, gahdemet, because what was the point of an armed forces without a commander-in-chief? Whereupon the listening marines broke into applause and cheered when the press and other military units garlanded the barracks front with flood and video lights and settled down for a long wait.

Three hours later, at the burning Administration Building, a black Mercedes-Benz disgorged two generals, picturesque with their brass stars, rows of multicolored ribbons, and swagger sticks. They looked at the flames devouring the building, which a forlorn fire truck was trying to douse, exchanged observations in low voices, and tracked by video and still cameras, marched down to the renegades' barracks. But the elite marines set up a drumroll of insults, shouting that the two weren't professionals, only reservists promoted through political patronage; they didn't even know how to parachute off airplanes, much less interrogate a subversive or two. They refused to come out. Impasse. It was a national emergency.

One of the discomfited generals cupped his hands about his mouth and yelled: *Who the hell do you want to mediate?* A pause during which the exploding of wood beams and glass in the burning building could be heard. Then, from the barracks, three hundred throats roared out the name in unison: *De Naval!*

It was a conspiracy, said the livid José Domínguez y García aka Blackie. The marines were in danger of court-martial—"at this very instant!"—and the president certainly would not consent to discuss anything until the men laid down their arms and surrendered.

Unfortunate words. "Like hell we will," the three hundred thundered.

What officers hadn't now joined the mutiny. Did this civilian president actually believe he could issue an ultimatum to marines, gahdemet? The much-imposed-upon Blackie then phoned every general he could manage but all refused to negotiate on his behalf. "Excuse my frankness," said one general, "Mr. President, but you don't ask marines to surrender." Blackie couldn't appreciate the fine point; who the hell then should negotiate? he demanded. The generals cleared their throats, went into if sos and whatevers, and finally admitted there was no helping it. No one knew how much firepower the marines had stashed, and short of pulverizing the barracks, there was no way of getting at them. "If you do," said a general succinctly, "you're done for. Every military man will rise up against you."

Blackie appealed for calm, even as the airwaves crackled with the voice of reporters detailing the latest in this newest crisis. Over and over again, the question was tossed around and tossed about: how did Blackie Domínguez y García propose to deal with the problem? "No matter," said Blackie, who had acquired blue hollows under his eyes, "which end of the Constitution one held up, there's nothing about the military having the right to concern itself with the current problem." Legal channels, like the legislature and COMELEC, existed to deal with it, he finished lamely.

At which the three captains, leaders, sirs, appeared before the press again, standing in a cleared and light-flooded space before the barracks, through whose windows protruded all manner of gun barrels. They were so "telegenic," as cameramen put it, that they were allowed a good fifteen minutes to reply to Blackie's statement. "We're the first to stake our lives," the handsomest of the three said, "for this country. We receive the most arduous training, not once but all our professional lives. We are prepared mentally, physically, and spiritually for leadership. How many politicians can say as much? Blackie Domínguez y García would have us deal with men we don't consider our equals. We believe it's time we end civilian interference in military affairs. That's how we read the Constitution."

Those words, carried to the barracks by radio and television, inspired a ten-minute nonstop cheering from the men within. DE NAVAL! DE NAVAL! they shouted.

By nine in the morning, when the business day started, groceries and supermarkets opened to an incredible crush of people hysterical but determined to be prepared for any eventuality. In two hours flat, the stores were cleaned out; all the shelves were emptied and nothing was left in the back rooms. Stocks plummeted, and the exchange considered closing for the day at noon. Meanwhile, within three hours, ten million pesos were withdrawn from banks all over the country. Endless problems. Government offices were empty, employees having chosen to stay at home, to attend to their own preparations, as men roamed the streets in search of food to purchase and women were busy boiling, frying, and freezing every sliver of meat and fish they could lay their hands on. The war, with its memories of famine, wasn't too far off to haunt everyone.

As dazed as Blackie, Armand, Teresa, and Katerina watched the unfolding of events on television. The telephones, both at the Basbas campaign headquarters and in the house, were in the hands of Armand's assistants, who'd been instructed to say that the Basbas family had no comment to make at this time. Only a call from de Naval could get through. But the Diablos had disappeared so completely not even their whores knew where they were. And though Armand located the blond Valkyrie, whom de Naval had hidden in the honeymoon suite of the Tagaytay resort, she didn't know where the Diablo was. Armand had to take comfort in spitting out the word "excessive" several times—admission enough that until and unless Hector rose from his bed, or rather Katerina's bed, there was no controlling the ex-captain.

The bad thing about it, Teresa said, was that they couldn't take pleasure in Blackie's discomfiture. They'd been sidelined by de Naval's gambit, perdition take the man, and that was worrisome. "They might try to make him president."

Only the children, kept out of school, greeted every mention of de Naval's name with jubilation.

By nightfall, more troops had mutinied, locking themselves in their barracks and swearing to shoot anyone who came within fifty yards of it. Intermittent gunfire crackled in the distance, puncturing the keening of ambulance sirens. What was being fired on, who was firing, no one knew. But hospitals took in bodies with bullet holes at the rate of one per hour. Blackie disappeared from the cameras, leaving the press secretary to offer, every so often, the unsatisfying explanation that a settlement was being worked out behind the scenes. Reporters guessed quickly enough that Blackie had decided to starve out the mutineers.

Senators and congressmen declared emergency marathon sessions and were in the process of denouncing everything under the heavens when they were warned they would be arrested by the mutineers. They promptly disappeared themselves, leaving the Legislative Building ghostly with lights and discarded paper.

Hector rested easily through all the commotion. Unmoving, flat on his back, the covers drawn to his chin, he nearly convinced Teresa he'd decided to join San Custodio in that mystical divide between life and death, managing thereby to abdicate from life's responsibilities while still breathing. She leaned over him and saw his eyelids flicker as her shadow fell on his face. Hector, she hissed at him, Hector. No response. Fatigued beyond belief, she returned to the living room and found Armand asleep in an armchair. She was about to waken him, to urge him to retire, when the private phone, the number used only by the Basbas inner circle and the Diablos, rang.

It was de Naval, chuckling, saying they shouldn't worry; enough food had been moved to the barracks to keep the men going for a whole month if necessary. Katerina, at the extension phone, cut in to say he was going too far, but de Naval brushed her aside, saying who was to say how far was far enough? "We want the senate president in there, don't we?" He'd worked it all out, he said, with Sunday Smith, calculating the risk of a downward spiral of the process. "By the best evaluation," he went on, "we can control it." Katerina trembled, hearing this strange echo of Hector's *fall-straight-down*. "What the hell are you talking about?" she snapped as Teresa, in a different manner, asked: "What downward spiral?" De Naval laughed. "Intelligence jargon," he said. "But keep watch over His Excellency. The 'Kano doesn't know his condition and thinks Hector's merely biding his time. Let's keep it that way."

He would not say when he was going to surface; at the moment, he was biding his time, keeping undercover, and what the hell did Armand think he was doing, scaring his blond girlfriend like that? He'd have to recognize the moment to reappear when it came, which was better than setting an arbitrary deadline. "But you're ruining the country!" Teresa shouted. Silence. She could almost see the slight but wiry ex-captain shrugging. "We'll patch it up later," he said. "Besides, it was ruined long ago." The line went dead. The two women had to admit defeat. Meeting in the corridor to the kitchen, they held hands. Katerina murmured that Hector had a way of speaking to de Naval that was equal parts contempt and approval. "I don't know how to do it," she said. "Hector makes de Naval want to please him." Teresa concurred; it was the way of men with men, a way which eluded women, who often had to bluster when confronted by creatures like de Naval. "We're at his mercy," she said, shamed by her helplessness.

Dawn broke with reports that snipers had positioned themselves along national highways and boulevards, taking potshots at cars, buses, and pushcarts. Streets emptied rapidly, to the grateful sigh of the banks, which, using the excuse that their employees were endangered, shut down all their branches, never mind the customers' howls. Armand, a glass of orange juice in hand, shook his head in admiration; Smith and de Naval had stopped the bank run just like that. "Let's see what happens next," he said, dropping to the sofa and stretching in a huge yawn. The phones rang intermittently; the assistants had begged leave to attend to their families. Calculating that most calls would be from panicked constituents and the media, Armand had given them his permission, saying the phones could ring to kingdom come in the meantime. "Better stay out of this," he said, "until the situation clears. We don't want Hector tainted. We don't want him connected to the mutiny." Katerina had argued against it, saying they were losing relevance each minute, but Armand eyed her from head to foot and asked, in a truly angry voice: "And what's so relevant about that zombie upstairs?"

Animal! *Tarantado!* Katerina hurled an ashtray at his head, just as the children were rounding the hallway corner from the kitchen. Without pausing, the three launched themselves at their father, pinning him down beneath their frail bodies, pummeling him with their fists, shrieking curses into his ears. Armand tried to laugh at first, pretending it was horseplay, but in the end, he shook them off like so many yapping terriers. Epee jumped, hands clawed to grab his hair—at which Armand backhanded her, sending her flying over the coffee table to slam down on the sofa. "Don't touch me," Armand screeched, voice thin with hysteria. "Don't ever touch me, you . . . Bah! Women!" He smoothed down his shirtfront and chin up, climbed the stairs to his bedroom.

Teresa shook her head, rang the bell to summon the help. Katerina swept the children with cold eyes. "I should pack you all off to boarding school," she said. She studied Epee and Inè intently. "You two are old enough. Remember that and don't get in my way again."

It wasn't a bad idea, she declared to Hector later. The clans sent their young at puberty's onset abroad, to Switzerland or England. An overseas education conferred sophistication, enough to distance the children from the volcanic temperament of the local people, who could thus always be manipulated with an appeal to sentiment by the unsentimental. Though Epee, of course, would never forgive her mother if she was sent away— "but we'll burn that bridge when we reach it," she said, not really hearing her words. She peered at him intently, half envying the peace in which he lay. Because of the disorder, the masseuses hadn't appeared; she had to do that for him now.

"You bloody coward," she muttered, pushing back the pajama

sleeve covering his left arm. She felt his skin, the loose tissues underneath. "You're losing it."

She couldn't decide whether she should step in as family head or not, jump into the fray as it were, issue a statement or something, and the longer she vacillated, the stronger Armand and de Naval grew. She wasn't sure anymore that Armand hadn't known about the mutiny. After all, he was the one who dealt with Smith. De Naval obviously was not taking instructions from her anymore, and the more he and Armand coalesced, the more Teresa and Herself were written out of the equation. Next thing one knew, Armand would be declaring his candidacy, perdition take him.

"I'm stalemated!" she shouted at Hector, flinging his arm back at his chest. "Wake up, you fool. We're going down!"

She found herself tumbling backward as he heaved himself from the pillows, his eyes agog, hair rising like snakes on his head. A humming filled her ears as a bitter ozone smell flooded the room. Hector fell back, his throat working; his arms and legs spasmed before his body settled back into immobility. But he was loose, his limbs straight, his torso no longer curled up. Katerina picked herself up from the floor and heard suddenly the pounding on the door. She opened it and found Armand, Teresa, and the children huddled outside. What was it? they asked. A thunderclap, the house hit by lightning, was he all right? They rushed to the bed and found Hector staring with wrath at the ceiling.

"He spoke," Katerina said. "I pleaded with him and he spoke."

"What did he say?" Teresa asked.

"He said *leave me alone, woman!* That's what . . ." Epee stopped when Teresa took a step forward, right hand drawn back.

But Katerina was smiling. "Yes, he said that."

Armand snapped his fingers. "Stimulus. That's what he needs. He needs to be stimulated."

Marmol, flapping tiny arms, brayed with laughter and, rising on tiptoe, leaped to the bed. Before the adults could react, he was perched on Hector's chest, legs straddling his torso, and was methodically *tickling* the Senate President. Hector's head and legs arched upward; a horrible honking ensued. Katerina screamed; Armand rushed to pluck the boy from the invalid while Teresa, stretching out a foot, deftly tripped Epee, stopping her rush to the bed.

It was Inè's voice which cut through the confusion. "He's awake!" she declared.

Awake, watching them with eyes whose pupils were contracted to pinpoints. Awake and enraged. His throat worked; he croaked, and Teresa, the first to unfreeze, snatched a glass of water from the bedside and held it to his lips. He gulped convulsively, water spilling down his jaws and staining the bedsheet.

"You'll drown him," Katerina yelled.

"Better drowned than half dead," Teresa snapped back.

Armand was on the intercom, demanding iced coffee, "lots of coffee!" They couldn't take the chance, he said, of his falling asleep again. For some reason, the three children were calmly opening the windows, drawing back the curtains to let the sunshine in. Hector had stopped drinking and turned his head away with a low wordless complaint. Teresa, returning the glass to the table and wiping dry her hands on the bedsheet, wondered if the same trick would work on San Custodio. It was worth a try; she could tickle him, poke his armpits, stroke his soles with a feather until a robust and virile laugh exploded from his mouth. But considering her luck, she thought, sighing, it probably wouldn't work. At least His Excellency (to-be) was with them again.

Who would have thought of it, they said to one another afterwards, that that was all that was needed—a huge bat of a child landing on his chest and prodding his ribs? Gathered in the sunroom, they laughed, united for once, and could not stop laughing, though through the house echoed ominous voices from radio and television detailing the country's "dire state of affairs." The children, lovable of a sudden, hugged and kissed the three, played tag with one another, and Marmol, the incoherent, had his hair rumpled fondly many, many times. For the first time since Hector's disappearance, the climate in the house warmed a few degrees as Katerina's frown unknotted.

That evening, when de Naval called, Katerina could tell him that Hector had managed ten full sentences and had begun to take in liquids—juice, coffee, tea . . . Nirvana! De Naval's shout nearly deafened her, but he simmered down at once, saying this was exceedingly good news, good news indeed, because he was getting worried, not knowing how much longer he could keep the whole thing up, it had already gone beyond the five-hour deadline which he and Smith had surmised would be enough to make Blackie cave in.

Within the next hour, two things happened. First, a disheveled and badly frightened doctor arrived, escorted by six Diablos. He was hustled to the bedroom and ordered to examine Hector, whom he pronounced stable and recovering rapidly. He'd removed the IVs from Hector's leg, and Mrs. Bas . . . uh, Gloriosa could proceed with puréed food. "Nothing fatty," he said. "Fruits mostly—bananas, oranges, avocados . . ." He was amply rewarded by the ecstatic Katerina.

Second, de Naval appeared, walked out of the shadows, just like that, into the circle of lights which marked the clump of media people hanging out at the marine barracks. "I'm de Naval," he said, facing the cameras, spine stiff, chin at a right angle to his neck. He wore his old uniform, his cap squeezed beneath his right arm. Having saluted the gathered officers smartly, he pivoted on his heels and marched to the barracks, ignoring the raucous cheers of the barricaded men. Truth to tell, he would say later, he nearly bolted out as soon as he stepped in; it was a total mess inside, with empty food tins, crumpled aluminum wrap and brown bags, beer bottles, potato chips and cheese sticks underfoot, half-clothed men lying bleary-eyed and half drunk on their double bunks. Had Blackie been more astute, he could've ordered an assault and taken the place just like that, for the men were bored, tipsy, and missing their wives and whores with a vengeance. Hard to do without women, the men said; next time they would smuggle in a WAC or two. If there was a next time. . . . "We got there in the nick," de Naval said. "The mutiny would've collapsed by dawn."

He took the precaution of staying for an hour and a half, listening to a radio voice saying every ten or so minutes that the "much-decorated and highly respected professional captain" was in the barracks "right now, ladies and gentlemen, in a parley with the mutineers, risking his own life," which made the men snicker and toast de Naval with warm beer. He drank beer, ate chips and smelly fried dried fish, and told them improbable stories about the war—which war, no one bothered to ask, the country having had so many. Occasionally they relieved themselves of heavy sentiment, clapping one another's shoulders and speaking gruffly about military brotherhood and solidarity, and what a shame there had to be civilians, and how they'd all been trained to be noble, pure, and obedient only to be messed up by a world without order. "Discipline," de Naval offered, fixing each man with a look until he got a nod of agreement, "that's what this country needs. No more, no less." For, Teresa, he was not so stupid as not to know that baffled men hankered for the quick and easy, for slogans so vague they seemed incontrovertible and required no further thought. Indeed, who would argue with such a word as "discipline"?

The outside world wasn't privy to this, of course; it remained within the Basbas mythology, for Katerina, Armand, and Teresa heard the details of de Naval's "complex and difficult negotiations," as the press put it, when he reported to a still weak but very much awake Hector, whose eyelids hooded as the story unfolded to his ears and who gave de Naval measuring sidelong glances. When the ex-captain walked out of the barracks, he had the soldiers' surrender in his hands, along with a list of what they wanted: across-the-board pay increases, exemption of rank promotions from the scrutiny of the Civil Service Commission, and quick resolution of the question of who won the election.

"Gentlemen," a precise de Naval told the microphones, "we enter a new age here—an age when the military can no longer be neglected but will have to be factored into each and every decision. These men have served notice. There will be no further toleration of any travesty of the Constitution. As a citizen, I urge every government official to search his conscience, to stop corruption and dedicate himself to the service of this country. If he expects soldiers like myself to stake our lives to protect him. And have no doubts, gentlemen, there are enemies out there." Having delivered himself of this warning, de Naval handed over the grievance list to a general and faded away from the cameras.

Well said, Hector whispered, his voice rasping, his eyes glinting. Congratulations.

20

Hard pressed though he was, Blackie had enough spleen left, as common talk put it, to denounce COMELEC's and Congress's decision to hold nonstop joint hearings until a winner was chosen. "Sheer capitulation," he declared, forefinger jabbing at the cameras. "Mark my words. We won't see the end of this." He was distracted by a report quoting (subsequently denied and then confirmed) an unidentified official of "a certain friendly power" ("That's Smith, yahoo!" Armand yelled, punching the air) to the effect that while this was a domestic matter, the country's foremost ally was interested in its speedy resolution. Blackie was done for, everyone agreed, since the phrase "speedy resolution" had become synonymous with the proclamation and swearing-in of His Excellency (to-be) Hector Basbas. Blackie could be forgiven for losing his temper and denouncing "foreign intervention," threatening to close "those interfering alien military bases." Even de Naval was impressed; nobody but nobody, he declared, dared to use such subversive words. One had to hand it to the old man, who was going down fighting, taking on all comers, the embassy by the sea included. He really had spleen, *apog* in the local slang. But Blackie had reserved ammo, it turned out. Two days after the hearings commenced, three Blackie columnists began clamoring for sight of Hector, just so the nation could be assured, they said, that he was, uh, physically capable of taking over the reins of government. Obviously, Blackie was on to something.

"Such bad prose" was Armand's reply, as he parried requests to interview His Excellency (to-be) Hector Basbas, Esq., all the while silently cursing his brother-in-law's refusal to heal immediately. "The president-elect," he said, "is keeping a low profile, as he doesn't want to prejudice the hearings." That convinced no one, though, and the media picked up on the demand. Hector's state of health rapidly became the sole topic of coffeeshop conversations—which reminded Armand of the lab results Smith had laid before him. Quietly, telling only Teresa, he called in de Naval for a consultation. The Diablo listened and nodded; he wouldn't be surprised, the ex-captain said, if certain doctors decided to immigrate overseas shortly. Armand was relieved.

Desperation inspired Teresa to arrive with her television crew one early morning at the Basbas house. "We have to stop this rumor," she said, for by then, three or four columnists were claiming that inside information had His Excellency (to-be) so brain-damaged he could be outsmarted by a lettuce. A forty-minute video, said Teresa, of Hector doing "recuperative exercises" should nail Blackie's coffin shut, so to speak. "Thank God for twentieth-century technology. An alternate reality is always possible."

It wasn't quite as easy as that, it turned out, for Hector collapsed after every five-minute session with the dumbbells and fell asleep to boot. The crew stayed for three days, snatching raw footage of His Excellency (to-be) doing sit-ups, touching his toes (despite the plaster cast on his left leg), waving dumbbells about, and shivered in the chill air of the president-elect's discomfort. When he managed to escape sleep, Hector hobbled about, gasping and whining tremulously that this was shit-work, what the hell was it for, anyway? Despite the sunlight, the terrace would then nearly ice over. "He's trying," said Armand after a while, "to avoid the work by freezing everyone to death." Hector had to be reposi-

tioned after every rest, told to pump away or strain himself at sit-
ups until a wheeze escaped his mouth, told to rest, repositioned
once again, and so on and so forth. Both Epee and Katerina were
barred from the gardens because they ruined constantly the film-
ing by dashing forward whenever Hector groaned. Armand had
to shepherd them away, patting Teresa's head when he passed
close to her and saying he was so glad that for a female, she was
so cold-blooded. Teresa bared her teeth at him and yelled sharply
at her crew to "get to it, boys, before he dies on our hands."
Everyone laughed a little nervously. Hector panted like an over-
heated dog.

Later, in a studio's editing room guarded by Diablos, Teresa
oversaw the editing and splicing of the tapes, making sure that
any awkwardness about the president-elect was scissored out. The
director and editor worked nonstop until what they had was a
thirty-minute strip of Hector doing fluid calisthenics, hefting
dumbbells, wiping his face with a white handtowel before grinning with appreciation into the camera. The crew applauded at
the end of the impromptu preview. "Done," Teresa called out
happily and signaled for lights. She was stupefied to find the
audience teary-eyed. The director looked wistful. It was, he said,
his finest work so far. Later, as she distributed cash-stuffed envelopes among them and listened to their fervent gratitude, Teresa was struck by how willingly people bought what they
themselves sold.

Of course she made sure first, she told the dreamy San Custodio that evening in her house, that she had retrieved all the
raw footage, stacking the cassettes like so many books on her desk
at the Basbas campaign headquarters. It being past midnight, the
building was empty, with the exception of security guards. In
this silence, she contemplated the cassettes and felt the idea
mushroom suddenly in her mind. What she had on her desk
was a weapon against the Basbas twins; the cassettes were both

history and commodity. She could keep them for the future (truth was always reserved for the future, as her father would say). Or trade them in the political market. They could finance an endless flight for herself and San Custodio, even to Bhutan. Or she could hide them for the opportune moment and save her father, herself, and—who knew who else?

But the idea died just as quickly; she shook her head, knowing the twins, knowing Himself in particular, who would not abide treachery from his own people. "He'd tear me apart," she said to the silent room, "with his bare hands." He would take away even this pittance of a happiness with her deaf, mute, and im-mobile lover. There was no helping it. She had made her choice, she reminded herself, years ago, when she picked up a scuffed black leather suitcase to follow Katerina. No one valued her as much. "Without the twins," she told San Custodio a little sheep-ishly, "my life would not have been as colorful. Between being dull and being evil—it's not much of a choice, no?" A little twinge of guilt compelled her to rearrange the plastic tubes that fed him, looping them into giant hearts.

Her mind then made up, she told him, she had her driver take her to the San Lazaro crematorium. Here she rang bells, demanded, proffered fistfuls of money until she was sold a child's coffin. Inside, she laid the cassettes in two neat rows. *Requiescat in pace,* she murmured as the coffin was swallowed by the fur-nace. The country had to be pulled together, she told herself as the muffled hunger of flames reached her.

The official video was an instant success, Blackie's acerbic comment that it should be marketed for the overweight ignored. Public curiosity about Senator Basbas's health waned. The family breathed easier for the time gained. In breathless gratitude, Ka-terina flung two rosaries ("heirlooms, *hija!*") at Teresa. One was of onyx; the other of jade. Hector could knit and heal in peace now, in Katerina's bed, in the warm cradle of her attention. She was good for him, even the house servants said; he was coming along nicely, but she—oh, she! Herself looked ten years younger, her skin as smooth as ripe mango, taut and glowing. She hummed as she puttered about the house, leaving the tedium of running the campaign to Teresa and Armand. Valero, who came often now, shepherding in decorators, chefs, flower arrangers, and other party experts, whispered slyly: "If I didn't know you better, I'd swear you were in love." Teresa was scandalized but Katerina only laughed.

Hector was getting used to the crutches. He stayed awake longer, surrounded by endless cups of coffee, the memory of his fall-straight-down dimming before the urgency of everyday problems. Locked in his study, he conferred with his guests: in the morning politicans and ward leaders, whom he urged to greater effort ("we need more *gasolina*, men"), in the evening the Diablos. Hector had changed, though; Teresa noticed how reserved and oblique he was with de Naval and the bodyguards.

One Sunday, Teresa awoke to find the black limo parked before the front gates of her house. Hector was sending for her, was insistent that she have breakfast at the Basbas residence. He had to discuss a small but urgent matter with Teresa. So said the Diablo who'd come with the car. A little impatient, because she did not like to leave San Custodio on the servants' day off, she dressed hurriedly and boarded the car, the sooner to be finished with business.

Armand met her at the front door, warned her with a shake of his head, and ushered her to the sunroom. Hector was there already, having coffee and toast; he waved Teresa to a chair, rang a silver bell for the maid, ordered another place set, and urged her to eat. "You're too thin," he said. He'd sent Katerina and the children off to some senator's birthday celebration. "Can't let our allies down, you know." Mystified, Teresa shot a questioning look at Armand, but he was being correctly neutral.

Hector waited until the French toast was before her. When she picked up knife and fork, however, he said quickly that he was sorry. Teresa froze and looked at him. "I've been so busy," he said, "I forgot to thank you." Her mouth opened, closed. "For the support, the video, and all your work." Fortunately, he went on, he was recovering fast and was sure occasions would arise which would enable him to show his appreciation. Teresa nearly choked. By those words, Hector had declared her passing over from Katerina's territory to his.

Without preamble then, Hector began cursing de Naval in the worst terms possible. "The man's dangerous," he said, licking a fleck of saliva off his lower lip. "We have to ease him away from our center." Armand, embarrassed, shifted in his chair. But Hector would not be stopped. "We'll have to deal with that strutting arrogant s.o.b." Frightened, Teresa opened her mouth to say she had nothing to do with this problem, but Armand cut in, forestalling her:

"He expects to be appointed defense secretary."

"Hell he does," Hector said and grinned.

Teresa shivered. No telling what the Diablos would do, nor what Smith would. As though tracking her thoughts, Hector said: "They're cooking something up, those two."

She had to try, she told herself, and inhaled audibly. Alarmed, Armand blinked at her. "They—he—did find you," she said. "It would not look good if you, ah, dispensed with him at this time. You owe him."

Hector studied her. After a while, he sighed. "That's true. You are invaluable indeed." And turning to Armand, he said his brother-in-law should watch Teresa and learn from her. "She has courage, this one."

A maid entered to announce that the other visitors had arrived. To Teresa's surprise, de Naval walked in, followed by four of his lieutenants. They had discarded their combat fatigues and were in formal *barong* shirts with silk embroidery, the loose hem hiding their handguns effectively. Hector called out to the maids to bring more chairs, coffee, and other things. "Let's treat our friends here well, very well," he said, and to Teresa's greater surprise, he started to praise the ex-captain extravagantly, calling him "son," confessing himself to be in eternal obligation to the man. "We were close before," he said to de Naval, "but now, we're just like this." Hector waved two fingers pressed together in de Naval's face.

The ex-captain peered at Teresa first and then at Armand. "So," he said, in a voice of displeasure. Teresa's heart sank; de Naval had concluded that whatever would happen next had been planned among them. Which was, she realized, Hector's intention. She had been set up; she was compromised.

De Naval smiled, sipped coffee, and abruptly giggled.

"I'd like you to be my defense secretary," Hector said quietly.

The Diablos jumped up from their chairs, applauding and crying out: "Oy! No better man! *Amigo!*" To his credit, de Naval waited blandly, his eyes on Hector's face.

"No thanks in order," Hector went on, ignoring the ex-captain's silence. "You're capable. And I owe you. However . . ." And Hector began to speak swiftly, saying there were objections from the military establishment, certain generals still angered by the mutiny, and so on and so forth. "They don't understand you, *amigo*," he said. "They see you only as a low-rank ex-captain. I tried to convince them. I spoke to them. But they said you weren't even a lieutenant general."

Dead silence. The Diablos sank back slowly, turning now to Hector, now to de Naval with quizzical frowns. De Naval did not remove his eyes from Hector. Teresa thought he looked murderous indeed, the more so for being so still.

"Tell me, friend," Hector went on, "what is this stupid thing about rank? I'm not a military man. I don't understand it."

De Naval said nothing. He was not, certainly, about to make it easier for Hector.

"But do tell," Hector said in a smooth voice. "Enlighten me."

Reluctantly, unable to resist complicity in his own execution, de Naval said through dead lips: "It's so much shit."

"Exactly," Hector said and beamed at the other Diablos. "So much shit. But in politics, we deal mostly with that, don't we, gentlemen?" He laughed and forced them to laugh back. They were really stupid, Teresa thought. "I do have a solution," Hector went on, and everyone breathed again. "There's this little war in a nearby country, thank God for little wars. We can send you over with a, uh, noncombatant force, to help out as it were. That way we can promote you—fast. Faster than the usual way."

Across the table, Armand winked secretly at Teresa. She nodded back, thinking that Smith had won this one after all, leaving Hector with the general discontent his decision would create. But since that involved only the public, it was of no consequence.

"It is agreed, then. You understand the process?" Hector asked sagely, signaling to his valet that his crutches should be brought now.

"But . . ." de Naval managed to croak, "who'll handle the defense department while I'm gone?"

A smile, innocent and open, stretched Hector's lips. "Why, I will. For a year or two or even longer, whatever it takes. Concurrent with the presidency. I'll baby-sit it for you, friend. Least I can do. And when you return, it will be there. All yours." He laughed and rose from the table while the men burst into an excited babble.

De Naval did not stir. "Who'll protect you while I'm gone?" he asked, his voice heavy.

At that, Hector looked him straight in the eye and said: "I'll have the presidential guards. And from here on, because you're away, you, my most trusted friend, no one will be admitted in my presence armed."

It was well done, Teresa had to admit. When de Naval returned from overseas, if he returned, he'd have to contend with a tight knit of officers handpicked by Hector. The same idea must've occurred to the ex-captain, for he lowered his head and gave a quick glance to his left and to his right, gauging the climate, she guessed. His shoulders jerked back, he raised a glass of water to his lips; his eyes were inexplicably hooded, and when he looked at Teresa, she saw that he had everything under control. He smiled then, said yes, indeed, that was the perfect solution.

So, she told San Custodio later, if Hector had expected the ex-captain to throw a fit—which would have been perfect excuse to dispense with him altogether—he was disappointed. By breakfast's end, de Naval was smiling, saying yes, it was a perfect solution. He even thanked Hector, his patron.

But Hector played it as coolly, explaining to Teresa when the Diablos had gone that he'd given de Naval to understand this was Smith's particular request. It was all the 'Kano's fault. "They will soon have a—shall we call it a minor falling-out?"

What an elaborate dance that was, Teresa said to San Custodio, far more complex than what she had planned for the inauguration—slide-step, slide-step; right shoulder forward, left shoulder forward; and will the rigodón stop at this point?—and all in the space of a few hours! If she could but choreograph it, if she could but stage it on the horizon, against the full moon's face, no lies would be left in this archipelago. She had to admire the genius with which Hector danced with one partner, pretending no one could be more preferred than the chosen, even while he was already wooing the next person and making eyes at a third. It was superb orchestration, for now Teresa stood next to Armand in Hector's glance, the spot usually occupied by the ex-captain. Worse, he knew that she knew it. And was terrified.

Before fear could compel her to action, however, news arrived from the Basbas campaign headquarters. Blackie Domínguez had sent feelers for a meeting with Hector—*mano a mano*; the problem, after all, could be resolved only by the two who had begun it. "He'll deal," Hector said when he was awake enough to appreciate the information. "It's all over—except for my vow." His eyes sliced about the room and fell upon Katerina. "Are you ready?" he asked her, excitement barely contained. What that meant Teresa didn't ask, and Armand only shrugged when she looked a question at him. "You," Hector said, pointing his nose at Armand, "set it up. Here. Tell him I'm unable to travel. That should make him curious." Better on his own turf, Teresa surmised.

So it was that at eight on a Saturday evening, when the whole nation was preoccupied with a basketball game, as Hector fortified himself with mugs of coffee, swallowing one mouthful after another as he leaned on Katerina's shoulder in the monstrous bed upstairs, a squad of presidential guards in civilian clothes descended upon the Basbas house. They were quite thorough, tapping on walls, checking out vases, sweeping rooms with detectors, and finally shooing all of the president-elect's bodyguards to the front yard. Katerina was scandalized when they walked into her bedroom, but Hector hushed her, offered the men coffee, and ignored their hands patting the bedcovers and pillows and opening drawers. But he called out as they left the room that this was "overkill. If I wanted to, I could've dispatched Blackie a long time ago."

He laughed and looked at Katerina fondly. They'd worked this out between them. Two beautiful white French chairs, satin-upholstered, silk-embroidered, were placed near the bed—one close to Hector's head, the other on the opposite side, near his feet. Blackie would be offered the first, because Hector didn't have the strength to raise his voice. Katerina would sit in the other, her presence justified by Hector, who would say to the incumbent but soon-to-be-ex president that this was as much his twin's life as his. She'd worked her fingers to the bone, so to speak, for him and was entitled to witness the end of the contest. Actually, Katerina had Marmol's silver .22 caliber, fully loaded this time, hidden in a fold of her chiffon gown, its bulge obscured by the swirl and drape of a blue silk scarf falling from her shoulders to her hips. "If he makes a move . . ." Hector had pointed to his face, indicating what she should aim for.

She was scared, Teresa, she would have to admit that; but at this nodal point of all their lives, she couldn't afford to vacillate. Valero had nearly finished the gowns; the floor of the inaugural stage was being inlaid with the sun and the moon; New Year's Eve was drawing near, and God help her, she couldn't imagine having the same old life for another four years. She needed respite, escape, to sail with the moon, the misshapen swollen December moon of this land of darkness. And so she held on to the gun, nestling it in her palm like a delicate but cold bird, breathing lightly, gently breathing, as she sat there and told herself that men never suspected women who breathed gently. She watched Blackie consider, halting for a moment in the doorway, flanked by two guards, dominating the room with a single glance as social grace prescribed men of power should. Hector held a cup and saucer and drank calmly, not spilling a coffee drop.

Blackie barked a laugh, tossed back his head, and aimed gimlet eyes at Katerina. "The deadlier of the twins," he said—which wasn't fair at all, Teresa would say later, hastily consoling Katerina, who turned out to have been extremely pleased by the remark. He stepped forward and waved his guards back, and the twin leaves of the bedroom door closed behind him like an irrevocable benediction. He walked to the empty chair, as designed, Katerina thought, his right hand feeling in his front shirt pocket for the usual cigar. Her muscles went rigid; she leaned forward, wondering if there was a knife there or . . . No. Only a cigar, cellophane-wrapped, which he proceeded to strip naked and pass under his nostrils as he took his seat.

"Well, senator," he said.

"Mr. President," was Hector's formal answer.

And like two weary warhorses, they lapsed into silence, eyeing each other.

She could've screamed, the tension being so palpable in the room it was a wonder they all remained civilized. But she understood, Teresa, that this was the way it was with men. They could murder each other and still grant their affinity to each other. How very, very strange. "If they'd been women," she said later, "they'd be clawing at each other's eyes. We're more honest, aren't we?"

Blackie glanced at her next and commented, in a dry voice, true, but gallantly, that she looked quite lovely. He hoped she understood it was only business, nothing personal. For if the truth be told, it was he who'd urged Hector to run for the senate and who'd backed him "all the way" at the time. "Hell, he would have no political career if not for me," he said. Katerina inclined her head, acknowledging the apology but refusing either to be disarmed or drawn in. But he'd already turned away, promptly forgetting her existence—for which, she vowed, he would pay someday.

More silence. Blackie smelled the cigar again, looked at Hector, eyebrows rising. Hector shook his head. He had terrible reactions to smoke, he said, and Katerina bit off a smile, because that was one of Hector's tricks: inconveniencing the other party so as to make him impatient, more eager to conclude the parley. Blackie shrugged and went on smelling the cigar. He'd given up smoking himself, he said, and simply amused himself with tobacco odor. His smile said he knew Hector only too well.

In which case, Hector said, he should consider marrying his daughter to a garlic-and-tobacco clan.

Blackie sighed. Sincerely, he wished he could; that was the crux of the matter, actually. He had only a daughter, no son, though not for lack of trying, sure guarantee he would have no dynasty but would see his family attached to another clan. Unfortunately, Hector's son was too young . . . Katerina nearly shot the stupid old man right there and then, but a glance from Hector nailed her to the chair. Besides which, Blackie went on, ignoring her sudden move, the fool girl had gone and done a stupid thing, namely, fallen head over heels in love with one of the Central Plains mayors now missing. Would Hector know anything about that?

Hector mulled that over and said not really, but then information could always be obtained. Blackie chuckled. "That leaves me pleading for the life of a prospective son-in-law of whom I disapprove." Hector looked puzzled. What exactly did Blackie want—a live son-in-law or a dead mayor? There was a terrible silence as hatred blossomed in Blackie's eyes. His head swiveled toward Katerina and then back to Hector. "The twins," he said after a while, his face flushing. "They say you're impossible to resist. I understand why. You name the secret desires people won't name even to themselves. You are very direct." Hector made a deprecating noise. Didn't he have such an excellent mentor? Blackie's eyes nearly smoked. Then the fire died and he laughed. Yes, indeed, the best. Hector said all he did was present Blackie with what, given the situation, seemed to be clear-cut choices. Blackie sighed again. "Yeah. No bullshit. A great temptation." He inhaled audibly. "But I'm an old man. I'll have to settle my accounts soon. I think we'll let this one go, for my daughter's happiness."

Hector nodded. He closed his eyes, and Katerina grew anxious that he was falling asleep. After a while, though, he murmured:

"Ah, Blackie, you're passing water."—by which he meant that the real man had lost his courage. And he looked the incumbent full in the face.

Such a grief descended on the old man's face even Katerina was touched. Still, he took that with grace. "There's a time for that as well, son." And leaning forward, he launched into such a long and complicated explication of what public service was all about, for the good of the people, a thankless job and so on and so forth, so pedestrian, Teresa, that Katerina barely suppressed a yawn. But Hector listened gravely, nodding once in a while, and when Blackie ran out of steam, he said softly that in other words, the president was broke and could use some *gasolina*.

Blackie's amazement turned into a huge laugh. "How sharp you are, Hector," he said. "So different from the callow youth I saw mouthing off at Defense. Amazing. But yes, yes, indeed. Truth to tell, I've been remiss. I've not provided for my family. In the last two years, I caught a glimmer of something so surprising, so entrancing, I forgot to prepare for my retirement. But then, once up there, you never believe you'll come down again. I thought I'd have more than four years."

"How much?" So soft were the words they seemed a declaration of love. Katerina felt so sorry for Blackie, so sorry indeed.

"A half million. In dollars."

She couldn't help grinning. Smith would shriek.

"Plus some guarantees."

Hector was frankly amazed. Of what? Blackie's shoulders twitched uncomfortably. "An honorable exit," he said finally.

Done! The two shook hands, Hector saying the president should plan this one; he'd simply go along, he and the rest of the nation. But before His Excellency could leave, would he share with his humble opponent what it was that he'd glimpsed in those two years?

Blackie was surprised. "Certainly," he said. "I didn't think you would be interested." A pause as he inhaled deeply and raised his eyes to the ceiling. "I saw a nation struggling to be born."

What a curious thing to say, Teresa; Katerina was so disappointed. She hadn't known that presidents could be as ignorant as that. Why, even the littlest grade-schooler knew, provided he wasn't too much of a moron, that the first republic was born at the turn of the century and the second right after WWII, so what the hell was Blackie talking about?

21

Well *done*. So did Provincial Governor Tikloptuhod confer his congratulations upon Teresa, his daughter, as they stood in the palace vestibule, the six-tiered chandelier of Venetian crystal tinkling overhead and couples in resplendent gowns and tuxedoes gliding through a corridor lighted by shaded beeswax candles scented with cinnamon. Well done indeed. José *Blackie* Domínguez y García, fifth and outgoing president of the latest republic of the archipelago, had withdrawn his petitions before COME-LEC, in the interest of national unity and reconciliation—for which the legislature, in joint session, voted him the Order of Lakandula, granting him the privilege to wear the red, blue, and yellow sash of honor whenever it pleased him. He was returning to private life with pension intact and with half a mil, as Hector said, in greenbacks, though he was foolish enough to deposit it in a local bank vault, tsk-tsk-tsk; the old man was losing his grip. Armand chuckled, saying bank vaults were so easy to pry open one might as well hide money in a shoe box.

Considering the preceding tumult, the new peace and order created such euphoria that the inauguration, planned on a scale never before witnessed in the land, acquired even more intense grandeur. Never before, as the media said, and never again, as Katerina said, waving to the crowd lining both sides of the street from the palace to the downtown park where all such inaugurations were held, never mind that the area had been an execution ground during the reign of the now long departed Spanish governor-generals and villains, bandits and heroes alike had been strangled, shot, knifed, and garroted there. She rode in an open limousine alone, Armand and the children in a closed Mercedes somewhere in the motorcade, Hector flying to the park by helicopter for security reasons, and though there were six inches of goose-down cushions beneath her rear to make sure she'd be visible, the crowd's roar, the music of the brass band, the lambent sunlight, and the fresh seabreeze blowing all the way from where such breezes were birthed to Manila so filled her with happiness that she waved, waved with both white-lace-gloved hands, and let her love beam, hotter than the noon sun, upon the multitude saluting her presence—Herself, Katerina Basbas Gloriosa. Someone had had the foresight to order this brand-new, gleaming limousine, just arrived from Germany, especially for her; was it Teresa, her dear, dear childhood confidante and friend? It was so beautifully balanced, this car, she could feel its tires crushing the ton of pale white rose petals flown in from Taiwan, petals released like a rain of congealed perfume by the crowd, as the cheering went on and on, drowning out a slight disturbance at the crowd's edge, over there near the outlying streets, a commotion of sudden placards and flags unfurled, oh, it was no more than a handful of students taking exception to His Excellency's announcement that yes, indeed, of course, the archipelago would come to the aid of its great northern ally and friend in that little war just beyond the seas, though Teresa, listening to the dismissive tones of the security men and de Naval, was assailed by a terrible foreboding and had visions of a gigantic throat arched, neck veins swollen, pouring its wrath to a blood-red sky, the crackle of flames and the crack of gunfire so different from the softness of the opening passage of the *rigodón de honor*, music wending its way among the couples standing stiffly, lissome youth self-conscious, awaiting the dance master's nod as the gathering guests about the cleared rectangle of the dance floor fluttered their hands, nodded, and whispered how beautiful everything was, just beautiful.

The Provincial Governor, Teresa's father, concurred, saying nice, nice, as he took her elbow and guided her through and between men and women in formal clothes in the main reception hall, on an aimless but amiable promenade. He wore his native shirt of the finest spun pineapple-fiber fabric, hand-embroidered with an elaborate and recurring motif of crossed garlic bulbs and a tobacco leaf, rather tongue-in-cheek, he confessed to Teresa, who couldn't appreciate the joke because, well, she was actually furious with him and would have preferred it if he hadn't come at all. For as soon as the signs were auspicious, the Governor had indeed sent his "evidence" to the president-elect, each sheet signed TIK, which had occasioned a terrific quarrel in the Basbas house. Hector had ensured, rather perversely as far as Teresa was concerned, that Katerina would know about the telegrams and the Governor's demand, at which Herself had lashed out at her dearest childhood friend and confidante, shrieking *Tik, Tik, traitor!* before rushing out for her fitting at Valero's. Hector and Armand had pinioned Teresa with their eyes and she could do nothing, only hang her head and shuffle her feet, trying not to cry, until His Excellency cleared his throat to say but of course, the Basbas twins honored obligations and debts of gratitude, the old goat could have his exclusive license to import cigarette filters, what the hell, it was such a minor thing, though it would make the man's corporation very, very valuable indeed. And did Teresa know who the old man's heir was? His sons, she'd answered bitterly and yet gladly. Armand whistled, said the corporation couldn't be allowed to fall into, uh, unfriendly hands. And did she know who her father's lawyers were? Such a delicate way of putting it, but she understood. She named the places where copies of her father's will were kept, including a law office in New York. Hector's eyebrows lifted. The careful son-of-a-goat,

he said, and turning to Armand, he asked, the Golden Arm?
Armand nodded. Later, she found out they were referring to a
master forger currently imprisoned at the old Bilibid compound.
She knew then that they'd wanted her privy to the plans for her
father's execution. They would have her named heiress in the
false will, and she would name Hector Basbas's children her
beneficiaries.

His mind wasn't at ease at all, the Governor said as he strolled
about with Teresa, occasionally halting a uniformed waiter with
a silver tray, spearing salmon bits with a toothpick, dipping endive
slivers into guacamole, or picking up a pâté-crusted cracker. That
morning, at the formal acceptance of congratulations in the presidential study, with Hector standing behind the desk, ramrod-
stiff and regal, the governor had come to tender his respects. And
to ask, of course, about the license. Oh, he was quite a sight,
His Excellency was, so miraculously recovered from his accident
that the Governor nearly asked what medicine he was taking,
flanked there by his nieces and his sister, who were decked out
in froths of chiffon, lace, bows, and flowers. There'd been a
slight tension when the ex-Excellency Blackie Domínguez y García had appeared, daughter and prospective son-in-law in tow.
Now, that young man was quite good-looking, and from everything the Governor had heard, was not slow on the uptake—
from which he surmised that Blackie had high hopes his daughter's future husband would manage to turn the wheel of fortune
one more time so he could be exactly where he'd stood before
and where Hector was standing now.

The Governor was contemplating this delicious and probable
soap opera from the neglected corner into which he'd tucked
himself adroitly when Hector caught sight of the former president
and his companions, stepped from behind the desk, and with
due humility welcomed his former rival. He smiled with such
pleasure and opened his arms, especially when the young man

was introduced. It was so charming only Governor Tikloptuhod cursed under his breath at such deviousness. He had no doubt at all Hector was planning to break Blackie, daughter, and son-in-law totally. "What have we loosed now, daughter?" he asked heavily.

So that was why Hector and Armand had shaken their heads over the greenbacks.

But that was neither here nor there, said the Governor, what did he care about this rivalry? What frightened him was Hector giving him exactly the same smile, exactly the same embrace, when he stepped up to the desk. "Is he planning something?" he asked straight out, and Teresa looked him in the eye and shook her head. No. Not that she knew of. Her father quivered between relief and suspicion, trying to read her face; but she was flesh of his flesh and blood of his blood, and while not totally convinced, he asked aloud whether he could trust anyone at all if he couldn't trust his daughter. Teresa could look him straight in the eye because she'd found out just that day, from a loud-mouthed and irritating reporter, that Herself had taken to calling her Miss Tik. Oh, ask Miss Tik that and check with Miss Tik please and give this to Miss Tik—which made her humiliation quite public, because the pun was difficult to resist and it was already being whispered naughtily at the press club that Herself meant Mistake, giggle, giggle.

As they rounded a pillar, the noise at the doorway grew and swelled. The archbishop of the Mystic Limb, resplendent in a red velvet cape and white soutane edged in gold-thread embroidery, identical, Armand was to say later, to the founder's, his late father's, funeral robes, had arrived, shoulder to shoulder with His Excellency Hector Basbas. The president's entrance, unheralded, drew attention away from the *rigodón* and all those searched-for couples who were moving forward, backward, skirts swishing, left shoulder profiled, right shoulder profiled, oh, how lovely they were, though not lovely enough, Teresa told herself, to dispel the memory of Hector's expression when he'd answered the archbishop's query yesterday afternoon, in the palace study room, when the old man had asked what the new president's policy would be over the next four years. Hector had brought his hands together, fingertip to fingertip, and over the apex of that steeple of flesh and bone, bent a gaze of such gravity on the sect leader before murmuring the word *alignment*. Just before the door closed and cut the two men off from the world, Teresa understood Hector would use the sect to dispossess the clans and then move in to cut down the Mystic Limb. For a minute, she had been assailed with the wild thought that Hector had died in the plane crash and what had returned was the devil.

But alignment was what she thought of when she had finally taken her seat, up there at the highest seat row of the Luneta Park Grandstand, as the stage had come to be known. She'd insisted on this, refusing seats closer to His Excellency and the First Family, because, despite an army of assistants, aides, and servants, a presidential inauguration was difficult to orchestrate and she, Teresa Tikloptuhod, had to hover like a hawk over this geography of celebration. She needed to see the length and breadth of the landscape of the ceremony, the continents of its joy, the better to describe it all later to her comatose lover. Down there, on the other side of the cement road running like a straight moat before the stage, like ants aligned with a sharp-edged ruler, was the bureaucracy, in alternating rows of green, blue, and red, per Armand's vision. Her eyes had to slide over the guests' heads, all seats being occupied by then, taken, not a single one left even for least-liked cousin Matrimonia Montelibano-Basbas, at the moment probably weeping her eyes out in chagrin and without her knowledge headed for ruin, since Katerina kept on her vanity, underneath an ivory-handled hairbrush, the list of her cousins' properties. The twins' close associates filled the last three rear

rows; clan scions and matrons were in the next four; foreign
diplomats sat in the next lower two; while government and military officials occupied the lowest tier, just before the empty space
where the sun-moon emblems, breathing out a fragrance, lay
underfoot and where two chairs, one mahogany and one white,
waited, facing a lectern and a bank of microphones. The chief
justice sweated in his black robes, but Armand and the children
were cool as ice, so relaxed in their seats down there in the front
row. They were so beautiful Teresa could have cried. An
unearthly roar fell just then from the heavens and a helicopter
descended, as fighter planes shrieked from horizon to horizon,
drowning out this chant, this intoxicating drumroll thundering
from the crowd: *Bas-bas! Bas-bas! Bas-bas!*—the name being the
Tagal root word meaning "to bless." Bless us, she murmured as
the noise crescendoed, chasing the fighter planes from the sky,
and Hector appeared on the left edge of the stage. He stopped,
scanned the crowd, and subdued it with a look. But the brittle
silence couldn't last; a blood-chilling scream erupted, a shriek
edged with hysteria, because Katerina Gloriosa, oh lovely Katerina, oh incomparable Herself, had appeared at the other side
of the stage, incredibly beautiful in a light blue gown all drape
and swirl, so simple in its classic design, wasn't that Valero simply
a genius, its folds gently defining her figure, which was all right
because she'd lost weight, Hector having restricted her to nothing
but diet pills in the last two weeks, and bringing the eyes to focus
on the impeccably high cheekbones of that perfect face. The
crowd screamed itself hoarse then, shouting *Bas-bas! Bas-bas!* in
recognition of being twice blessed, blessed by His strength and
Her loveliness, as fireworks etched ephemeral flame blossoms
against a darkening sky. In synchronized steps, the twins moved
toward each other, met and embraced at center stage, traded
cheek-kisses, and then repaired to their respective seats, Katerina
toeing the pale moon beneath her white rattan peacock chair

prettily before fixing her eyes on the crowd. Only Teresa noted Epee's quick glare of hatred at her mother—or perhaps de Naval noted it, too, for the bantam cock of an ex-captain was there, roaming the back of the stage with a swagger stick squeezed beneath his right armpit. He winked at her and then grinned, but the signal's meaning escaped her.

The dancing couples froze and the music died along with the lights just as a spotlight drenched the curving stairs where six boys dressed as court pages (weren't they cute in their little red capes?) were stationed on the last three steps, a pair each. The boys lifted trumpets to their lips, as the guests exclaimed in pleased surprise, ravished by such originality in the proceedings, and out blared the fanfaronade. There she was, Katerina Gloriosa, Herself coming down the steps, slowly, carefully, a slide-step, slide-step gliding, because of her stiletto heels and the weight of her pearl-encrusted gown, its angel-wing whiteness disturbed by a tricolored sash, a duplicate of Blackie's Order of Lakandula—which caused the Governor's scotch to go down the wrong way, and he hacked and coughed so much Teresa had to pound his back while the ex-president turned as pale as his dark complexion would allow him. Herself had the last laugh, after all.

Amazing. Truly amazing. The whisper reached her despite the applause and the trumpet blast. De Naval, in white ducks and spats, gave her an okay signal, thumb and forefinger forming a circle. The Governor had to hide himself behind a pillar to stifle his rasping while she watched de Naval and became convinced that the man would survive the little war, would return from "over there" loaded with black-market loot and a bevy of medals, to hound the Basbas twins, Armand, and herself for the rest of their lives. He winked again and turned away. She realized with a shock that the man with de Naval was Blackie's future son-in-law; and such hatred sizzled in her bones that she saw herself in this very room, empty save for herself and a military man who was whispering, whispering, urgently, irritatingly, about this same young man, who'd become a gadfly, a thorn in their side, with his endless repetition of a mindless claim that the twins, the Basbas family, and Hector himself had no right to stay on beyond his term, so many, many years beyond his term, and she was feeling quite unable to take any more of this, feeling flustered and fatigued beyond endurance because Hector was undergoing surgery, his second or third, somewhere in the bowels of the palace, which had grown labyrinthine and enclosed with all of Katerina's remodeling, and she was feeling so imposed upon, that to clear her chest of a dark mass of wrath, she blurted out that they should "do away" with the fellow, and that was that; she precipitated the end; while the demise of a clan supporter was of no consequence, the murder of a clan member was. She was, would be, responsible—and yet that, too, would not be the whole truth, for the whole country would be rampaging by then, twisting and turning like a huge serpent trying to get at the Basbas family's throat.

A final flourish from the trumpets; Katerina reached the bottom step and Hector stepped forward, right arm akimbo, to escort her deeper into the reception hall. The lights over the dance floor brightened as the frozen couples stirred with the initial measures of the Salute. Oh, she'd worked that out pretty well, Teresa had, mixing tradition and innovation. Not even the awkwardness of having the couples immobile as mannequins destroyed the moment. It was a minor distraction, on the same scale as Hector's slurring the words of his oath of office that afternoon, what the hell, he was thereafter His Excellency, sir, so twenty-one booms of artillery proclaimed, though Armand frowned and worriedly cornered Teresa just before the state banquet to whisper well, he's at it again, and she whispering back what, what, and he hissing *steroids* just as she caught a glimpse of Katerina plucking two, three pâté-and-crackers from a passing tray borne by a waiter, not even mindful of the guests' eyes.

The *rigodón* was ending and the live rock band at the lower end of the hall was on its feet, because Teresa had decreed there would be nonstop music throughout, the better to prevent men and women from pouring woes and pleas into the presidential ear. As designed, the chandeliers winked out, as the globe of mirror descended from the hexagonal ceiling, which, as Katerina had noted, was shaped like a gigantic coffin, and strobe lights flashed blue, green, and red rays throughout the room, setting the guests squealing and jumping, while in the turning, turning globe, one caught reflections of the revelry below. The guests shook off official formality, scattering protocol to the winds, and spilled to the dance floor, knocking askew the stiff pattern of the *rigodón* dancers, and Teresa saw Hector leading Epee to the center of the room as the emphatic beat of electric guitars and drums ricocheted from the walls.

Well done. Very well done. That accolade was hers, no one else's. She turned her back on the celebration, the image of San Custodio a weight in the bottom of her heart, heard a rising murmur from stray guests at the broad back terrace overlooking the city's only river, whose waters came from way up there, in the mountains, which were blue shadows because they were so far away, seemingly in another country where there were no lights, no music, no wine, and boys didn't play trumpets but bent their backs to the plow. The same terrace had so disturbed Katerina during the two women's first visit that she'd murmured it wouldn't do, it was too open, too open, why a man could stand on the other bank and train who knew what—binoculars, a rifle, cameras—on the palace and spy on the family; it would have to be walled up, the whole place walled in, windows shuttered, everything closed, no exits and entrances. There was no convincing her that her fears were without basis, not even when

Teresa said that the other side of the river was a military camp, the headquarters of the presidential guards, nor even when she pointed out that the terrace's ceiling-to-floor doors were the palace's main means of ventilation. Katerina had snapped she'd air-condition the whole place; it was that hot, humid, and dismal anyway. Teresa understood then that the Basbas twins would begin shearing off their remnant connection with the world, with that faraway country of blue-shadowed mountains beyond the river. She thought of how the lovely summer retreat of Spanish governor-generals now long gone would be transformed into a fort, its windows boarded up, sunlight and breeze vanquished, guests turned away, reality itself denied. She murmured that Katerina should consider how the structure had stood untouched for two centuries plus. Well, time to touch it, Katerina had retorted.

A ghastly light spilled on the river now and she saw what had inspired the guests' awed murmuring. To the north, the firecrackers had been set off and huge starbursts of flames were igniting the dark sky. Suddenly, there was a terrific splash of light and the red outline of two human figures, half-overlapping, loomed over the horizon. The Sign of the Gemini was rampant over the land. A faint cheering, perhaps of an exultant crowd, came from the distance and lasted as long as the sky-twins' brief existence.

The full moon, eclipsed before by so much brilliance, held sway now over the night, so huge and clear it seemed to hang just beyond the terrace's fluted iron rails, to lean forward to kiss the river. She raised her face to it, arching her throat, letting moonrays cool her cheeks and shoulders; she allowed herself to yield, just this once and only for this minute, to temptation. She could kick off her shoes, she told herself, climb the rails, prod the moon with her toes. She could ease her weight upon it slowly, right foot first, then the left, the way children rode rolling barrels, and let it bear her away, while there was still time, heaven help her, in this night of celebration, and she could leave behind that sinister globe of mirrors which threw back—what?—images of the past and·the future, oh, if she could leave now, before dawn broke over palace, city, and archipelago and everyone awoke to find his nightmares loose upon the land.

Manhattan and Cincinnati, 1990

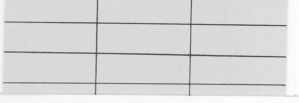

Rosca
    Twice blessed.   cop.1 "Fic